ALCHEMY OF SECRETS

ALCHEMY
OF
SECRETS

A Novel

STEPHANIE GARBER

FLATIRON BOOKS
NEW YORK

This is a work of fiction. All the characters, organizations, and events portrayed in this novel are either products of the author's imagination or used fictitiously.

ALCHEMY OF SECRETS. Copyright © 2025 by Stephanie Garber. All rights reserved. Printed in the United States of America. For information, address Flatiron Books, 120 Broadway, New York, NY 10271. EU Representative: Macmillan Publishers Ireland Ltd., 1st Floor, The Liffey Trust Centre, 117–126 Sheriff Street Upper, Dublin 1, DO1 YC43.

Designed by Donna Sinisgalli Noetzel

ISBN 978-1-250-78915-0

This one is for my dad.

You told me not to write this one for you,
but I did it anyway.

I love you, Dad!

ALCHEMY OF SECRETS

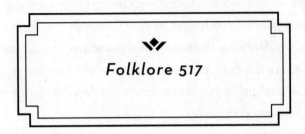

Folklore 517

t started with a whisper you heard while in line at a coffee shop, a story you probably should have ignored. But the rumor stuck in your head like a song, it plagued you like an unsolved riddle. Until, at last, it led you here. A parking lot, which had clearly not paid attention to the weather report.

They said it would be all stars, no clouds tonight, but you feel the rain on your toes. The wet hits in eager droplets as you dash across the pavement in sandals. Around you, streetlamps flicker, a staticky chorus to your damp footfalls.

You're not out of breath, but you slow, stopping under a marquee. The words COMING SOON sizzle in red block letters, throwing neon shadows on a retro cashier's booth, covered in washed-out posters for attractions that have already come and gone. Veronica Lake's name splashes across the top of one poster in faded yellow letters, while a black-and-white Loretta Young smiles at you from another. Loretta's poster is for *A Night to Remember*, and you hope tonight will be one of those nights.

You don't know for certain if the stories are true, but you half expect to fall through a rabbit hole as you step through the theater door into the lobby.

Your excitement varnishes everything in an extra layer of shine. On your right, there's a bank of gleaming pay phones in neat wood and glass boxes. You've never seen a line of so many. You're almost tempted to snap a photo, but you don't. And you couldn't have even if you'd tried. By now your phone is no longer working, though you don't know that yet. You're suddenly too distracted by the ancient concession stand to your left, where the dust looks like nostalgia and you barely notice the chips in the gold paint that make up the art deco border of geometric suns and jumping dolphins.

The sign above says:

10 cents for popcorn
15 cents for popcorn with butter
25 cents for cigarettes

You were unaware they used to sell cigarettes in theaters, but for a moment you can smell the smoke and the popcorn. You can almost taste the butter, too. But you don't linger in the lobby. There's only one theater—one attraction—that you wish to find, and you walk directly toward it.

Your chest is tight. Your heart is already racing. And you're still hoping for the rabbit hole that will take you to another world. You're starry-eyed and optimistic, an overexposed picture made of too much light, as you step through the double doors.

It still smells like smoke and popcorn, but there's something else, too. Maybe it's just the scent of old velvet mixed with lingering hints of petrichor, but it makes you think of Technicolor dreams as you stretch your neck to take in the impossibly tall ceiling. It's all ivory and gold, and it's covered in more art deco designs that look as if they could be cousins to the zodiac.

Beneath the elaborate dome, a fraction of the seats are already occupied. Twenty-five? Maybe fifty? You're too nervous to properly count as you take a chair near the back. It rocks, and the worn velvet is soft, but it feels too far from the stage.

You decide to move closer, sneaking more looks at the others as you do. You want to see who else made it inside, if there's anyone you recognize. But given the scant number of people you know at school, it's unsurprising these faces are all strangers. Some are whispering, some are giggling, a few like you say nothing, but there's a thread that ties you all together: expectation.

This has to be it. The curtains on the stage are deep, lush pink, and when they part you hold your breath.

Gentlemen, kindly remove your hats, flickers across the silver screen.

Then another slide replaces it: *Loud whistles and talking are not allowed.*

This, of course, elicits a number of whistles. But then it's all quiet and hush as the image leaves the screen and a tiny star appears in the upper-right-hand corner. It blinks once, twice. Then every light in the theater goes out.

It's darker than the night outside. You hear people pulling out their phones, but none of them are working, including yours. No signal. No light. No digital clock to tell you how much time is passing.

You don't know how long you sit there before you hear the first person leave. They've decided this class is not for them, if it even is a class. A few others follow.

You hate that you're tempted to do the same.

Your toes are no longer wet, but your skin is prickly with cold. You feel as if someone's watching you, though it's too dark for anyone to see.

More time ticks by, and you go over the stories you've heard, the rumors and the whispers about a very particular class that can't be found in any online catalog, taught by a professor who's not on any website. And suddenly you think it's for a good reason. You think maybe you should go. You think—

A light flickers on the stage. Just a tiny thing, but the shine gets you. You close your eyes, then open them. And when you can see again, she's there.

She's sitting on a wooden stool in the center of the stage.

You don't know how long she's been there, but you have the impression she's been waiting for hours, just like the two dozen or so of you who remain. She's shorter than you'd imagined. The way people talked about her always made her sound tall, statuesque, literally larger than life. But she looks like someone's grandmother. Bobbed silver hair frames a round, barely smiling face, as she says words that make you feel as if all the cold and the damp and the waiting have been worth it.

"You're here because of a story," she says. "Now I'm going to tell you another one."

CHAPTER ONE

Holland St. James had been counting down the minutes until tonight. She had tried on seven different dresses and five different pairs of shoes, she had curled her hair, she had even put on new eye makeup. And now she was about to ruin it all.

"I thought we were going for ice cream?" Jake asked, perfectly nice. Because Jake might have been the nicest guy Holland had ever dated.

When Jake had first come into the Santa Monica Coffee Lab a couple weeks ago, Holland had thought he was the perfect kind of cute. He looked more Clark Kent than Superman, with the type of dark-rimmed glasses that had always been her personal kryptonite. Then, he'd bumped into her, spilling some of his cold brew, and Holland had seen the textbooks he was holding. Jake was in grad school, studying to teach ESL.

On their first date, she learned he also volunteered at the Los Angeles Animal Rescue and the Echo Park Time Travel Mart, which was actually a nonprofit that helped children with their creative writing. On their second date, she learned Jake had recently become a vegetarian, and he rode a bike instead of driving a car because he wanted to do whatever he could for the environment.

Jake was genuinely a good guy.

Maybe there was a tiny part of Holland that thought he was a little too perfect, like an email without a typo or an airbrushed picture that needed one wrinkle. But that could have just been Holland looking for red flags that didn't exist.

This was only their third date, but Holland hadn't made it to a fourth date in two years. She really didn't want to screw this up. And she was afraid she might have already done that minutes ago, when she hadn't been able to stop herself from dragging Jake down this grimy alley, after seeing a poster that made her think of one of the Professor's stories.

The poster had been plastered to the side of a cement wall. It was one of those vintage numbers, the kind that looked as if it should have been on one of the wooden postcards they sold on the Santa Monica Pier. Palm trees in sun-washed brown and green framed the charcoal silhouette of a man wearing a fedora and looking down at his watch. There were no logos, no brand names. There were actually no words at all to identify what exactly the poster was selling. There were just two initials on the faceless man's cuff links: W.M.

The Watch Man.

It was the first thought that had entered her mind. Then she had taken Jake down this alley. She hadn't been able to stop herself.

Holland had been raised on her father's treasure hunts. As a child, she'd learned to look for clues the way other children learned to play with blocks or each other. Perhaps that was why Holland had never felt as if she quite fit in, until she found the Professor's folklore class. Her stories made Holland feel as if she was on one of her father's hunts again.

She hadn't actually expected to discover anything tonight. Things around LA were always reminding her of the Professor's stories, and Holland always felt compelled to chase them. She was perpetually darting down alleys she swore she'd never seen before, only to find a bar or a coffee shop or a bookstore she'd actually already visited.

But not tonight. Tonight, Holland knew she'd never been down this alley. She would have remembered the sign.

Curios & Clockwork
Inquire Within

The words hung from a sleek copper hook that shone against a door Holland wanted to believe was vintage but might have just been dirty. One glance at Jake and she could tell he was thinking *dirty*. He was possibly rethinking his choice to go on this date as well. She wanted to change his mind. She also really wanted to go through that door, and she wanted to convince him to come with her.

"Do you like urban myths?" she asked.

"Yeah—I actually love them." Jake gave her smile that was far more Superman than Clark Kent. Holland felt a spark of hope that she was headed in the right direction again.

And yet . . . she hesitated.

The Professor had a rule about not sharing her stories with people outside of her class. No one broke this rule. The class required too much effort from students for them to then give the stories away for free, and the Professor always warned students there could be serious consequences to doing so. But Holland wasn't a Folklore 517 student anymore, and it was only one story. But . . .

"Before I say anything else," she said quietly, "I need you to swear on the life of your dog, or your bike, or that houseplant you've been working so hard to keep alive, that you won't tell anyone what I'm about to say."

Jake grinned wider. "I swear." He leaned in and kissed her lightly on the lips, as if to seal the promise. "So, is this like a family secret?"

Holland froze.

She reminded herself that Jake came from a large family that was always calling him and sharing even the most mundane details of their day. Talking about family was normal for him. He wasn't fishing for information.

Yet it took her several seconds to smile in a way she hoped looked playful. "It's not a family secret, but it is something I'm not supposed to talk about. When I was doing my undergrad, I took this class called Folklore 517: Local Legends and Urban Myths. The class itself is sort of a local legend. You can't register for it. It's not on any website. You have to find it by word of mouth. Then if you pass the class, at the end of the semester, it shows up on your transcript."

Jake looked all in. "So, it's like a secret society version of a class?"

Holland nodded nervously, or maybe she was feeling excited. It wasn't as if sharing this little secret was going to hurt anyone. "Each week, the Professor would talk about a different local legend or urban myth, and we'd have to swear never to share them. One of the Professor's legends is about someone called the Watch Man. Supposedly, there are signs that lead to him around Los Angeles. If you follow the signs and you manage to find him, you can ask him the time, and the Watch Man will tell you when you'll die."

Jake's expression shifted, a tiny worry line forming between his brows.

"It's not as morbid as it sounds," Holland hurried to say. "The Professor also said that you can make a deal with him to get more time, to live longer than you would have."

"And you *really* believe this?" Jake asked. There was something in his voice Holland couldn't quite place, but suddenly she feared she'd been a little too optimistic about his interest in legends. He was a normal guy who was probably used to going on very normal dates. And most likely he wanted a very normal girl.

Of course not.

It's just for fun.

No—not even a little.

Any of these would have been excellent answers to his question; these were all things a normal girl would have said.

"Just come inside with me," Holland hedged.

"Sure," Jake said. And because he was a nice guy, he reached out and opened the door with the *Curios & Clockwork* sign for her.

Everything on the other side was milk glass and gold. A perfect row of milk-glass lights on golden cords lit a perfect floor of milk-glass penny tile with a number of shimmering golden tiles that spelled out the words *tick tock*.

There were no footprints, no smudges, just the glittering words, which winked like the flutter of a second hand under the glassy lights.

It almost felt like *magic*. Not big, miraculous magic but the simple magic of timeless things. Of two-dollar bills and handwritten letters, typewriters and rotary phones.

Holland might have said as much out loud. But Jake looked as if he wasn't sure what to make of this uncanny room in the back of a strange alley. This wasn't what he'd signed up for when he'd suggested they go for ice cream. He wanted a date who would look good in an Instagram photograph, not one who could end up on Dating Hell Reddit.

Holland had definitely misread this one, but she couldn't go back now. This felt like the closest she'd ever been to finding one of the Professor's myths in real life.

There were two doors across from them, and they were milk glass as well, glossy white, with golden handles and simple rectangular golden plaques in the center. One plaque said *curios*. The other said *clockwork*.

Holland reached for the *clockwork* door, hoping it was for the Watch Man. If she was ruining this date, it needed to be for a good reason.

The doorknob didn't budge.

She tugged again. "I think it's locked."

Jake reached over her shoulder and knocked. Two loud raps of his knuckles.

"May I help you?" The voice came from the other door. The one labeled *curios*.

In the yawning doorway now stood a girl. She had pixie-cut platinum hair and a small nose ring, and she wore a fitted white dress the same shade as the milk glass. At first glance, she looked young, but there was something about the way the girl stood and stared that made Holland think her appearance might be deceiving.

Holland tried to see behind her, to get a glimpse of the curios inside, but there was only more white light.

The girl drummed her squared-off nails on the doorframe impatiently.

"We're looking for the Watch Man," Holland said.

"I'm sorry. I can't help you." The girl immediately stepped back to shut the door.

"I just want to ask him the time," Holland blurted.

The girl froze. "Are you sure about that, hon?" She followed her question with a look that said Holland would be wise to walk away right now and take the cute boy with her.

"She's sure," Jake said. "I want to know the time, too."

"Really?" Holland asked.

He wrapped an arm around her shoulder, his skin warm against hers. "If you're doing it, I'm in, too."

She wanted to ask what had changed his mind, but she was suddenly feeling too much nervous excitement.

The girl in white muttered something under her breath. It sounded like the word *fools*. Then she disappeared behind the door.

Time slowed inside the milk-glass hall as Holland waited for the girl to come back. Jake's arm grew hot against her shoulder. This time, she felt like the uncomfortable one, hoping the girl would actually return.

Finally, the *curios* door reopened. The girl emerged, holding out pens and slips of paper that had carbon attached to the back. She pursed her lips. "If you two are certain about this, write down your names, along with the requested information, and the Watch Man will be in touch."

CHAPTER TWO

The next morning arrived slowly, reluctant to perform a job it had grown tired of doing.

Holland woke up to thick silence. There were no chirping birds, no cars rushing down the street, no creaking floorboards as her house stretched awake. For a second, she swore her heart didn't even beat.

Her head spun as she finally sat up in bed. She felt vaguely nauseated all of a sudden. It wasn't a hangover, at least she didn't think so.

She tried to remember what she had done last night. But for a moment she couldn't even recall what day it was. She felt like a piece of paper that was slightly stuck to the page before.

Holland groggily leaned over to check her phone.

It was Thursday.

Yesterday had been Wednesday.

Her third date with Jake.

The details came back in a slow parade of grainy off-white pictures that made her think of old home videos. She remembered the alley . . . the milk glass . . . Jake's arm around her shoulder . . . sheets of carbon paper . . . the simple magic of timeless things . . . the Watch Man . . .

Everything had felt so electric at the time.

But now the night felt strangely dull and far away as she replayed the events.

After leaving the alley, she and Jake had finally picked up peanut butter and bacon ice cream, and then he'd kissed her at her car. They'd kissed for a while. But maybe he felt differently about all the kissing than she did because this was the first morning since she'd met him that she hadn't woken up to a text from him.

It wasn't that late. He could still text Good morning.

Her phone chimed, as if on cue.

But it wasn't a message from Jake.

2:00 Meeting with Adam Bishop

Holland dropped her phone back on the bed.

Adam Bishop was a new faculty member who had recently come over from the UC Berkeley Folklore Program. Holland hadn't met him in real life, but she'd heard other grad students chattering about him. Everyone seemed to love him.

The email he'd sent her on Monday was brief, requesting her presence this afternoon. When she'd followed up to ask why, Adam Bishop had cryptically responded that it would be easier to explain in person.

She wondered if maybe he was looking for a teaching assistant, and the Professor had given him Holland's name. Holland might have been behind on finishing her thesis, but she was an excellent assistant. She'd been the Professor's TA for two years—one year during undergrad and one year during grad school—and everyone knew it required a lot of patience, along with a number of skills that weren't usually found on résumés. She actually really missed that job. But she had another job now. A fantastic job.

Every Friday night, Holland showed classic films in the loft of the Santa Monica Coffee Lab, then followed them up with a discussion. It was like teaching without the grading, and everyone got to drink.

She loved it.

She loved the Coffee Lab. She loved the people who showed up each week. But most of all, she loved the old movies.

Holland had loved movies ever since she was four and her father had introduced her and her twin sister to *The Wizard of Oz*. When they'd finished the film, her sister had taken off with a broom and Holland had immediately asked for a pair of ruby slippers.

Her father had said, "I thought you might say that, Hollybells." Then he'd told her the slippers were already waiting for her somewhere in the house; she just had to find them.

That had been her first treasure hunt.

Her father had always connected his hunts to movies. Showing old films at the Coffee Lab made her feel close to him now. She was currently doing a film noir series, and she loved the history behind the films. She loved how the movies had a way of making her believe there was a hidden black-and-white corner of the world, where private eyes lined the streets instead of fast food joints, and at least once a week a femme fatale with a peek-a-boo hairstyle would walk through the door and take someone's life down a dark, twisty path.

If Adam Bishop was looking to hire her as his assistant, she didn't think she'd be interested. But Holland was still curious. She was always curious.

After getting up, she went for a run and tried to imagine what else Adam Bishop could possibly want from her. But as the run turned into a walk and the morning disappeared into noon, her thoughts kept returning to Jake.

He still hadn't texted.

Holland wanted to regret taking him down that alley. She wanted to think it would have all gone differently, and she would have woken up to a good morning text, if they'd just gone straight to ice cream and she hadn't messed it up by chasing an urban myth about death.

But what Holland really wanted was for Jake to like her in spite of—or maybe even because of—the myth. The irony was, the Watch Man wasn't even one of Holland's favorite myths. She didn't really care to know when she would die, she just wanted to know that the myths were true.

It was now nearly time for her meeting. Holland checked her phone one last time.

Nothing.

She knew this didn't mean it was over, but in that moment, it didn't feel as if it was going anywhere. She considered texting Jake, but she'd been the last one to text, last night after she'd gotten home.

If only January was there.

Holland knew what her twin sister would say—something along the lines of *Forget any guy who doesn't want you.* Only January would have used a different *F* word than *forget.*

The sisters might have been identical in appearance, but in most other ways they couldn't have been more different. And yet, January was Holland's best friend. The one person she told everything to.

Holland darted down her staircase to leave for her meeting. Like so many things Holland loved, her house was old, built in the 1940s, full of real wood, white walls, and lots of windows that let in the light. Halfway down the steps, she called her sister.

Normally Holland and January talked every day, but since the beginning of October, January's job had been keeping her busier than usual. For the past three weeks, there had only been the occasional text or photo from Spain.

Right after college, January had gotten a job as a rare book collector. People were willing to pay exorbitant amounts of money to have something no one else did, and it was January's job to track those somethings down. It was truly the perfect job for her. She'd always wanted to travel the world, and like Holland, she'd been raised on their father's treasure hunts. But Holland missed her whenever she was gone.

January's phone rang once before it went to voicemail. "Hello. You've reached January St. James. I'm traveling internationally at the moment—"

The recording was interrupted by January answering the phone. "Hey—" she sounded out of breath but wide awake.

"Is this a bad time?" Holland asked.

"No, but I only have a second." Traffic rumbled in the background, making it sound closer to midday than midnight.

"What are you doing?" Holland asked.

"Boring work stuff. I just finished meeting with a client who really liked hearing the sound of his own voice." January always tried to make her job sound far less interesting than it was, probably to keep Holland from feeling jealous. But tonight, January actually sounded a little worn out. "I miss you, kid."

January never said *I miss you*.

"I miss you, too," Holland said. "My house has been far too clean, since you haven't visited. When is your trip over?"

"Not soon enough . . ." The phone went quiet for a second. Holland briefly thought she might have dropped the call, then January said, "I wish I was there with you . . ." Her voice was so soft, it didn't even really sound like her.

"Is everything okay?" Holland asked. "You almost sound sappy." Usually, Holland was the sappy one.

"I'm just tired," January said, and she really must have been because she didn't even scoff at being called *sappy*. "It's late here and I wish I could talk longer, but I need to dash. I—"

Holland's doorbell rang, muffling January's last words.

Then her sister was gone.

Holland glanced out the windows flanking her door. No one ever rang the doorbell, except for the occasional person selling pest control or solar panels. But this gentleman didn't look like he was selling anything.

There were wisps of silver hair peeking out from his hat and wrinkles on his light-brown cheeks. His shirt was white, and his pants were khaki, held up by a pair of brilliant red-and-white checkered suspenders that made everything else on Holland's quiet street appear dull.

Holland didn't have any minutes to waste if she wanted to make her meeting on time. But as she looked through the window, she was struck by a bolt of déjà vu. *I've met him before,* she thought. Only she couldn't place how.

It might have just been that the suspenders reminded her of an old picture of her grandfather, who had died before she was born.

Whatever it was, it was enough to make her open the door.

"Hello, Holland." The gentleman smiled, an easy grin that made her think of hard candies in shiny wrappers and exaggerated bedtime stories.

"Do I know you?" she asked.

"No, I'm afraid you don't." His smile remained, but his brown eyes lost some of their twinkle as he held out a package wrapped in brown paper and string.

"What's this?" she asked.

"I found it on your doorstep."

Holland took a second look at the parcel. There was no return address, only a blocky orange *Happy Halloween* stamp in the corner and her full name, Holland St. James, typed across the middle in smudgy, old-fashioned letters.

It must have been from the Professor. She loved sending packages and, of course, she never put her name on the return address because she liked them to be mysterious.

Holland's palms tingled as she held the brown paper box in her hands. She was curious about what the Professor had mailed her this time. They were usually esoteric books or manuscripts related to the devil, which the Professor thought might be helpful for Holland's thesis.

Unfortunately, Holland really didn't have time to open anything right now. She set the package down in her hallway.

"Thank you for grabbing this," she told the man. "But I'm afraid I have to—"

"I know you don't have much time, but I'll only take a minute," he promised, and then he held out a pale cream business card with foiled emerald-green printing.

MANUEL VARGAS
Senior Banker and Inheritance Specialist
First Bank of Centennial City

There was a phone number at the bottom.

The opposite side of the card contained a map that marked the bank's location with a star, and underneath it were the words *By Appointment Only*.

"I've never heard of this bank," Holland said. The Professor told a story in her classes about a bank, which was also *by appointment only*. But it was the one story Holland could never seem to remember, and, for some reason, instead of being excited by the idea that this man might be from that bank, Holland was feeling unusually skeptical.

Centennial City, where this man's bank was supposedly located, wasn't even an actual city. Holland had never been, but she knew it was a very old, very wealthy neighborhood within Los Angeles, mostly comprised of an exclusive gated community and a sprawling park where rich people did rich-people things like play polo. She'd heard that, once upon a time, Centennial City was home to a boutique hotel, but the neighborhood residents had used their collective wealth and will to shut it down.

"Did you not receive my letters?" he asked.

Holland raised her eyebrows. "I've never received anything from this bank."

"I'm so sorry. They must have gone astray. My apologies. I had thought you were simply ignoring them, which is why I chose to stop by today, as a sort of last plea." Mr. Vargas somberly took off his hat, revealing more of his fluffy white hair. "Fifteen years ago, one of my clients leased a safety deposit box. Shortly after, this person passed away. The box was already bought and paid for, and therefore it has sat untouched. But its lease is now about to expire." Mr. Vargas paused to check his watch. "The lease will end in twenty-four hours. If the box is not claimed before this time, then, per the original owner's contract, the box and all its contents will be incinerated."

"And let me guess," Holland said, "you're going to tell me that I can claim this mystery box?"

Mr. Vargas nodded gravely before wiping a line of sweat from his brow.

"You know," Holland said, "this is an excellent story." And it was. It was just the sort of mystery Holland usually would have found difficult to resist.

But suddenly she realized why she was feeling skeptical.

It seemed like a hell of a coincidence that last night she'd given out her personal information to a stranger, after following one of the Professor's urban myths, and then today, a different urban myth showed up on her porch.

Maybe this was why the girl from last night had muttered *fools*. Not because Holland and Jake were fooling around with actual myths and magic, but because their belief in them had made them stupid enough to share their personal information.

"I'd really love to believe you," Holland went on. "But this all sort of feels like a real-life version of one of those Nigerian Prince emails, where someone tells me I have a long-lost uncle with an embargoed fortune and all I need to do to secure it is give you my Social Security number, bank account access, and five pints of blood."

Mr. Vargas frowned. "I'm not a con man."

"You said *con man*, not me." Holland moved to shut the door.

Mr. Vargas grabbed the edge with surprising speed. "You're wise to be wary. But we both know who you and your sister actually lost almost fifteen years ago."

For the second time that day, Holland swore her heart stopped beating.

This man is a fraud.

A con man.

He's a liar, Holland told herself.

Most of her friends knew she had a twin sister. And a lot of people died fifteen years ago. This Mr. Vargas could have just picked that number of years to be dramatic. It didn't mean he actually knew who she had lost.

Holland could practically hear her sister's voice, sternly telling her to throw away the business card and let whatever was inside the box burn—if there even was a box. *Leave the dead where they belong,* January would say.

The problem was, Holland had never felt as if her parents belonged among the dead. Maybe this man was a liar, and a con man, and a fraud. But Holland couldn't help herself from asking, "*If* I were to go to your bank, what would you need from me to open up this box?"

"They'll just need to identify you. However . . ." Mr. Vargas paused and lowered his voice. "If you do make an appointment, please do me a favor. Do not tell anyone else. Even if you don't call this number, it would be best that you not mention my visit, or this box, to anyone."

The First Bank of Centennial City did not have a website. And Holland couldn't find an email address for Mr. Vargas, either.

Holland paced around her entryway, knowing she needed to leave for her meeting with Adam Bishop but feeling too distracted to drive.

Usually, she was all for chasing the clues, but this definitely felt like a scam. Why else would this Mr. Vargas tell her not to mention his visit to anyone? And, if it had been real, all he would have had to do was say her real last name, or one of her parents' names, instead of alluding to a mysterious death.

Holland never said her parents' names out loud. As far as everyone who knew her in LA was concerned, her name was Holland St. James. Her real last name was her best-kept secret.

When her parents had died almost fifteen years ago, it had been her aunt and uncle's suggestion to change it. Everyone had known who her parents were. Their death was the sort of sensational story people still talked about today. If anyone found out who Holland and January's parents had been, that's all they would think about when they met them—how their parents had died, and what their deaths must have done to these girls. The sisters would never have their own identities. They would just be stories for others to repeat, or subjects of media specials.

She thought back to last night, when she'd foolishly given her name and number to the girl in the alley. Maybe the girl was a former student of the Professor's and, after hearing the legend of the Watch Man, had come up with an idea to set up a scam to sell personal information to people who would use it for profit. It made sense that students who believed in myths might also believe strangers showing up at their doors telling them they'd been left mysterious safety deposit boxes.

Holland didn't want to be naive. If one of her parents had left her something, she would have found out about it before today.

She couldn't call Mr. Vargas's number, even if she was tempted to. Holland knew herself too well. Once she started down a rabbit hole, she couldn't stop herself from going all the way to the very end. Falling never scared her as much as failing to find out the truth.

Folklore 517:
the Best Sidecar in Town

I t's the second night of class.

You're once again in the old theater. Tonight, it smells slightly sweet. Caramel corn—or is it Cracker Jack?

The scent is so sticky and strong you half expect to see the student closest to you munching on a box of the classic candy. But everyone is transfixed by what's happening on the stage. No one is drinking their coffees or typing on their laptops. Of course, laptops are not allowed, just pens and notebooks—*thank you very much*—but no one is using those, either.

The Professor has already begun.

A tiny click echoes, and she smiles as a slide appears on the silver screen. It's a photograph of a rectangular business card. Black, with a series of gold art deco–style lines around the edges. It looks as if there was once writing in the center of the card, but it's blurred now.

The next slide is clearly older; the gold and the black are duller. The design of the business card is unmistakably the same, only there doesn't seem to be any writing in the middle, blurred or otherwise.

A few more slides take their turns, each one more aged than the last. But the gold-and-black business card in each picture is always the same.

You never thought you cared for art deco before, but you're mesmerized by the elegance of the border when the slides turn to black and white.

At the bottom of one slide is typed 1942.

Then 1936.

Followed by 1927.

The entire time, the Professor doesn't speak.

You keep expecting her to say something—she promised to tell a story—but she's just standing there with a Mona Lisa smile.

Finally, someone raises his hand and, without waiting to be called on, says, "Are we supposed to find one of these cards?"

The Professor laughs, dry and raspy. Not quite amused. "You do not find these cards, young man. There's only one way to obtain one." Finally, she launches into her story. "There are a number of haunted hotels in Los Angeles, and there is one in particular that the devil favors. It's said he enjoys drinking their sidecars."

The person next to you whispers, "What's a sidecar?"

"I think it's a drink," you murmur.

"It's a cocktail," the Professor says, looking right at you. "Made of cognac and citrus, the sidecar has been around for over a century, and if you buy one of these for the devil, he'll give you one of his business cards. Each card may be used only once for an appointment with the devil, where you can make a deal for whatever you want, and then—"

She waves her fingers in a gesture that universally means *magic*, as she explains that this is why the cards are all blank—they have been used for deals with the devil, and thus the writing has disappeared.

You're skeptical. Her only proof is the photographs, and you're not even sure they're real. Anyone could have created these images.

The devil is a myth. One you don't believe in.

But when you walk out of the theater, you want one of those cards.

CHAPTER THREE

For the past year, all Holland's graduate classes had been in the evening. It felt different to walk around campus now, when it was still light out.

Everything smelled like freshly cut grass and looked like the glossy cover of an admissions brochure. The late October sun was shining on students riding bikes and playing frisbee. Trees shaded a couple who were laughing in between sips of iced coffee, while a portable speaker played a familiar song on repeat. It was a little unnerving to hear the song over and over as she walked, but perhaps that was the point?

It was the day before Halloween.

The music faded as Holland stepped inside the building that housed the Folklore department. Her cork heels softly tapped against the tile as she made her way toward the stairs. Holland had always loved the sound. But every time she wore high heels, she remembered why she never liked to wear them.

Unfortunately, the cork heels were the closest thing she had to anything professional. The Coffee Lab didn't have a dress code, so Holland usually just wore flowy skirts until the weather got too cold. She was wearing one now, a knee-length white one, paired with a pale pink cropped blouse that barely skimmed the waist of her skirt. A leather messenger bag hung from her shoulder. January had bought it for her the first time she'd gone to Italy for work, and Holland took it everywhere.

The sound of Holland's heels disappeared as she reached the second floor, which was covered in unfortunate green carpet that didn't allow for clicking. The hallway was decorated with a few plastic pumpkins and lined with closed doors bearing dull bronze name plaques.

Adam Bishop's door was at the far end, and it was already cracked.

"Hello!" Holland knocked. The door stretched open wider, welcoming her into an empty office. The air conditioner must have been broken, because it was warmer here than it was outside. It felt like a summer day that had been left behind.

There were no Halloween decorations in here. There wasn't much of anything. The walls were white and bare, save for a trio of diplomas from very posh and impressive schools.

"Either this new professor hasn't finished unpacking, or all he wants people to know about him are the overpriced schools he attended," muttered Holland.

"I was just thinking the same thing," said a soft voice from behind her.

Holland spun around.

In the doorway stood another grad student, in ripped jeans and a plaid shirt. He looked about her age—and, for lack of a better word, he was *hot*. Unfairly hot. Even for LA standards, where everyone was some level of attractive. He must have been from a different department, because she definitely would have remembered seeing him before. He had tousled golden hair, tan skin, and nice arms—the kind of arms that said he worked out, he cared, but not too much.

Not that she should have been looking at his arms.

But he appeared to be checking her out as well. His eyes were on the necklace dangling just above the neckline of her top. She started to follow his gaze, but then she stopped herself.

Holland was dating Jake. Although, even as she thought it, their brief relationship already felt as if it had ended a long time ago. She remembered him the way she remembered the people she'd met when she'd first moved back to LA, the ones who had only spent a few chapters in her life.

"So which one do you think it is?" the grad student asked, motioning toward the black lacquered frames.

Holland's gut said that only hanging these diplomas was an intentional choice. But she felt the stupid urge to impress this guy, so she opted for the kinder response. "I'm going to guess Professor Bishop hasn't finished unpacking."

"Then you'd be wrong. He's a pretentious bastard." The grad student said it like a statement, not a guess.

Holland was surprised. So far she'd only heard positive things about Professor Adam Bishop. "Why don't you like him?"

"I didn't say I don't like him."

"You called him a pretentious asshole."

The grad student quirked a brow. "I actually think I called him a bastard."

"No, you—" She swore he'd said the word *asshole*, but now as she replayed the last few seconds, she heard him saying, *You'd be wrong. He's a pretentious bastard. Bastard. Bastard. Asshole. Bastard. Asshole.* The words skipped through her head like a broken track of music. Until she felt something that wasn't in her head.

Drip.

Drip.

Drip.

Holland lifted her fingers to catch the blood falling from her nose. Red drops landed on her palm before staining her white skirt.

"Here, use this—" The grad student pulled a red handkerchief from his back pocket. Because of course he would have a handkerchief. It was perfectly normal to have a handkerchief—*sixty years ago.*

Holland might have thought the handkerchief was part of his Halloween costume. But Halloween wasn't until tomorrow, and the rest of him appeared normal.

"Who are you?" she asked.

He flashed an absolutely perfect grin. "I'm Adam Bishop."

Holland laughed. "Oh really." She had a quick thought that being hot and funny was a fantastic combination. But he wasn't smiling. Instead, he was nodding, unnervingly serious. And she felt a sudden, painful flash of embarrassment.

"Maybe you should take a seat," he said. And now he sounded serious, too. There were no more smiles or grins, and she felt ridiculous for thinking he'd maybe been flirting with her. Except . . .

This was not how she had pictured Adam Bishop. Ripped jeans, plaid shirt, sexy smirk. Strike that. He was a professor. He didn't have a sexy smirk. Except he absolutely did, even if he was no longer wearing it.

She tried not to stare at his mouth. But then she made the mistake of looking up, at the dash of freckles across the bridge of his nose. And then there were his eyes. Hazel, with lots of green, flecks of gold, and a dark circle of blue, and she was definitely staring now.

"I really think you should take a seat," he said. "You're looking a little flushed."

"I'm not flushed. Just surprised." But she was definitely flushed. She could feel it, and she knew he could see it.

He shoved his hands in his pockets. A gesture clearly meant to show he was closing himself off to her because she'd definitely misread the situation. Then he took an intentional step back toward the desk. "Let's start over. I'm Adam and I asked to meet because I'm going to be your new thesis adviser."

"I'm sorry. What?" she blurted.

"I'm going to be your new thesis adviser," he repeated.

"But I already have an adviser."

"That's why I said I was going to be your *new* one."

"You can't be."

"Why?" he asked innocently, but then she saw it again. A new smirk that briefly seemed to ask, *Is this because you find me attractive?*

"I think there's been a mistake," she managed calmly. "Professor Kim has been my adviser since I started the program."

Adam frowned at the mention of the Professor. "That's why I asked you to come here in person. I've been told the two of you were close."

"What do you mean *were*?" Holland asked nervously. "Did something happen to her?"

Holland thought back to the last time she'd seen the Professor. It was near the beginning of the month. Holland remembered the Professor being unusually excited that it was finally October. She hadn't seen her in person since then, but earlier that day she'd received a package from her.

"Far as I know she's fine," Adam said.

"Then why are you replacing her?"

"You really have no idea?" He suddenly looked sorry for Holland, and for a second he didn't say anything, as if he wasn't sure how to phrase whatever he needed to say next.

"Has the Professor been fired?" Holland asked.

"No," he said carefully. "I'm not at liberty to say anything else about it, but she can't be your adviser anymore."

"Wait—why?" Holland interrupted. "The Professor is one of the most beloved faculty members in this department."

"But her classes are full of lies," Adam cut in.

Holland flinched at the sudden sharpness in his tone.

"I'm sorry to say this," he said more softly. "I know you look up to her, but you really shouldn't. That woman is a liar and a fraud."

He said something else along the lines of not being allowed to answer any more questions on the subject, but Holland was having a difficult time focusing. She needed to get a hold of the Professor and find out exactly what was going on.

Holland knew there were some faculty members who didn't take the Professor seriously. But most of those people considered her classes harmless fun. And they didn't usually call her a liar.

"Well, thank you for this information. It was nice to meet you," she lied.

"Wait," Adam said. "We still need to talk about your thesis."

"I'm good." Holland was already backing away. If she stayed, she was either going to get into a fight with him or burst into tears, neither of which she wanted to do.

"This isn't an optional conversation," he said. He reached behind him and grabbed a manila folder from the desk. It was blank, save for Holland's name in one corner, written in severe capital letters.

Holland had the sudden impression that she was in trouble now, too. And this time she didn't need to ask why.

Her palms started sweating and her fingers started toying with the chain around her neck as she watched Adam open the folder.

Holland was extremely proud of what she'd written, but her thesis was supposed to be between her and the Professor. She'd shared pieces of it with January, which actually hadn't gone very well, and she had a feeling things wouldn't go much better with Adam Bishop.

After opening the folder, Adam looked inside for what felt like an eternity, then finally said, "What you've written is good."

"Really?" Holland asked, relieved.

"You're an excellent writer," he said sincerely. "The Professor's notes mention that you were briefly a Storytelling major in your undergrad, and it shows. You pulled me in right away with your version of Natalia West's death. The way you connected her rapid rise to fame in the 1950s with her mysterious death was smart, and you did a clever job of drawing parallels between the strange details of her death and those of other celebrities who died under tragic or unexplainable circumstances."

Adam flipped through a few more pages. Holland tried not to grin. She was still upset by everything he'd said about the Professor. But she also couldn't help thinking that maybe there was more nuance to Adam Bishop than she had given him credit for. He seemed to really understand what she was doing. And he'd called her smart.

"Unfortunately"—Adam shut the folder and looked up at Holland with eyes that had lost their smile—"you can't use any of this."

"But—wait—" she stammered. "You just said it was good."

"It is. Your theory that some of the most famous deaths in Hollywood were actually murders committed by the devil is extremely entertaining, for fiction."

The word *fiction* hit her like a slap. For the second time since meeting Adam, she could feel her cheeks turning red. She wasn't sure if he was doing it on purpose or if he was just a jerk, but she felt like he kept tricking her.

"You've been in this department since undergrad, so I don't think I need to explain what we do here. I just need you to come up with a new topic."

"What if I can prove I haven't made any of this up?" Holland asked.

Adam looked at her as if this was not what he'd expected her to say. For a second, she swore he looked impressed, but, like his enigmatic smirk, the expression was there and then gone. "You want to prove the devil is real?"

"Yes." Holland felt a terrified thrill as she said it. It was the same way she felt whenever she worked on her thesis. It was a dark topic—delving into old Hollywood deaths and connecting them to deals with the devil that were never paid back. Holland struggled mentally with researching it for extended stretches of time, which is why she was behind. If not for all the Professor's encouragement, and for the fact that this topic meant so much to Holland personally, she would have given up on it.

"I get it," Adam finally said. "The Professor is very convincing. But I think chasing after any of her stories is a dangerous idea. So, no. I'm not giving you the chance to prove the devil exists. I need you to submit a new potential topic to me by next Wednesday."

"That's not enough time," Holland protested.

"That's why I've already come up with a suggestion for you." Adam gallantly pulled a page from the folder and held it out to Holland.

"No thank you," she said, refusing to even touch the paper.

Shock flitted across Adam's handsome face, as if, once again, her response was not what he'd anticipated. "Take it just in case," he insisted.

"I don't want your help," she said. And she didn't need it. Holland didn't care what he'd just said. The Professor wasn't a liar. Holland wasn't naive and she was going to prove it, for her mentor and for her parents.

As soon as she left Adam Bishop's office, Holland pulled out her phone and called the Professor.

"Hello, you have reached the voicemail of M. Madeleine Kim. I am not in the habit of returning calls, I prefer meetings in person. If you truly wish to reach me, I can be found during my office hours, or I can be reached via physical correspondence sent to my house—if you are lucky enough to have the address. You may also send letters, telegrams, or packages to my office." Her final word was punctuated with a long slow beep.

Holland hung up and sent her a text.

During the three years Holland had known the Professor, she had never replied to a text, and truthfully she was terrible at answering her phone.

That's when Holland remembered the business card from Manuel Vargas. She pulled it out from her messenger bag. The emerald ink shimmered in the low hall light.

Earlier, Holland had convinced herself it was all a scam. But what if it wasn't?

In Holland's mind, the Professor's Folklore 517 stories were all connected. She always imagined they lived in a world together, similar to that of the Brothers Grimm fairytales. If she was right, then it could make sense that finding the Watch Man didn't unlock a door just to him, but to the Professor's entire world of myths and legends.

Holland dialed the phone number on the card.

"Good afternoon, thank you for calling the First Bank of Centennial City," chirped an automated voice. "If you know your party's extension, please say it out loud or enter it now using your keypad or rotary phone.

If you do not know your party's extension, please say the last five digits of your account number."

The voice continued to list selections that didn't apply to Holland, until finally she was given the option of leaving a message.

"Hello, my name is Holland, and I'd like to make an appointment tomorrow, with Mr. Manuel Vargas," she said. "I just found out that there is a safety deposit box in your bank that was willed to me, and I would like to open it."

Folklore 517:
Hollywood Forever Cemetery

t's supposed to be a perfect day, sunny with a light breeze, but you don't feel the breeze, just the sun, as you reach the towering iron gates of the Hollywood Forever Cemetery. It's pretty beyond them: green grass, tall trees, stained glass, and marble buildings.

It feels more like a movie set than a cemetery. In fact, you think they might be filming something to the right. You see a series of black pop-up tents, a few golf carts, and a number of people strutting around importantly, much like the many peacocks that call this place home. You avoid them—the people and the peacocks—choosing to walk straight down the middle of the cemetery.

The back of your neck is sweating. You always thought graveyards were cold, but this one is hot, all sunshine and palm trees. And yet you have the prickly sense you're being watched.

A dried palm frond drops to the ground behind you and you turn. That's when you notice the view. The center path you're on is lined in dark graves and spindly palm trees; they point straight toward the hills in the distance, where the famed *HOLLYWOOD* sign looks down on the dead.

It's a great view of the iconic sign, but you don't linger. You're running late for class.

Everyone else must have already found the right grave because you don't see any other students. To your left, your eye snags on a tombstone with an unexpectedly familiar phrase. Above the name *Mel Blanc* are his famous words *"THAT'S ALL FOLKS."* The phrase always seemed cheerful to you in cartoons, but now it feels sad. The sorrow stays with you as you make your way toward the mausoleum in the back.

Finally, you see a dozen other classmates just beyond the entrance. Each week there are fewer students. Week by week the classes have gotten more difficult to find, as the Professor's clues have become more complicated. You feel proud of yourself for piecing together the clues and making it here.

The mausoleum doors are already open, but you notice there are heavy chains for when they're closed. One of your classmates rattles the chains as you walk past. You say you don't believe in ghosts, yet you can't help briefly wondering if the chains are there to keep people out or to lock the spirits in.

The first thing you see inside is a dusty piano. Though you probably shouldn't, you can't resist tapping a yellowed key. It's soundless. Dead, like all the people laid to rest here.

To your right and to your left are halls of marble squares with bronze name plaques and matching vase sconces on both sides. Most of the vases are empty, but you pause at one that holds fresh gerbera daisies, with a number of lipstick kisses lining the marble around it.

It's the grave of Benjamin "Bugsy" Siegel.

This isn't the Benjamin you're looking for, but you're not the only one of your classmates who takes note of the famous gangster. One of them leaves a penny at the grave, while another adds to the collection of lipstick kisses.

You move on toward the back.

There's a large fan embedded in the wall, but it slows to an unfortunate stop as you reach the end and find the names you're looking for: Isla Saint and Benjamin James Tierney.

The graves are side by side. Isla doesn't have any vases or an epitaph, but Benjamin does.

Loving Father, brilliant mind, gone too soon.

You're familiar with his story, so you don't expect to feel choked up, but you do.

"Usually, I take students to the hotel where Isla and Ben both died, but those ghosts are not as friendly." The Professor sighs loudly, as you turn to see her now sitting on the dusty piano bench.

She's dressed in heavy black; she even has a hat with a little net veil. At first you think it's theatrical, but then you wonder if maybe she knew Isla Saint and Benjamin J. Tierney. They died more recently than most of the cemetery's inhabitants—almost fifteen years ago—and they are far more famous as well.

The Professor gives you all a minute to come closer before she continues.

Benjamin J. Tierney and Isla Saint were once *the* Hollywood royals. Their fame and their love story began in 1996, when twenty-five-year-old Tierney's time-bending masterpiece, *Mirrorland*, which starred Saint, became the top-grossing film of the year. It outsold the second-highest-grossing film of that year, *Independence Day*, by over $250 million.

You know this because you read the Wonderpage before coming to class—and you've seen the movies.

During the filming of the *Mirrorland* sequel, *Puppet Kingdom*, Tierney and Saint cemented their fame by leaving their significant others (Victoria Monroe and Sebastian Friday) and eloping halfway through production. It was all anyone talked about, until *Puppet Kingdom* was released in late 1997 and became an even greater success than its predecessor. In 1999, the third film in the trilogy, *Lostland*, broke every box office record and spawned a universe of spinoffs. Although, in your opinion, none of the spinoffs are as good.

Benjamin J. Tierney was a genius. There has never been another like him.

After the original Mirrorland films, he signed on to write and direct another trilogy for Jericho Monroe Entertainment. The first two films, *Price of Magic* and *Symphony of Death*, were financially on par with the Mirrorland films. However, the productions were so fraught with misfortune, many believed the franchise was cursed. There were fires on set, multiple car accidents involving cast and crew members, several reports of amnesia, and one day, during outdoor filming, an entire flock of doves died midflight and fell from the sky.

The third film, which was supposed to be released in early 2007, was initially delayed for a year. Tierney said he needed more time to research the script and finish writing, but no one has ever seen a single page. It has long been suspected that Tierney's true reason for the delay was that he believed the Price of Magic trilogy was cursed, and he was afraid to finish it.

Around this time, Saint, who had taken a break from acting to spend time with her and Benjamin's twin daughters, made her grand return to Hollywood by starring in the gritty 2010 drama *Conclavity*. This film earned Isla Saint her first Academy Award. It's said she cried during her entire acceptance speech.

You tried to find the speech online, but there are no recordings of it. When you looked for it, you found videos of everyone else who won an Oscar. But all that came up for Isla Saint were articles about how, that same night—February 27, 2011—she murdered her husband.

Even before reading the Wonderpage, you knew this. You might have just been a toddler when it happened, but everyone knows how their love story ended.

"The official crime report says that Isla shot Benjamin with a gun just like this," says the Professor as she stands, opens the lid of the piano, and pulls out a dull black revolver. "Don't worry, this weapon is merely a prop." She smiles her Mona Lisa smile, and you're not sure you believe her. "Isla shot her husband twice—once in the heart and once in the head—before turning the gun on herself." The Professor points the gun at her head, making you flinch. "The tabloids said it was all because of another woman. A young unknown actress named Jessica Travers, who Benjamin was having an affair with. Of course, Jessica never confirmed these rumors because she died by suicide the same night."

There's a click. The Professor has pulled the trigger.

Your heart stutters and stops before starting again.

The gun is just a prop after all. The Professor's head is intact, or at least it looks that way on the outside.

"Don't worry, my dears. I have no wish to die, and I don't think that Isla Saint did, either." The Professor sets her gun on the bench. "How many of you have heard the Hollywood Rule of Three—that if one celebrity dies, two are certain to follow? I'm not sure when it began, but I can tell you it's a lie. All three of these deaths are part of a cover-up, a bit of misdirection, to hide the real reason Isla and Ben were killed."

The Professor lowers her voice to a whisper that makes all of you move closer. "By now, I'm sure many of you have tried to find the devil at a hotel bar, and I probably should have said this before: Be very careful. Hollywood was not built on dreams, it was built on favors from the devil, and the devil does not handle it well when those favors aren't paid back."

CHAPTER FOUR

Visiting the Hollywood Roosevelt always made Holland feel as if she was stepping back into the 1920s. She didn't know if it was the ocher light, the tawny Spanish tiles, the potted palm trees, the etched champagne coupes, or something else entirely. If maybe *time* was more alive than anyone realized, and a piece of it was trapped inside the lobby of the Hollywood Roosevelt.

Her love affair with the Roosevelt began the year she took Folklore 517. There had been a small group of students who had decided they would visit every hotel bar in Los Angeles in an attempt to buy the devil a drink. They went to three hotels before they tried the Roosevelt.

Holland had fallen a little in love with the iconic building even before she'd visited, when she'd read up on its history. The Roosevelt was built in 1927. Its architecture was Spanish colonial revival. Its ballroom had hosted the first-ever Academy Awards. There was an old-timey gaming parlor with a bowling alley. And it was rumored to be the home of a number of ghosts. A man in a white tuxedo was said to haunt the mezzanine level. And Marilyn Monroe—who lived in the hotel for two years—supposedly appeared from time to time.

Holland believed this had to be the place the devil would frequent, if the devil actually existed.

Her friends weren't immediately convinced. After their first trip to the Roosevelt, they'd wanted to visit other hotels, ones with trendy rooftop bars and outlandish cocktails that came with batteries on the side. But eventually they'd realized what Holland had known right away: The Roosevelt was special—and it didn't need electric cocktails to prove it.

Now they met in the Roosevelt lobby on the final Thursday of each month.

Over the last few years, Holland's friends had all bought drinks for various men and women who they thought might be the devil—or who they had just wanted to flirt with. Holland was the only one who had never bought anyone a sidecar. She planned to only buy one once, and when she did, she wanted to be certain.

Every month, she arrived at the Roosevelt a little early in case she finally saw him. Tonight, she was earlier than usual. And, after her meeting with Adam, she was in the mood to buy a stranger a drink. She wanted to prove that her faith in the Professor wasn't misplaced, and more than ever, she wanted to prove the stories about the devil were real.

If she could prove the devil made deals with people that led to their deaths, then she could prove her mother had never murdered her father. She could rewrite their story, change the ending. She could turn Isla Saint from Hollywood villain back to leading lady. And maybe Holland could save someone else from making the same mistake as her parents and countless others.

Holland couldn't be absolutely certain as to which former stars had made deals with the devil and then failed to pay him back. But she had very strong ideas about it. While working on her thesis, Holland had been unsettled to discover that there seemed to be a similar tragic pattern to a number of Hollywood deaths: awards, fame, the kind of success that made people rich and powerful and adored, until it all came crashing down in a devastating turn of mysterious events no one could ever fully explain.

Holland felt a familiar stab of sadness as she grabbed the first open table she could find. It was covered in flyers for tomorrow's Halloween party and was right next to the fireplace. It was far too hot a day to sit

next to a fire, but half of the lobby was closed off with covered-up instal-
lations for the party, and the rest of it was already buzzing with people.

The music of clinking glasses mingled with tipsy laughter that
floated up toward the mezzanine. Usually, the sound made her think of
rising champagne bubbles, and Holland would try to picture how the
Roosevelt must have looked once upon a time, full of gentlemen in hats
and ladies in gloves with rows of iridescent pearl buttons.

Tonight, though, she wasn't feeling the magic of the Roosevelt the
way she usually did. As she sat in the lobby, she felt antsy, unsettled. Her
heart was racing as if it knew something she didn't.

Holland checked her phone to see if the Professor had returned her
call.

No new notifications. Not from the Professor and not from Jake.
Although by now Holland had given up on hearing from Jake.

She shoved her phone back into her messenger bag and tried to take
a proper look around to see if anyone resembling the devil had arrived.

She had been raised by her Aunt Beth, who believed in God and Je-
sus, and usually Holland did, too. She wasn't a biblical expert, but she'd
looked into the name *Lucifer*. Bringer of light. That's what the name
meant, which made Holland think the devil would look golden. Skin
that ranged from tan to bronze. Hair that could be either gold or blond.
Light eyes—she wasn't certain of the color, but she knew they would be
beautiful.

Suddenly she had a picture of Adam Bishop, smirking at her over a
cocktail glass.

She tried to shake it from her head. Adam wasn't that hot, except . . .
he really was. He had that lean tall build, the kind that made her think
he'd look young and healthy forever. If she'd first met him at the Roosevelt, she would have considered buying him a drink.

Although Holland was convinced the devil would wear a suit. He
wouldn't look like a grad student. And he definitely wouldn't be a tourist, which the lobby was full of that night. There were lots of people

taking pictures of their drinks and themselves—something the devil would never do.

Her eyes drifted up toward the mezzanine level. The area was empty. There was nothing to see that she hadn't seen before, but her skin felt suddenly hot. Her unsettled feeling was back with a vengeance. Sweat beaded on the back of her neck.

"Hey you!"

Holland turned to find her friend Cat, sauntering toward the table, all long dark legs and long black braids swishing behind her.

Holland's anxious feeling dissipated at the sight of her dear friend's smile.

"How was your date last night?" Cat asked excitedly, because Cat pursued love the same way Holland chased after myths and legends.

For Cat—whose full name was Charlotte Elizabeth Davis—searching for the devil had always been purely an excuse to buy cute strangers drinks. During undergrad, she had taken Folklore 517 because of her girlfriend at the time. Holland didn't think that Cat believed in any of the Professor's myths, including the one about the devil. Cat simply believed in love, and in doing whatever it took to find it. And Holland adored her for it.

"I think I'm destined to be a spinster," Holland said, joking but also a little bit serious. "I've decided my new goal is to get over my cat allergy, since I don't think there are going to be any men in my future. Or maybe I'm just not meant to date nice, normal guys."

Cat's eyes immediately filled with pity and a flare of anger because Cat was the sort of friend who couldn't imagine anything being wrong with Holland.

"*Nice* and *normal* are both such boring words," Cat said heatedly, full of that wonderful good-friend righteous fury. "I'm not sure why you're trying so hard to make that your type."

"It is my type. I'm nice."

"Yes, you're an absolute sweetheart. But—" Cat's expression softened. "*Nice* just isn't the first word I'd use to describe you. You are so much *more* than nice. You're like a sunbeam with all your boho skirts and your smiles and your long blond hair and your corny jokes. But you don't have a soft sweet center. The first time I met you, the way you believed in the Professor's myths made me wonder if you were a little insane."

Holland's eyebrows shot up.

"Only for a second!" Cat clarified. "Then I immediately wanted to be your friend."

But all Holland could think was that this was her problem: her endless chasing after the Professor's myths and legends. It was what had botched things up last night. It was what always did, because she wanted to chase them more than she wanted anything else.

"Hey, please don't feel bad," Cat said. "You know I think you're amazing. The way you see the world is so different and surprising, and it makes you a far more interesting person. I just wonder . . ." Cat paused and pursed her scarlet lips, as if she thought she should stop there.

"It's all right," Holland said. "I probably need to hear this."

Cat reached out and put a hand over Holland's. "I feel like you're going after the wrong type of guy. I don't think you actually want someone safe and *nice*. I think you want someone who scares you a little, like the Professor's myths. And I think you *need* someone who won't make you feel as if you have to hide those dark and twisty parts of you."

And this was the other reason Holland loved Cat. Even though Holland kept secrets from her friend, Cat could still see so much of what was going on inside of her.

For a second, Holland wondered what it would be like if she told Cat the reason why. If she spilled her guts about her parents, if she confessed her real last name and told Cat the actual reason she'd taken the Professor's class.

She imagined Cat would hold her in the world's tightest hug and then make it her new crusade to find the devil as well. Holland could almost hear Cat yelling, "I'm buying everyone in here a sidecar!"

And for a moment, the ever-present ache inside of Holland would vanish. For a moment she'd feel like she might not spend the rest of her life alone, haunted by questions she couldn't quite answer.

But one of the great joys of Cat was also one of the reasons Holland could never tell her. Cat didn't have any secrets, which made her tragically bad at keeping other people's. And this wasn't just Holland's secret. It was January's, too.

"I love that you see me this way," Holland said. "But I really don't want to be scared."

Cat raised a disbelieving brow. "Then why do you get here early every week to look for the devil?"

"I'm the only one who's never bought him a drink."

"Let's change that tonight!" Cat declared.

Just then a burst of giggles erupted from a table at the other end of the lobby. Holland and Cat both turned their heads. Chance Garcia had arrived.

Yes—*that* Chance Garcia.

Chance, of course, already had a drink in his hand. Servers always brought Chance drinks almost as soon as he entered the lobby.

Chance had never explicitly stated why he'd taken Folklore 517, but Holland always imagined it had something to do with *The Magic Attic*. Not that Chance ever talked about *The Magic Attic*. It was the one subject he never touched.

But he was always kind and generous to any fans who recognized him from the show. And, even after all these years, he was still easily recognizable. More so now that he was making an unexpected return to acting in the newest Vic VanVleet film, which was premiering on Thanksgiving.

The giggling girls had clearly been excited to spot him, and now they were all taking pictures near a potted palm tree.

"I don't know how he deals with it," Eileen huffed, as she took a seat at the table.

Holland hadn't even seen her enter, but suddenly Eileen was there, dressed as if she'd come straight from work, in a pair of tailored slacks and a smart, long-sleeve cream blouse, with a navy ribbon threaded under her collar and tied into a neat bow.

During undergrad, Eileen Cheng had been a business major, and she'd taken Folklore 517 to round out her educational experience. Now, she was an overworked personal assistant for someone she refused to name. Cat and Holland both imagined Eileen's employer was a celebrity, but an NDA prevented Eileen from revealing which one.

Every week, Cat tried to guess who Eileen worked for—she believed NDAs should really be FrienDAs. But Eileen was a vault. She was the friend whom everyone agreed they would call if they ever needed to hide a dead body. In fact, her name was in Holland's phone under the words In Case of Lethal Emergency.

"How do you always do that?" Cat asked. "You just appear like magic."

"Magic is mostly misdirection," Eileen said coolly. "Both of you were busy staring at Chance and his newest fan club."

"Should we rescue him?" Holland asked.

Cat and Eileen both made a show of checking out the giggling girls to see if any were pretty. Chance had repeatedly told them never to rescue him if the fans were pretty.

Chance really was a solid friend. He was the guy to call if you wanted to go out for drinks at a new bar, go for a jog along the beach, or move furniture that was too heavy. But he could be a little shallow.

"I think we should leave him tonight," Cat said. "He seems to be smiling at the blonde who looks a little like you, Holland."

Holland wrinkled her nose. "I don't think she looks like me."

"I agree." Eileen took a second to eye the blonde. "She looks like the sort of person who has never had anything bad happen to her." Eileen's eyes narrowed. "I would bet she only buys books to use as props in photos, and her version of news is celebrity gossip."

"I enjoy celebrity gossip," said Cat.

Holland's phone chimed. She glanced down quickly, hoping the Professor or Jake had finally texted (because despite what she kept telling herself, she hadn't completely given up hope that there would be more than cats in her future).

Still nothing from either of them.

Instead, she had a missed call from a number that came up as FIRST BANK OF CENTENNIAL CITY.

Holland's skin went cold.

The bank had left a voice message. But all her phone said was Unable to transcribe.

"What's wrong?" Eileen asked.

"I'm sorry, guys. There's a message I just need to check—" Holland quickly shoved up from her seat. "I'll be right back."

The lobby was too loud. Holland made her way up to the mezzanine, where the sound of the crowd below was dimmed enough that she could hear her footsteps on the old Spanish tile.

She tried not to pace, but Holland couldn't help it as she hit *Play* on the message.

"Good evening. I'm Padme Davani, assistant to the Manager of the First Bank of Centennial City. I'm calling to inform you that I've been able to secure you a fifteen-minute slot on the calendar tomorrow at 9:45 a.m. As I believe this is your first appointment at the Bank, I suggest you arrive five minutes early, and do not be late or you may not have enough time to open up your father's box."

Folklore 517:
the Bank

t's the morning. You wake up, bleary-eyed and hangover-lethargic, although you don't recall drinking. You rub your eyes as the walls stop spinning.

Now you remember, you had class last night, or you think you had class. Trying to play it all back is like attempting to hold on to a vanishing dream.

You can hear the Professor's raspy voice, but you can't remember anything she said. And you don't remember leaving.

You text a friend.

Hey! Were you in class last night?

Dots appear as your friend begins to type. They stop. Then they start again.

The dots follow this pattern several times until, finally, three words appear:

I don't remember

You open your notebook, the one you take to class every week. There are scribbled notes from the week before. But after that there's . . . nothing.

You're about to close the book when you see it. It looks like erased pencil marks—more of an impression than actual writing, but you make out a string of lines that give you the impression of a story you tried to erase.

THE BANK.

Impenetrable.

Most secure vaults in the world.

No one has ever stolen from it. No one ever dares break into it.

By appointment only.

CHAPTER FIVE

t was real.

Holland had been afraid to get her hopes up. But she hadn't mentioned her father when she'd left her message, she'd just said she'd been left a box.

She could practically hear her father's voice now, telling her, *Good job, Hollybells, keep following the clues.* Because this felt like a clue.

Holland wondered what her father could have left her. She hoped it was maybe the start of another treasure hunt. But even if it wasn't, she'd be happy to have anything from her dad.

Holland needed to call her sister. She knew it was past midnight in Spain, and Mr. Vargas had warned her not to tell anyone about the box. But everyone knew the rules were that if you had a secret, you got to tell your person, and January was Holland's person.

She pressed her sister's name, but the call went straight to her all-too-familiar voicemail.

"Hey JJ, it's me. Something has happened. I was just contacted by a bank. I think Dad left us something in a—"

Her phone rang halfway through the message. Jake's name flashed across the screen. *Finally.* Holland wanted to answer. But this was the worst possible time. She sent Jake to voicemail with a text that said Can I call you later?

No, he replied immediately. The Watch Man called.

Her heart skipped a beat.

Jake called again. This time, Holland answered on the first ring.

"Tell me this is all a joke," Jake demanded, before she could even say hello.

"What ha—"

"He called," Jake cut in. "The Watch Man. He—" Jake stammered and swallowed loudly enough for Holland to hear through the phone. "He told me that I would die tonight. Unless—" Jake broke off. For a second, all Holland could hear was a ragged sound that might have been a sob.

Holland wanted to tell him it was going to be okay, that it couldn't be real. But the message she'd just received from the bank made her feel that the Professor's stories were more real than ever.

Then she thought about Adam Bishop. She heard his voice saying, *I know you look up to her, but you really shouldn't. That woman is a liar and a fraud.* And suddenly Holland hoped he was right.

It physically hurt to imagine being so wrong about the Professor, to think that the Watch Man was a scam, which would mean the bank was definitely a scam as well, and there was no box from her father.

But if the Professor was everything Holland believed, then that meant Jake was going to die.

"What did the Watch Man tell you?" Holland asked.

"He said that I would die at 6:47 p.m. unless—" Jake cut off again. Then, so soft she almost didn't hear it over the laughter and the footsteps and the tourists talking too loudly in the lobby below: "I can't do what he says, Holland."

"What does he want you to do?"

"I don't want to say. I just—I don't want to be alone right now. Can you come over?"

"I . . ." Holland trailed off. Something in Jake's voice made her nervous. But what kind of person said no to someone's dying wish? *No*— she corrected herself. Jake wasn't going to die tonight. Only, Holland wasn't sure she actually believed that.

All she knew was that she'd had a bad feeling since she'd stepped into the Roosevelt, and she wondered if this was why.

"Please," Jake begged softly. "I only filled out that paper last night because I was trying to impress you."

Holland felt a stab of guilt. He was right about this basically being her fault, and if the situation was reversed, she wouldn't want to be alone, either. "All right," she said. "Just tell me where you are."

Her phone pinged with a text showing an apartment complex address that was ten minutes away. "Hurry," Jake said. "If this guy is right, I only have about an hour left."

Holland jogged down the stairs back to the lobby. She might have gone without saying a proper goodbye, but she'd left her messenger bag at the table, and she knew her friends would worry if she just abandoned them.

"Please tell me you bought that man a drink before running away like Cinderella," said Cat as soon as Holland approached.

"What are you talking about?" Holland asked.

Cat slyly inclined her head toward the mezzanine.

When Holland had been upstairs, the mezzanine level had been empty. But someone was there now. Standing in the grainy hotel light, leaning against the low wall, was a man in a white dinner jacket with an undone bow tie hanging around his neck.

Holland knew the stories about the different spirits who haunted the hotel, including a man in a white tuxedo. But the man she saw now wasn't wearing a full-on tux. He also looked real, and just like Adam Bishop.

Something like ice crept up her spine. What the hell was going on? Had Adam followed her? But on second glance, it was clear he wasn't actually Adam. There was definitely a resemblance, but this guy looked a little older, harder, and colder. His skin was a little lighter and his hair was a little darker. He was the looking-glass version of Adam.

Immediately, the stranger turned his head. His eyes locked onto Holland's and the atmosphere charged, as if a bolt of electricity had escaped its bulb and now crackled through the air.

He didn't stare at her the way a stranger might. This look was intimate. As if he knew her, as if he'd known her for a very long time. But Holland would have remembered a face like his.

Cat whistled through her teeth. "If you didn't buy that man a drink, then I will."

"No—" Holland said, although it came out a little like a shout. And for a second, she couldn't say why. Earlier that night all she'd wanted to do was buy a stranger a drink, to prove the devil was real. And this guy definitely seemed as if he could fit the job description.

But for the first time in Holland's life, she didn't feel as if following the clues was a good idea. She thought about Adam's earlier warning: *The Professor is very convincing. But I think chasing after any of her stories is a very dangerous idea.*

If Jake's call wasn't proof of this, Holland didn't know what was.

Both Cat and Eileen stared at her with slightly bewildered expressions. "What's wrong?" they asked at the same time.

"Don't buy him a drink," Holland said.

"Don't buy who a drink?" asked Eileen.

"The white dinner jacket guy on the mezzanine."

Cat's eyes lit up. "What white dinner jacket guy?"

"The one we were just talking about!" Holland turned and pointed, but he was already gone.

Holland felt it then.

Drip.

Drip.

Drip.

Her nose was bleeding. Again.

"Holland, are you all right?" Eileen quickly handed her a napkin.

Holland brought the cloth to her face, dizzy. Although she didn't know if she was dizzy from the blood or because she was seeing and hearing things that no one else was. This was her second nosebleed today. She almost never got them, so she wasn't an expert, but she didn't think they usually came with a side of hallucinations.

"Sweetie, why don't you sit down," said Cat.

"I can't." Holland swiped her nose once more with the napkin. Thankfully it wasn't much blood. She was still feeling wobbly, but she tried to act as if she was fine for her friends. "I hate this, but I actually have to run. I'm so sorry—I love you both."

Her friends both said they loved her too.

"And don't forget about the party tomorrow!" Cat held up one of the flyers on the table for the Hollywood Roosevelt's Halloween Ball. "If you need a costume, I can still hook you up—and I can get one for Clark Kent, too, if he comes to his senses!"

Holland tried to smile at her friend's eternal optimism. Then she spun around and immediately crashed into something solid.

"Whoa, Holly—" Chance put one of his hands on each of her shoulders. "Please tell me you're not running away from me." He flashed his irresistible smile. And Holland knew he wasn't even trying to dazzle her. Chance was one of those very lucky child actors who grew up to be an even more beautiful adult.

"I'd never run from you," Holland said. Normally she would add a teasing line about how she knew he was the one who liked to be chased. But she didn't have it in her tonight.

Chance twisted his mouth. He might not have known her secrets, but he knew her well enough to know when something was wrong. "Is everything all right?"

I don't know, she wanted to say. *I feel like I made a mistake, or like I'm about to make a mistake.* Then she thought again that if there was one person in her life who could possibly understand everything she was feeling and help make sense of what was going on, it would be Chance.

They had met after the class where the Professor had told everyone the myth about the devil and the sidecar. That night, in the parking lot, Holland had been talking to a small group about checking out various hotel bars, and suddenly Chance Garcia was there.

Can I join? he'd asked, and then he'd smiled as if he were just the boy next door—if the boy next door was a former child actor, with a face that had never stopped being cute. He had dimples, big eyes, and a smile made of pure charm.

Holland remembered being skeptical at first.

Sammy Sanchez had been her childhood crush, but this wasn't Sammy Sanchez, she'd told herself. That was just the role Chance had played on television. Chance wasn't an orphan with a heart of gold and undying loyalty to his friends. He was a former child actor with a very dark past. And yet, it was the dark past that had eventually drawn her toward him.

One night, after too many drinks at a hotel bar, after everyone else had left, Chance had confessed that he believed in all the Professor's myths. His smile had vanished, his eyes had lost their spark, and she had seen that the demons that had ruined Chance's childhood still haunted him.

Now Holland was almost tempted to tell him that the guy she was dating thought he was going to die in an hour because the Watch Man had given him a call.

But she feared that if she did tell Chance, he wasn't going to let her leave. Even now, as he looked at the bloody napkin in her hand, she felt him gripping her shoulders tighter. "What happened?"

"Just a nosebleed."

Her phone chimed with a text from Jake: Get here soon.

Chance's eyes cut toward the screen. He dropped one hand from her shoulder, but for a second he kept the other one there.

"Chance, I need to go."

"I know. But—" He squeezed her shoulder, and the last remnants of his dazzling smile disappeared. "Ever since I walked in here tonight, I've had a bad feeling. I don't know what's going on, but do me a favor and just be careful."

CHAPTER SIX

Ten minutes.

Holland was nearly out of time when she arrived at an apartment complex made of Hollywood dreams that hadn't turned into reality, full of actors and musicians masquerading as fitness instructors and baristas.

The sun was on the edge of setting, but the shade from the trees lining the walkway made the complex darker. Lights flickered, blinking in and out before coming to life and coloring her steps an unnatural shade of yellow.

Holland had always been someone who felt certain about what she believed. But all she felt now was scared. Her heart pounded as she climbed the steps to the apartment number Jake had texted.

Ten minutes from now, Jake was either going to be alive—and Holland would know for certain that the Professor's stories were lies—or he was going to be dead—and Holland would regret ever hearing the stories.

She knocked on the door.

Jake opened it immediately.

He looked awful. His eyes were shot with blood, his Clark Kent hair was flat and a little greasy. Behind him, the only light came from a television in the corner. He looked smaller than he did in her memories, dressed in a washed-out red USC shirt that made him look faded as well.

"Do you want to come in?" He smiled, but it wasn't the superhero grin from the night before. Even if it had been, Holland didn't think she'd want to step inside. This version of Jake didn't feel like the guy she'd been dating.

"I think I'm good out here," she said, and she tried to make her voice sound light. The last thing he needed was to think she was feeling uncomfortable. "This way I can stand between you and anyone who wants to hurt you."

"Please." He looked at her with the saddest pair of eyes she'd ever seen.

Holland felt another stab of guilt. Then she felt as shallow as Chance for judging Jake when someone had just told him he was going to die. "Yeah, of course." She took a cautious step inside.

"Wait—don't—" Jake put a hand out as if to stop her. "Don't come in."

"You just asked me to . . ." Holland looked at him questioningly.

He cursed under his breath and ran a nervous hand through his hair. "Holland—I—I think you're a really good person. And I'm sorry. I'm so sorry. I—"

"Jake . . . you're making me nervous."

His bloodshot eyes met hers. "Jake isn't my real name."

"What?" Her heart pounded.

His expression changed from scared to guilty as hell. "I'm so sorry, Holland. They made it sound like a simple job."

So many alarm bells went off in her head. She shouldn't have come here. She had no idea what he was saying, but she knew this was when she needed to leave. She backed away.

"Wait—" He grabbed her arm.

"Let me go or I'll scream."

"Just let me explain," he said quickly. "I know I lied to you—but you're not safe out there."

"Says the guy who won't even tell me his name. Who was hired for—I don't even know what!"

Guilt creased his features once again. "I didn't mean to hurt you. But you're really not safe. Someone wants you dead." He took a deep, ragged breath. "The Watch Man—or whoever called me earlier—told me that was how I could get more time, by killing you tonight."

Holland went cold all over. Then she tore her arm from *Jake* and ran, nearly tripping on her stupid heels.

"Holland!" he called.

She didn't stop.

"Holland, don't—"

She kicked off her heels and ran until she reached the parking lot. But she must have gotten turned around because she couldn't find her car.

With shaking hands, she pulled out her phone. Someone needed to know where she was. January was half a world away; there was nothing she could do but worry.

The next person who came to mind was Chance. If she'd just been honest with him at the hotel, she might not have even come here.

She was an idiot.

Chance answered on the first ring. "Miss me already?"

"I'm so stupid, so so so stupid," she said.

"Whoa—slow down, Holly. What happened?"

"I—I—don't know where to start." Holland could barely speak, but she didn't want to get off the phone as she anxiously turned back toward the complex to find the right parking lot.

Everything looked different. It was darker than when she'd arrived, the patches of sky above her quickly shifting from blue to night.

Someone wants you dead.

Jake's words echoed in her ears as she cautiously retraced her steps, desperate to find her car. She saw the heels she'd kicked off and her heart pounded harder. This was where she'd first run from Jake. Was he hiding in the shadows?

"Where are you?" Chance asked. "I'm going to come get you."

"I have my car," she whispered, "I just—" Her words broke off at the sight of a shadow lying a few feet down the path.

Only it wasn't a shadow, it was a person.

He wasn't moving.

Holland froze, except for her shaking hands. She couldn't make them still, and she couldn't make the rest of her move.

She could see dark hair and a faded red USC T-shirt.

"Jake—"

"Who is Jake?" Chance asked through the phone.

Sprinklers sputtered to life, popping out of the ground next to the path. Water sprayed on ferns that bent under the weight. They sprayed on Jake as well, wetting his hair and dampening his shirt.

Holland inched closer, to see if he was breathing. If his chest was moving up and down, if—

"Oh God, Oh God, Oh God," Holland repeated. But not even God could help Jake now.

CHAPTER SEVEN

Sprinklers had always sounded innocent to her. They made her think of childhood summers, of playing in bright green grass, of running through sprays of water on days when the sunlight took over the whole sky.

Now the sputtering noise sounded staticky, broken.

Chance cursed through the phone and repeated, "What did he do?"

"He didn't do anything," she said. "He's dead."

Holland's vision darkened at the corners until all she could see was the water that continued to soak through Jake's shirt. Or was it blood?

She hadn't heard a gunshot. It must have been a knife. There was definitely blood pouring from his back. She didn't dare get close enough to see a blade. But did it matter? She knew who had done this.

The Watch Man.

Holland numbly pulled her phone from her ear to check the time. 6:53. Six minutes after the time of death that the Watch Man had given Jake.

Quickly, she tried to do the math, to see if it added up. She'd been standing here at least two minutes, and she'd been lost a few minutes before then. Jake must have chased after her, and then he could have died at 6:47. Right after she'd kicked off her heels.

The Watch Man was real.

The Professor's myths were true.

And Holland felt as if she'd fallen into a world of trouble.

She'd been chasing after the Professor's myths with the guileless faith of a child following a breadcrumb trail, so fixated on the clues and the stories that she never paused to think about where they might eventually lead her.

"Holly—are you still there?" Chance yelled through the phone.

"Sorry . . . I'm here . . . I'm here," she repeated. She didn't know what else to say. She could feel her body returning to her, the water running under her bare feet, but parts of her head felt numb, unsure of what to do next.

Should she call the police? Should she try to run from the person who had murdered Jake? His blood was mixing with the water from the sprinklers, seeping to her toes. She didn't feel safe just standing there in the growing puddle, but what if she ran into the killer?

Holland's knuckles turned white as she gripped the phone tighter, thinking that *killer* was such an ugly word. She still couldn't believe someone had murdered Jake.

Why would someone want him dead?

Then she remembered something else Jake had said.

They made it sound like a simple job.

Who were *they*? What was the job? Suddenly Holland had so many questions, and if the police arrived soon, she knew she might never get answers. While researching her thesis, she had been shocked to uncover just how many Hollywood deaths had alternate versions of what could have happened; detective work was imprecise and sometimes full of outright lies.

If she wanted answers about Jake, she was going to have to find them herself.

"Listen to me," Chance said. "If someone is dead, if you think you're in danger, you need to get out of there."

"I have to go back to his apartment," Holland said.

"Do not do that," Chance growled. "Just tell me where you are and wait until I get there."

But Holland couldn't help herself. This was so much more than a rabbit hole. There was a mystery right in front of her. Holland ran up the stairs, bare feet slapping against the cold metal. "I'll stay on the phone."

"Are you out of your mind?"

"Probably," she admitted.

"Don't go in there!"

But it was too late. Jake's door was wide open. She was in.

"Holly, please just get somewhere safe," Chance pleaded. His voice through the phone was the only sound in the apartment.

She frantically scanned the space. Thankfully it was small, but it was dark apart from the muted TV, and it was messy.

"Please get out of there," Chance begged.

"I'm not going to touch anything."

This wasn't really the sort of place where she wanted to touch anything anyway. The living room smelled like a locker room, musty and stale. The carpet was matted underneath her bare feet. Jake was kind of a slob.

No. Not Jake.

Jake didn't exist. This became clearer the longer Holland stood in his chaotic apartment. Take-out wrappers littered his coffee table, along with piles of mail all bearing a different name.

"Axel Jorgenson."

"Who is Axel Jorgenson?" Chance asked.

"It's Jake's real name. It's on all his mail."

"Why are you going through his mail? You need to get out of there!"

"I just . . ."

Holland trailed off at the sight of a glossy black folder tucked under an In-N-Out wrapper covering a half-eaten burger. Unlike the rest of the apartment, the folder was pristine, and it appeared to have a shimmering gold art deco border.

Just like the devil's business card.

This couldn't be a coincidence. Holland wasn't sure what it meant, but it made her think Jake might somehow be connected to the world of the Professor's stories, only now the thought did not excite her.

Numbly, she picked up the glossy folder. It was thin. There didn't seem to be a lot of pages inside. She wanted to open it right away. But she didn't need Chance yelling at her through the phone to know that hanging out in a dead guy's apartment was a bad idea. Holland darted back down the stairs.

Jake was still motionless on the ground. Her steps faltered at the sight of him. She supposed some of the initial shock was wearing off and all this was becoming very real.

"Holland, are you still there?" Chance asked. But his voice sounded far away, and she was feeling far away as well.

Earlier, she'd felt pure terror, but now as she stood beside Jake, she felt grief slipping in. She knew his name was really Axel, but she didn't have the bandwidth to process the change. In this moment, he was still Jake. And she could still remember what it felt like to kiss him, how sweet he'd been on their first date, how much hope he'd made her feel when he'd put his arm around her, and maybe none of that was real—maybe it had only been a job to him—but he'd still been a real person. He didn't deserve this.

Holland really needed to call the police. She needed to dial 911, or scream for help, or do any of the things people did when they found someone dead.

"Chance, I have to go."

"Holland, don't ha—"

She ended the call.

She had every intention of dialing 911. But her eyes went to the glossy black folder clutched in her hands.

She had read enough about crimes and murders to know that when the police showed up, they'd take everything she had. They definitely would take this folder, and depending on what information the folder contained, they might take her away as well.

She couldn't call the police until she found out what was inside of it.

The sunlight was fading, covering the complex in old VHS colors, but it was still light enough to clearly see the folder's contents as Holland pulled it open.

CHAPTER EIGHT

Holland half expected a black business card to fall out of the folder, but there was just a small pile of pages, held together by a shiny gold paper clip. *We're civilized criminals*, it seemed to say, as she flipped past the first blank page and found a photograph of herself.

Holland already had the impression that Jake's job had something to do with her, but it was still alarming to see the photo. It was a candid. Her blond hair was blowing across her face as she looked off into the distance. Someone had clearly taken it when she wasn't watching, and it appeared to be recent.

The next page was even more disturbing, full of all sorts of information about her. Date of birth, where she went to school, how much she loved movies and what her favorites were, where she liked to shop for groceries, how often she ate out, her usual jogging route, how she drank her coffee.

A part of Holland regretted opening the folder—this didn't feel like a clue to follow, this felt like something to run from—but she couldn't stop turning the pages. The formatting shifted on the next page, which wasn't about her at all.

Role: Jacob Smith (Jake for short)
Jacob Smith is a graduate student studying to teach ESL. He tutors kids after school, he doesn't eat meat, he rides his bike everywhere.

He cares about the world and about others. He's someone whom Holland St. James will believe she can trust.

Objective: Enter into a dating relationship with Holland St. James and find out everything you can about her and her family.

Her family.

Jake was an actor—it wasn't just his name that was lie, the person she'd been dating wasn't real, he'd tricked her, used her—all to find out information about her family. Which meant it was very likely someone in Los Angeles knew who Holland really was.

Holland wondered who? How? She had changed her name almost fifteen years ago, long before she'd moved back here.

Her head spinning, she took in the glossy black folder with the art deco border, and once more she thought about the devil's business card. Was it possible *he* had hired Jake?

Her phone rang again.

Chance had been calling over and over since she hung up. She probably needed to put him out of his misery. "I'm still alive," she answered.

"For now," said a man who was definitely not Chance. The words were followed by a buzzing sound and a burst of static that made Holland think of a voice moving through an old radio.

"Who is this?"

"I believe you already know. You were asking for me last evening."

There was another pop of static as a chill slid down Holland's spine.

"Would you still like to know the time?" the Watch Man asked.

"You killed Jake!" she cried.

"I did not kill anyone," he said, affronted. The static paused whenever the Watch Man spoke, revealing a posh mid-Atlantic accent, which, like the static, sounded as if it had been stolen from another time. "Contrary to what some of the stories say, people cannot make deals with me to live longer. I merely tell people the time that they will die and, when applicable, I tell them what they can do to extend their time. I often simply suggest getting a dog, exercising more, and refraining from leaving mean comments on the internet. Unfortunately, none of that advice applies to you. Although, if you do manage to get yourself some more time, I highly recommend a dog."

"Are you kidding me?"

"I do not kid on these calls, and generally speaking, if you need to ask if it's a joke, it's not a very good one, which is another reason why I'm not known for joking." Although, for a second, it sounded as if he was joking. The accent made him sound like a character from an old black-and-white comedy. "I tend to frighten people," he went on, "but I assure you, I am not the one who wants you dead."

"Then why did you tell Jake to kill me?"

More static prickled through the phone as the Watch Man sighed. "I did not tell him *to* kill you. I told him killing you would prolong his life. But I didn't say it was a wise idea."

"Then maybe you shouldn't have said it at all!"

"He asked the time," the Watch Man said patiently, but the static on the line was growing thicker. "It is my job to tell him what he wanted to know. And now I must tell you that you will die tomorrow, Halloween, at 11:59 p.m."

Tomorrow. It was more time than Jake, but not by much. The puddles of water on the sidewalk were making their way toward Holland's feet, and now she could feel the wet soaking through her skin, into her blood.

"Are you still with me?" the Watch Man asked.

Holland wanted to hang up, or scream, or hang up and scream. This couldn't be happening.

"This might be a good time for you to ask how you can get more time," the Watch Man prodded.

"I don't want to kill anyone," she managed.

"That's good to hear. The world does not need more murderers. And it wouldn't get you any extra time. The only way to live past tomorrow is to find the Alchemical Heart."

Holland tried to remember if this was something the Professor had ever mentioned in her stories. For a second, she almost thought it sounded familiar. It made her think of an overheard conversation, something mentioned once in whispers, but she couldn't remember when or where or why. "What's the Alchemical Heart?" she asked.

"I cannot tell you that—" Another chorus of static burst through the phone. "But—Holland—it *is* a wise idea to find the Heart—"

The other side of the phone crackled and buzzed.

The Watch Man stopped speaking.

The line crackled again.

"Hello?" Holland said. "Are you still there?"

"Please insert five cents if you would like to continue your call." The tinny words warred with the static that had taken over the other side of the line. "Please insert five cents to continue—"

Sirens wailed in the distance, overwhelming the voice. The blares sounded far away for a second. More of an idea than an arrival.

"Please insert five—"

She hung up the phone with a whispered curse. Quickly, she typed the words *Alchemical Heart* into Google, but nothing useful came up. She found only pages about meditation or links to the novel *The Alchemist*. The cry of the sirens moved closer. Someone else in the complex must have seen Jake's body and called the police. The wailing sounded too close to be a coincidence, and Holland just wasn't that lucky tonight.

Her eyes darted from the body at her feet to the time on her phone. 6:59 p.m.

Twenty-nine hours left until midnight on Halloween. Or she would end up just like Jake.

Holland's heart raced faster, cold blood pumping until it turned hot in her veins. She knew the right thing to do would be to stay and talk to the police. But that could take hours. More, if they saw that she was the last person Jake had called or if they found the folder in her hand, which possibly gave her motive for a heat-of-passion murder.

Holland hadn't done anything wrong, but the cops wouldn't know that right away. And she made a sensational suspect—that was another thing she'd learned from her research into Hollywood murders. Sometimes the most well-known suspect wasn't the best one, just the most interesting one.

Holland had to get out of there. Her ticking clock had already started. She only had twenty-eight hours and fifty-nine minutes left to find this Alchemical Heart, and there was only one person she knew who might be able to tell her what it was.

Car doors slammed.

Voices shouted out directions.

And Holland's feet slapped against the pavement as she fled.

CHAPTER NINE

The Professor owned a very old and very large collection of clocks. Wall clocks. Table clocks. Clocks that were part of things clocks weren't generally part of, like cookie jars and porcelain dolls. Holland really disliked the Professor's clockwork doll, although it was one of the Professor's favorites.

Once a semester, the Professor taught a class at her house, and she always sat the clockwork doll beside her. Its glass eyes watched nothing and everything as students filled the sofas and chairs, and the rest of the clocks cheerfully *tick-tock*ed all around the room.

This was how she taught her class on the Watch Man, in a room buzzing with synchronized second hands.

When Holland had been the Professor's TA, it had been her job to position all the clocks in the same sitting room, sync all their times, and then set their alarms so they would all go off at the exact same moment. When the Professor revealed what happened when a person asked the Watch Man for the time, all the clocks went off at once, filling the room with an ungodly trill that made every student jump or curse or some combination of both.

Holland could hear that trill now as she ran to her car.

She finally found her car on the far side of a crammed parking lot, its hood practically against the cement wall, its sides sandwiched between two cars she didn't remember being so close. Everything felt closer than it should have, as if the cars, the apartment complex, all of Los Angeles were pressing in on her.

She squeezed in on her driver's side and reached for the door handle, but it didn't open. She tugged again. The door stayed locked. She fumbled in her bag for her keys. But even when she pressed the fob, her car wouldn't come to life.

She swore she could hear a swarm of police officers in the distance. According to police procedure, they'd start canvassing the area. She needed to get out of there.

A dark SUV approached, window rolled down on the passenger side. "Having trouble?" the driver asked.

Holland shook her head. "I'm good." She tried her fob again, hoping the driver would keep going—this guy was better off getting away from her—but he rolled to a stop, right behind her car, boxing Holland in.

"It doesn't matter how many times you press that button. I made sure it's not going to start."

Holland's stomach dropped.

"Now be a good girl and get in the car." He opened the passenger door. Interior lights glowed, revealing a guy who could have been the reason you had to warn women they weren't supposed to go off with strangers. He had an attractive face, wore an impeccable suit, and his square jaw was covered in just the right amount of dark stubble.

Holland backed up as much as she could.

The stranger didn't take his eyes off her. They were dark and a little tortured. She got the impression he didn't feel great about kidnapping her, but it wasn't going to stop him. "That wall isn't going to save you, sweetheart. And before you waste more time protesting, it's either me or the cops. Or you can take your chances with whoever murdered your boyfriend."

She didn't bother to correct him about Jake being her boyfriend. She was more concerned that this guy knew about his death. "How do I know that you didn't murder him?"

"You don't know. But I didn't." The stranger gave her a hard look that said he wasn't a liar. As if that sin was even worse than kidnapping or murder. "We're running out of time." He impatiently motioned toward the empty passenger seat.

That's when she saw it, on the underside of his wrist: an indigo tattoo of an antiquity eye, with the symbol for tin—♃—on top and the symbol for sulfur— ♄ —below.

Her breath caught at the familiar combination. Instinctively her fingers went to the chain around her neck. "You have the exact same tattoo as my sister."

"Who do you think asked me to come here?" he said, and he looked as if he regretted saying yes to the request. "I'm doing this as a favor to January, but I'm only staying thirty more seconds. Then it's you and the cops."

There was a very strong part of Holland that wanted to jump over the car beside her and start running. She needed to get to the Professor's house. She needed to find the Alchemical Heart. But he'd said her sister's name, and he had the same tattoo.

Right after January had gotten her tattoo, Holland had thought it would be fun to get a matching one. But January had said she actually rather regretted it, and then she'd bought Holland a necklace like it instead. She'd given Holland an antiquity eye with the symbol for tin hanging from the bottom, and she'd bought herself the same necklace, except with the symbol for sulfur. January had promised to never take it off, and Holland did the same. Her fingers were now clutching the symbol for tin, as they did whenever she was nervous.

Even if this man knew her sister, he felt like a wolf in a suit, and she didn't want to be his Little Red Riding Hood.

He sighed. "I swear, I'm not going to lay a hand on you." He said it the same way he said he wasn't a liar, as if there were some lines he wouldn't cross, but not very many. "I only killed your car because I needed to get you to come with me."

"Why not just ask like a normal, nonthreatening person?"

"Because I am not very good at pretending," he said gruffly. "I'm here because I owe your sister. January told me to keep you alive, but I can't do that if you won't get in." He cut a glance to his rearview mirror. "You have five seconds," he warned. "If you want to live and find out who actually killed your boyfriend, come with me."

The patter of footsteps sounded in the distance, followed by voices that made her think the cops were close. If they found her now, they'd have all kinds of questions about why she ran from the scene. She was trapped between two bad choices.

Get eaten by a wolf or questioned by the cops.

Holland knew she wasn't thinking clearly. But that didn't help her think more clearly, it just made her more aware that she was probably making a very bad decision as she got inside the car.

Folklore 517:
the Chained Library

Driving through the Hollywood Hills makes you feel as if you're playing a real-life video game designed by a sadistic city planner.

The roads are steep and dangerously narrow, cars going the other direction are always moving too fast. Then there are all the driveways, which always seem to have construction vehicles or moving trucks spilling out onto the street.

A red ball bounces in front of you. You slam on your brakes, afraid a child might chase after it. But it's just the ball. It *bounce-bounce-bounces* down the road.

You drive a little slower, which is all right because you're practically there. A few cars are already parked. You recognize one of your classmates' vehicles; it has an old bumper sticker that says *Birds aren't real.* You feel relieved at the sight of it. You're in the correct place.

The Professor has been getting more cryptic with her clues. The last one you pieced together said *There will be an Earthquake in China-town on Halloween.* It's October, and you'd wondered briefly if this was a prediction, not a clue. Then you noticed *Earthquake* was unnecessarily capitalized. You did some digging and discovered that all three of the capitalized nouns are names of movies with scenes filmed at the Holly-wood Reservoir.

You visited here once, when you first moved to Los Angeles. They say it has the best view of the *HOLLYWOOD* sign, and you have to agree.

It's the sort of place that makes you want to take up jogging. You imagine running along the water, a resurrected song from the '80s playing in the background, making you feel as if you're living inside one of those movie montages.

There's no music today, just dry wind and heat. You feel closer to the sun at the top of the hill. The Professor is wearing round black sunglasses that cover half her face. Her back is to the water and the mountains and the perfect view of the *HOLLYWOOD* sign. The rest of the class forms an eager horseshoe around her. There are now only nine of you left.

Everyone is waiting for her to speak and she is waiting for you. She stays still for a full minute after you arrive, so the rest of the class knows you're the cause of the delay. Then, so quietly that everyone has to move in a little closer, she begins. "There are several places in Los Angeles where time moves differently. LAX is one of them. All of you have probably noticed how time often slows to a crawl in those terminals."

The student next to you giggles. The Professor ignores her and continues.

"It slows down here as well. People attribute the peaceful, unhurried feeling of the reservoir to the water and the view, but I'm here to tell you that it's magic. Real magic that dates back to the story I'm going to share today. Have any of you ever heard of the Chained Library at the Hereford Cathedral?"

Three hands go up. It sounds so obscure, you're surprised a third of the class is familiar with it.

The Professor looks disappointed. "In the Middle Ages, books were extraordinarily valuable, and it was common practice to chain them up to protect them from theft. About five hundred years ago, a large number of these chained-up books and manuscripts began to mysteriously arrive at the Hereford Cathedral. No one knew why, but so many of them appeared that someone decided to form a library.

"Most people consider it a curiosity, a place to take pictures that can be posted with pithy captions. However, my dear students, there's a reason all those chained manuscripts showed up at that particular cathedral. The Hereford Cathedral is dedicated to two saints, one of whom is Saint Æthelberht the King. I'd ask if any of you know who he is, but I don't want to be disappointed again, so I will just tell you. Æthelberht was a ruler during the Middle Ages who was betrayed and murdered by the parents of his betrothed."

The Professor mimes a knife slashing across her throat. And you feel slightly disturbed by how animated she becomes whenever she speaks of someone's demise.

"Recordkeeping was abysmal in the Middle Ages, so Æthelberht's life would have been forgotten by history, except that the events after his death are quite remarkable. As Æthelberht's body was on its way to be buried, the stories say his severed head rolled out of a cart and restored the sight of a blind man. Even more miracles were reported at the location of his grave.

"Rumors spread that the grave was magic. A church was built there, which turned into the Hereford Cathedral, and then the chained books began to arrive. But it was not all by happenstance, as the stories say. There was one chained book in the library that was locked up not to keep it safe, but to protect the world from what had been hidden inside it. The other chained books were all just decoys to camouflage the existence of this volume and the magic that it concealed.

"But even bound in chains, protected by a dead saint, and hidden among stacks of other chained volumes, the magic locked inside this book made its presence known. Stories started spreading around England about people who visited the library receiving preternatural gifts. The most notable of these was a woman from Dewchurch named Mary Young—although it's doubtful that was her actual surname. After visiting the Chained Library, Mary Young didn't age a day. Eventually, she was labeled a witch and killed for this, but not before her story traveled across England. Other stories spread as well, until one day the book disappeared from the shelves."

The Professor pauses dramatically, letting her story sink in. This is the first time she's told a tale that doesn't relate to Los Angeles. But you're already imagining how she'll bring it back around.

"To this day, no one knows who took it," she continues. "But after it vanished, there were more stories of peculiar magics all over England. There were whispers of time stopping, of loved ones returning from the dead, of a young boy who could kill with his mere words. For one hundred years, there were stories of ordinary people receiving extraordinary magical gifts, until one day the stories stopped. The book that had been stolen reappeared at the Chained Library. Only now the volume was without chains, and it was completely hollowed out. The magical object inside was gone. All that remained was a slip of parchment with a series of numbers on it. I don't usually share this next part with students, but let's just say the time feels right."

The Professor begins to rattle off a list of numbers. It's a long list. Finally you think she's near the end, because she pauses and then she finishes with "One zero two zero two five."

You're working on doing some math in your head when the person beside you says, "The numbers are dates. Months and years."

Someone else says, "The last one is *this* month."

The Professor's expression is difficult to read with her giant sunglasses, but you think she sounds pleased as she says, "You're both correct. The list is indeed a series of dates, and each of those dates has coincided with the reappearance of the object that was hidden inside the book."

"What was hidden?" asks the same student who first figured out the numbers were dates.

The Professor scowls. "I just told you. The most powerful object in the world."

"Are we supposed to find it?" you ask boldly.

"My advice would actually be to stay away from this particular item, but if you hear any rumors about it, please let me know."

CHAPTER TEN

The stranger drove fast and sharp, as if car crashes only happened to mortals, and he wasn't one of them. Holland hadn't even finished shutting the door before he sped away. Engine revving. Tires taking corners too fast.

"Are you trying to kill me?" she wheezed, fumbling to buckle her seatbelt. The vehicle was cold, pouring out aggressive California air conditioning. Yet her palms were clammy and her skin was burning, and she wasn't entirely sure if it was because she'd just gotten into a car with a complete stranger or because of everything else that had just happened.

Maybe it was both.

Her heart was racing faster than the car. She felt as if it would never slow. It raced as if she needed to move, as if she needed to outrun everything. She needed to outrun Jake's death and the sirens and the words of the Watch Man.

You will die tomorrow, Halloween, at 11:59 p.m. . . . The only way to live past tomorrow is to find the Alchemical Heart.

That's what she needed to focus on—finding the Alchemical Heart.

"Where are you taking me?" she asked.

"Somewhere safe," the stranger replied.

"No," Holland argued. "We need to go to the Professor's house." She rattled off the name of her street, along with the exit he needed to take.

"Yeah, that's not going to happen." He careened onto the 405, accelerating to an ungodly speed that made Holland grip the armrests so tightly she worried her fingernails would break.

"Listen, I'm not sure why my sister sent you. But . . ." She didn't know how to finish the sentence because for a second she couldn't help wondering if her sister actually had sent him.

Yes, they had the same tattoo, which felt significant. And Holland could absolutely picture her sister sending a bodyguard—even though they were twins, January had always taken on the older, more responsible sister role. But that didn't help explain why she had sent *him*.

Holland carefully pulled out her phone.

The stranger grabbed it from her hands, rolled down the window, and threw it onto the freeway.

Holland let out an involuntary shriek. "Why would you do that?"

He shook his head, as if she was the one who'd just done something wrong. "January told me to keep you safe."

"January is who I was trying to call." Holland glared at him. "I wanted to make sure you're not a sociopath."

"Here." He tossed something onto Holland's lap. It looked like one of those pay-as-you-go phones, with actual buttons instead of a touch screen. "Go ahead, call your sister. She's in my contacts under *J*. Ask her whatever you want about me."

"It might help if I knew your name."

"It's Gabe."

"Do you have a last name, Gabe?"

"January knows who I am."

Holland didn't doubt it. Gabe was the sort of guy you didn't forget. In the car's dim light, Holland couldn't tell if he had scars, but he seemed like the sort who would—she imagined one on his right cheek, just below his eye. His jaw was square and hard, as if he exercised it by munching on rocks. His brows were thick and she imagined his eyes were lined in thick, dark lashes as well. But she still said, "Gabe is actually a pretty common name, and my sister knows a lot of people."

A muscle ticked in Gabe's jaw. And she felt a small amount of triumph that, for a second, she wasn't the only one who was uncomfortable. "It's Cabral," he muttered.

Gabe Cabral.

Holland had a sudden feeling she'd heard the name before, but she couldn't remember how. Could January have mentioned him after all?

She opened Gabe's contacts. There were only five of them. All were either letters or numbers, as if he wasn't mysterious enough. "Do you have something against names?"

"No, just against women who snoop through my phone."

Ignoring the barb, Holland pressed the letter *J*. For the third time that day, she reached her sister's voicemail. At least Gabe actually knew her sister. "Hey JJ, it's me, Holland. I need to talk to you. I'm calling from the phone of your *friend* Gabe Cabral. Call me back as soon as you can at—"

Gabe rattled off a number, which she repeated.

As soon as she finished, he took the phone back. "Better?" he asked.

Holland laughed. "You think that letting me make one call after you destroyed my phone and killed my car is going to make me feel better?"

Gabe twisted his mouth. He looked as if he wanted to say yes. As if for him, acting like an actual human was a colossally good deed.

"You basically kidnapped me." Holland opened the glove box.

"Hey, stop snooping," he ordered.

"As an abductee, it's my job to look for any clues I can." Sadly, the glove box was immaculate, aside from an insurance slip that belonged to Rita Meeker. She held it out for him. "Thought you said your name was Gabe Cabral."

He glared. "Would it make you feel better if I said I'll give her back the car when I'm done?"

"Only if I believed you." Holland still had a number of questions as to why her sister had sent him. "Only half of this even makes sense. How did my sister know I was in trouble?"

Traffic came to a halt. Gabe scowled as he checked all the mirrors.

"This is what your sister left for me." He handed Holland a slip of paper. She immediately recognized January's handwriting.

KEEP MY SISTER SAFE.
If he doesn't get what he wants, he'll come for her next.

It looked as if there might have been more words below, but the bottom was ripped off.

"What else did it say?" Holland asked. "Why was this page torn? And who is *he*? When she did leave this?"

Gabe briefly looked as if he regretted handing over the paper. "What has January told you about her boyfriend?"

"January doesn't have a boyfriend." After a man whom Holland had promised never to mention again, January had sworn off dating. *I don't do boyfriends. I only sleep with ugly men,* she liked to say. But she didn't even do that. January had her job. She traveled the world. Holland didn't think her sister was happy, but this was how she kept her head above water.

"So, she didn't tell you about him?" Gabe asked.

"My sister doesn't have a boyfriend," Holland repeated.

Gabe's frown deepened. "She met him on her latest job. He told her he was a tourist, and the last time I saw her, she told me they were in love."

"That doesn't sound like January."

"I know," Gabe agreed. There was a note of something in his voice Holland couldn't quite place.

"Why was she telling you this?" Holland asked. "Did you two used to date?"

"No," Gabe said immediately, as if the idea offended him. "I work freelance. I'm good at acquiring difficult-to-find things. Sometimes, when she's working a challenging job, your sister calls me. Recently, I needed a favor, so I called her, and when I saw her, I knew right away that something was off. Then I saw the engagement ring on her finger."

"My sister isn't engaged. She doesn't even have a boyfriend," Holland repeated yet again. "She would have told me."

"I'm just telling you what I saw," said Gabe. "But I agree. The whole conversation made me think that whoever this guy was, he was doing some sort of mind job on her. When January talked about him, she sounded like a sappy greeting card." Gabe scowled, as if both sap and greeting cards left a bad taste in his mouth.

Holland had a bad taste in her mouth as well. Her sister was never sappy, but earlier that day she'd sounded just that way on the phone.

January was a force. She was smart and clever and ruthless in a way that Holland had never been capable of. But there was a reason she didn't date.

In college, January had fallen for the wrong guy. It was the first time she'd ever been in love, and when it had ended, January had disappeared for a month. Holland didn't know all the details, only that her sister had nearly failed out of school. Then she'd come back, but she hadn't been the same. January had never been as sensitive as Holland, but anything soft about her had been carved away and replaced by something hard that hadn't cracked since. At least until now.

"The next day, January called me," Gabe continued. "This time she sounded shaky, nervous. She asked me to meet her again, but all I found was that note."

Holland looked at the torn page again, and another set of questions rushed through her head. Why would January send Gabe? Why wouldn't she just tell Holland this message directly? They had talked earlier that day, and January hadn't said a thing.

Although . . . Holland once again thought about how January hadn't sounded like herself, with the *I miss you* and the *I wish I was there.* "What does this guy want from us?" Holland asked.

"That's what I was going to ask you," Gabe said. "Has your sister sent you anything? Or told you anything strange or unexpected?"

"No," Holland replied. January hadn't told her anything significant recently. But—

Holland reached into her messenger bag and pulled out the gold-and-black folder she'd taken from Jake's apartment. "I found this tonight. The guy I had been dating, the one who died—he had been hired to become a part of my life and look into my family. It makes me wonder if maybe the person January was dating was doing the same thing."

"That folder—does it say what the guy was after?"

"No." But it seemed to Holland that it was very likely Jake had died because of it, which made her think it had to be something valuable.

"You have any idea what he would want?" Gabe prodded.

She started to say no, but then she thought about Mr. Vargas and the safety deposit box left to her. She had no idea what could be in it, but maybe that's what he'd been after? She thought about telling Gabe, but Mr. Vargas had made a point of telling her not to mention the box to anyone.

"What aren't you telling me?" he asked.

"Considering I don't trust you—a lot of things."

Gabe stepped harder on the gas, pushing the car to go faster. "I'm just trying to keep you alive, sweetheart."

She might have told him to stop calling her sweetheart, but as soon as he said the word *alive*, her ears filled with crackling static and the Watch Man's words—*The only way to live past tomorrow is to find the Alchemical Heart.* "Have you ever heard of the Alchemical Heart?" she asked.

Gabe's gaze immediately shot her way, as if she'd just become a lot more interesting. "Is that what you think they're after?"

"I don't know," she answered honestly. "I don't even know what the Alchemical Heart is."

His expression turned skeptical. "Then why did you ask about it?"

Holland really didn't want to answer that question, but he had just said he'd been sent to help keep her alive, and he clearly knew what this heart was. "I need to find it."

Gabe laughed. It was a slightly disturbing sound.

"Why are you laughing?"

"Because, sweetheart"—his laughter died, but his expression remained an unnerving sort of amused—"everyone would *love* to find the Alchemical Heart."

"Why do you say it that way? What is it?"

"It doesn't matter. It's not something you're ever going to find," he said with an air of finality that made her feel as if he'd just torn the last few pages from her favorite notebook so she couldn't write any more words. His eyes were back on the road, and Holland knew that if she didn't change his mind quickly, she'd never find the Professor, she'd never figure out what the Alchemical Heart was, and she would never live past tomorrow.

"Listen, Mr. Killing Cars and Kidnapping Women Is My Hobby."

"Don't ever call me that again."

"I'm just trying to get you to listen to me," she said impatiently. "Earlier tonight, right before you showed up, I was told that I have a little over twenty-four hours to find the Alchemical Heart. If I don't, I'm going to die."

"Who told you that?" he asked.

Holland considered telling him about the Watch Man, but the last person she'd told the story to was dead. "It doesn't matter," she murmured. "I believe him."

Gabe narrowed his eyes. "Did this person threaten to kill you, or did he tell you the *time* you're going to die?" He put extra emphasis on the word *time*, and Holland wondered then if maybe somehow Gabe already knew the legend of the Watch Man.

"The time," Holland said. "One minute before midnight on Halloween—unless I find the Alchemical Heart."

"Fuck," Gabe muttered. "You're screwed."

CHAPTER ELEVEN

When Holland was younger, whenever she got sick enough to miss school, she always told Aunt Beth that she thought she was going to die. Then, of course, Aunt Beth would reassure her she wasn't going to be killed by a cough or the sniffles or horrible cramps.

Holland wanted Gabe to reassure her now. She wanted him to tell her that, despite what he'd just said, she didn't need to worry, she wasn't going to die, not as long as she had him to keep her alive.

But Gabe didn't say any of those things. He looked as if this was not what he'd signed up for when January had asked for help.

"I'm just telling you the truth," he said. "The Watch Man is always right."

"Wait—how do *you* know about the Watch Man?"

"The better question is, how do you?" Gabe looked at her again, as if he found her less than impressive, and he couldn't understand how she knew much of anything, let alone an obscure myth.

Holland straightened her spine and met his dismissive gaze straight on. "I might not be good at fleeing crime scenes and burying all my emotions, but I know a lot about folklore, and the Professor I want to visit is an expert on urban myths and legends. If anyone would know where to find this Alchemical Heart, it's her. I tried to Google it but—"

Gabe scoffed. "You can't Google the Alchemical Heart."

Holland felt her face go red once more. "I know that *now*. So will you please tell me what it is?"

He sighed. "It's a myth."

Normally, Holland loved the word *myth*. When she heard *myth*, she imagined her world was about to get bigger. She believed there was always some truth to every story. Myths and legends had to come from somewhere. But Gabe didn't sound as if he believed that. He said the word *myth* the way a parent might say *fairytale* to a very small child.

"I still want to hear about it," Holland said.

"All right," said Gabe begrudgingly. "Have you ever heard of the Sacred Order of the Parallel Dawn?"

Holland had a sudden flash of a shiny brochure that read, *Welcome, new recruit!* But she was fairly certain it was a product of her overactive mind trying to find a connection to a class she'd taken on secret societies, because this definitely had the sound of one. "I don't think I've ever heard of it," she said. "But I am familiar with the Order of the Solar Temple and the Hermetic Order of the Golden Dawn."

Gabe looked less than impressed. "This secret society is far older than either of those. It was formed at the start of the Middle Ages by a group who believed in a parallel world that contained magic. The story goes that after one of the members died and then came back to life in a ritual, they claimed to have visited this parallel world and brought back proof in the form of an object that later would become known as the Alchemical Heart."

The traffic on the freeway came to a halt. Gabe's eyes darted around the neighboring cars, and then he checked all his windows and mirrors before saying, "No one knows what the Alchemical Heart looks like, but it's said to be so powerful that any person it comes near gains an ability, and any object it touches fills with magic. The Sacred Order realized too late that once any form of magic was created, it could not be destroyed. The magic or ability would simply be passed on to another person or object. This is when the Sacred Order of the Parallel Dawn began to fracture. One faction wanted to destroy the Alchemical Heart."

"Wait," Holland interrupted. "I thought you said magic can't be destroyed."

"It can't be," Gabe said. "But the Alchemical Heart is said to be the source of all magic, and some people believe that if the Alchemical Heart is destroyed, all the magic it has created will be destroyed as well."

"This sounds like the most powerful object in the world," said Holland.

Gabe shot her a look that seemed to say, *Thanks for stating the obvious, toots.*

"I'm not just stating the obvious. The Professor taught a class on this. She talked about an object hidden away in a chained library." Holland gave him a quick recap, finishing with how the chained book was returned, hollow and empty. "She never called it the Alchemical Heart, though—she just said it was the most powerful object in the world."

"That could definitely be it." Gabe looked at Holland as if she wasn't completely useless after all.

She tried to hide her grin. She really didn't care about impressing him. It just felt good to finally have some sort of grip on what was happening. "I just wonder why the Professor didn't mention it by name?"

"Probably because there is an entire organization dedicated to erasing the Alchemical Heart from history," Gabe replied. "The Professor's story sounds vague enough that it wouldn't draw their notice. But they might kill you for hearing the story I told you."

"Then how do you know it?"

Gabe scowled. "You ask a lot of questions."

"I'm just trying to stay alive."

"I hate to tell you this, but the chances of that aren't very good. Like I said, the Alchemical Heart is a myth. There's a rumor about a list of dates—months and years—that say when it's going to pop up, but as far as I know, all that list does is get people who search for the Alchemical Heart killed."

Holland had never heard about such a list. Although if it really did get people killed, she could understand why the Professor never shared it.

"If you're afraid of dying, you don't have to help me," Holland said. "All you have to do is drop me off at the Professor's house."

Gabe sighed. Holland couldn't tell if it was an *I need to get rid of her* sigh or an *I don't actually care about dying* sigh. "You really trust this Professor of yours?"

"With my life," Holland said.

"Tell me where she lives again."

"It's actually the next exit." The cars on the freeway started moving once more and Holland quickly recited the directions.

"I'll take you there," Gabe said. "But once we're there, if I say we go, we go, no questions asked."

Holland nodded. Although he really was insane if he thought she was ever getting in a car with him again.

CHAPTER TWELVE

The Professor lived in one of those classic Americana neighborhoods that always smelled like freshly cut grass and looked like a 1950s film set. Almost every porch light was on, every sidewalk was swept, and most homes were ready for Halloween. Stoops were covered in plump orange pumpkins, and friendly ghosts made of sheets swayed from old trees.

If it had been earlier in the night, neighbors would have probably been out walking their dogs, and someone would have definitely noticed a young woman without any shoes stepping out of a car that had parked in front of the only house on the street without the porch light on.

Every window was dark and the house was quiet as Gabe exited after her. He was taller than she'd realized in the car. She could feel him towering over her, walking too close. Close enough that she imagined if she were to take more than one step away, he'd grab hold of her and pull her back to him.

His knuckles brushed against her fingers. "Don't even think about running," he whispered.

"I'm barefoot. You think I could get very far?" Holland kicked and wiggled her toes.

Gabe's eyes dropped to her legs. He looked unamused, but she swore his eyes lingered on her bare calf before traveling up to where her skirt had hitched up on her thigh.

For a second, Holland lost her balance.

Gabe immediately grabbed her arm, steadying her. Then just as quickly, he dropped it, as if he didn't want to touch her. "Just don't," he ordered. "I can't keep you safe if you run."

"According to what you just said in the car, you can't keep me safe at all." Her voice came out snappier than she'd intended. If it had been anyone else, she would have apologized, but she was fairly certain Gabe was half the reason she felt snappy.

A gust of wind pushed a rocking chair forward and back as Holland and Gabe reached the Professor's door. Unlike her neighbors, the Professor hadn't decorated. There wasn't so much as a miniature pumpkin, just the rocking chair and a doormat that read *Of All the Gin Joints.*

The Professor didn't decorate for Christmas, but she loved Halloween. Usually, she went all out for the holiday. She made elaborate jack-o'-lanterns and hung strings of candy corn lights. Last year, she even put up one of those fake door knockers shaped like a skeletal hand. Holland found it more than a little worrisome that she hadn't done anything this year.

"Doesn't look like your Professor is home," said Gabe.

Holland knocked on the door. She knew he was probably right. The house was too dark and too quiet, but she couldn't help hoping. Hope was all she had tonight.

"Professor, it's me, Holland," she cried. Then she rang the doorbell and knocked harder.

The house creaked. A ghost made of sheets swayed in a nearby tree.

Gabe darted a sharp look up and down the street. "We should get out of here."

"That's not a real ghost," Holland scolded.

"I'm not afraid of a sheet in a tree."

"Good, because we can't leave yet."

A dark shadow covered his face. "Remember when I said, if I say go, we go?" He wrapped his hand around her wrist.

He tugged, but Holland stood her ground, toes digging into the

Professor's doormat. "She has a journal. She calls it her sacred note-book. It's where she takes notes on every myth and legend she teaches, as well as a few she doesn't share with students. There's probably in-formation in there that could help us find the Alchemical Heart."

Gabe looked unwillingly intrigued. "You know where she keeps it?"

"In her library, at the back of the house."

"So, you want to break in?" He reached underneath his suit coat. At first, Holland wasn't sure what he was doing. Then she saw a distinct flash of metal.

"Oh no! No guns."

"We're breaking into a house."

"We are not breaking in. I know where the spare key is."

Gabe looked as if he wanted to argue, but Holland couldn't let him win this fight.

"The house is empty, and if someone does find us, it will probably be an elderly neighbor, and then you'll end up killing someone's grand-parent. Do you really want to be that guy? Gabe the Grandma Killer?"

He looked at her as if he'd never heard a more ridiculous argument or seen a more ridiculous person. But he left the gun where it was, tucked underneath his jacket.

Fallen leaves stuck to Holland's feet as she let herself into the Pro-fessor's backyard. In the daytime, it was full of flowers and tinkling fountains. But tonight, there was only the unsettling sound of glass light bulbs being knocked together by the wind.

Holland used to wonder what genre her life would be if it were a movie. Growing up on her aunt and uncle's farm in Northern Califor-nia made her childhood feel like one of those dramas that won lots of awards but were a little slow and boring. Holland had vowed that when she grew up, her life would be a television show with oversaturated colors, perky pop music, and lots of kissing.

That was the path she'd been on before she'd heard about the Pro-fessor's class.

She wasn't sure what genre she was in now, but the colors were grittier, there was no pop music soundtrack, and it didn't have nearly enough kissing.

Her eyes drifted toward Gabe.

Just standing this close to him felt like going the wrong way down a one-way street. She definitely didn't want to kiss him. But for a second it was all she could imagine. It wouldn't be soft. His arms would hold tight. Painful tight. Keep her from breaking to pieces tight, until he let go, sudden and harsh, and pieces were all that was left. Guys like Gabe broke girls like Holland.

That wasn't what she wanted at all. Cat was wrong when she'd said Holland wanted someone who scared her a little. Holland wanted someone who made her feel safe. Who made her feel like even if the world came crashing down around her, he wouldn't stop holding her.

But that guy wasn't Gabe. Minutes ago, he hadn't been able to hold on to her wrist for more than a second. Holland quickened her steps to get ahead of him.

The Professor's personal office was reachable by two antique French doors that led onto a brick patio surrounded by overgrown roses, hardy fuchsias, and Japanese maple trees strung up with tiny glass lights that kept clanging in the wind. The Professor hid her spare key under a grumpy garden gnome that glared at Holland as she picked it up.

"You don't need that," Gabe said, as Holland retrieved the key.

"I told you we're not breaking in," she argued.

"We're also not the first ones here." He pressed two fingers against one of the Professor's French doors, easily pushing it open.

A second later, all the lights switched on.

And then, everything was chaos.

Folklore 517:
Until Further Notice

I t smells like urine.

You keep walking, kicking up dust from the dirt trails, but the scent only grows stronger. You think about leaving, about skipping this class, but everyone who's taken the course before says this one is important.

The words are always followed by a hush.

You're impressed by the loyalty the Professor's old students all seem to have. But you understand it; you don't share secrets of the class, either. These stories are things you feel you've earned, and you don't want to give them away for free.

And so here you are at the Old LA Zoo in Griffith Park.

You're not sure how long the zoo was open, but after passing by the tragically small cages, you can't believe it was open at all. You've seen closets bigger than these pens. No wonder the animals who once lived here are said to still haunt it.

You think it was built in the early 1900s, but unlike other parts of LA that were constructed during that time, these small iron and stone enclosures don't seem to hold any magic. If anything, they feel cursed.

This place has more ghosts than it does trees. You think about the poor couple who died on a picnic table while making love. Then you think about all the people over the years who've shown up here with amnesia. It happens about once a month. Sometimes they forget days, sometimes years, and no one has ever been able to figure out why. You wonder if maybe this is what the class will be about as you stop behind one of the cages, where the few remaining students are gathered.

"Ahem," says someone behind you. Everyone slowly turns.

It's not the Professor. But this young woman is clearly one of her protégés. Her posture is rigidly straight. Her eyes don't blink quite as much as they should. And you immediately dislike her because you fear her presence means the Professor isn't coming. She's sent a proxy.

The proxy waits until all eyes are on her before she says, "I'm here to inform everyone that all the Professor's classes have been suspended until further notice."

She turns and leaves before you can ask any questions.

CHAPTER THIRTEEN

Framed newspapers had been torn from walls. Books had been ripped off shelves. Drawers had been ruthlessly pulled out of desks. Cushions had been yanked from chairs. The entire house was ransacked.

Gabe said something, but his voice sounded far away. Holland could barely hear it over the staticky buzzing of light bulbs—or maybe the sound was only in her head.

Holland had always loved the Professor's office. It was one of those spaces, like the milk-glass room, that was full of the magic of simple, timeless things. Most of the Professor's treasures were related to her myths. Her bookshelves were full of blueprints for haunted Hollywood hotels, elaborately framed recipes for sidecars, original ticket stubs to the Old LA Zoo, windup clocks from her collection. One of the clocks appeared to be broken. The minute hand was spinning like a second hand, and the hour hand was ticking like a minute hand and echoing through the battered room.

"We need to find the Professor," Holland said. "We need to make sure she's *okay*." Holland couldn't bring herself to say the word *alive*. She didn't want to entertain the idea that the Professor might be dead, like Jake.

Holland didn't know how much more she could handle tonight, but she definitely couldn't handle losing the Professor.

Gabe pressed his lips into a tight line as his eyes landed on a trashed copy of *Murder at San Simeon*—one of the Professor's favorite conspiracy novels. His expression seemed to say, *If your Professor is here, then she's not going to be okay.*

"She might be injured," Holland said. She started toward the door, which led to the rest of the house. She tried to avoid stepping on any books or shards of broken glass, but her legs were unsteady and her movements were sloppy.

Gabe grabbed her wrist and quickly pulled her back with a force that nearly made her trip. "I'll look. You stay."

"But—"

"No," he said sharply. "We do it this way, or we leave."

"I'm not leaving."

"You think I can't make you?" His fingers tightened, sending a line of heat up her arm. "Stay," he ordered. Then he let her go.

The light seemed dimmer as soon as he was gone. Holland had thought the overhead chandelier was on, but now there was just the glow of the Professor's tipped-over Tiffany lamp. It was on the desk, next to a shiny green rotary phone that was making the noise phones make when they've been taken off the hook.

Holland walked to the desk to put the phone back on the receiver, and that's when she saw it, tucked under the handle: a pale cream business card with emerald-green lettering.

JANUARY ST. JAMES
Rare Book & Artifact Collections

Holland's head began to spin. January and the Professor didn't know each other. They had never met. And January had been in Spain for all of October, so she couldn't have been here. Unless she'd stopped by last month. But then why hadn't either January or the Professor mentioned it?

Holland wanted to tell herself that she was reading too much into this. The Professor loved rare books and artifacts. Maybe she'd gotten hold of January to track something down, and both of them had forgotten to mention it to Holland. Or there was a bigger connection Holland wasn't seeing.

She thought about Gabe. He knew about the Watch Man and the Alchemical Heart. It made her wonder if January did as well. But then why wouldn't she have mentioned any of it to Holland?

Before Jake, Holland had never shared the Professor's myths and legends with anyone, except for January. After starting her thesis, Holland had shared a draft of it with her sister. Then she'd told her the Professor's myth about the devil and the sidecar. Holland had tried to forget what her sister had said because her words hurt too much.

You need to grow up, Holland. They're gone. They aren't coming back, and making up stories about them won't change that.

The fight about the thesis had turned into a fight about their parents. Holland had been mad at January for never talking about them, and January had been angry at Holland for refusing to let them go. Then somehow it had turned into January telling Holland she needed to scrap the thesis and end her relationship with the Professor, whom January had then called a crackpot.

It was the worst argument they'd ever had. They'd gone for a full month without speaking. Then, one night, January had come over to Holland's house unannounced with an overnight backpack and a bottle of wine with a label that read, *I'm sorry, I suck.*

They didn't revisit the topic of the thesis or the Professor. But knowing how stubborn January could be, Holland doubted that she had changed her mind on the subject. Which made Holland wonder once again: Where had the Professor gotten January's business card? And why did she have it?

Holland had spent the last few years studying stories, and she knew that no matter how complicated something appeared, at the heart of every story was always one simple truth that tied everything together. So, either Holland still didn't have all the pieces of this story, or she was putting them together incorrectly.

Holland shoved January's business card into her messenger bag as she turned away from the desk. Maybe she'd ask Gabe about it when he came back. Holland literally didn't have the time to figure it out now.

Every single book had been ripped from the Professor's shelves, as though whoever had done this was looking for her journal. Holland felt her heart break as she took in the damage to the Professor's most prized things. Very little of it looked salvageable, but Holland couldn't stop herself from trying.

After putting a few books back up on the Professor's shelf, she picked up a *Price of Magic* film poster that usually hung on the Professor's wall. Holland had often wondered how the Professor had gotten her hands on it. Holland's father had been very particular about replicas never being made of his original posters because he liked to hide Easter eggs in them.

At the top of this poster, the title blazed in fiery letters above a windswept picture of the film's main couple, Red and Sophia Westcott. They were holding hands, but if you looked closely, you would see it was really Sophia holding on to Red.

Behind him, it looked as if the sun had finished setting, but again, upon closer inspection, Red was actually standing in front of a pair of shadowy black gates. Behind Sophia was a group of children. A more prominent child with perfect blond ringlets was holding on to a dog with a sprig of holly and a pair of bells attached to its collar along with a heart-shaped red name tag with the letters *JJ*.

The bells and the holly were for Holland, because of her nickname Hollybells, and the *JJ* was for January. Their dad had put little *gifts* for his daughters in both Price of Magic films, which had then led them on two of their favorite treasure hunts. As Holland held the poster now, she wondered if perhaps it contained another Easter egg she had never seen. She knew—

The house creaked.

Holland froze.

Then she heard footsteps.

Gabe was returning. At least she hoped it was Gabe. Maybe she was being paranoid, but she swore these footsteps sounded different, lighter. Someone was trying to be quiet. Holland wished there was something more substantial in her hands than an old movie poster.

The footsteps were outside the office.

Holland lunged for the rotary phone, just as Adam Bishop sauntered through the door.

CHAPTER FOURTEEN

Adam looked almost the same as when Holland had met him in his office: ripped jeans, plaid shirt, perfect arms, freckles across the bridge of his nose. He made her think of a grad student once again. Someone like her, someone she could trust. But there was no reason for Adam to be in the Professor's ransacked house. Not any good one.

"I can explain." Adam stopped just past the doorway, as if he didn't want to frighten her. But it was too late for that.

"What are you doing here?" She tried to sound demanding, but the words came out breathless and scared.

Adam ran a hand through his golden hair, turning it more disheveled than tousled, no doubt trying to make himself look even more disarming. "January said you wouldn't be able to let the Professor go."

"Wait—what—" Holland stammered. "How do you know January?"

"She's the reason I'm here." He took another cautious step.

"No—no—no—no—no—" Holland backed farther away.

"She asked me to look out for you," Adam said.

"No," Holland repeated. January wouldn't have sent two people into Holland's life. Unless she was really scared for Holland, or . . .

One of them was lying. After the night she'd been having, that seemed like the more likely answer.

"January said that you were attached to your mentor, so she thought that might be a good role for me."

"A role?" Holland repeated, her skepticism growing.

Adam looked half-apologetic, half-surprised she'd actually believed him, and Holland felt incredibly foolish. Of course he wasn't a professor, he was just another guy trying to trick her.

"I didn't want to lie to you." Adam's eyes were now entirely apologetic. "She asked me to protect you from a distance, so I tried. But"—he paused and took a look around the demolished office—"it doesn't really seem to be working." He took another step closer.

"No—" Holland put out her hand as she moved closer to the garden door. "Stop right there."

"Holland, we don't have time for this. We need to get out of here."

"I'm not going anywhere with you. You already lied to me once today. If you want me to believe this story, I need proof. Let me see your wrist." Holland's eyes shot to the thick watch band covering the space where January and Gabe had matching tattoos.

"What will that prove?"

"Just do it."

Adam took off his watch, and there it was. A tattoo just like Gabe's and January's. Adam watched her impatiently as she stared at it. "Is this proof enough?"

Holland shook her head. "It doesn't make sense. Why would January send you and Gabe?"

Adam's expression turned alarmed. "Your sister only sent me. Whoever Gabe is, you can't trust him."

"That's funny, I was about to tell her the same thing." Gabe stepped in from the open garden door and quickly pushed Holland behind his back. "*Run*," he muttered.

"He's the one you need to get away from," Adam said.

"You need to run," Gabe repeated.

"I don't think she wants to listen to you." Adam took another step toward her.

"Don't move." Gabe reached inside his coat and pulled out his gun.

Across from him, Adam moved incredibly fast, and then he was holding a weapon, too.

"No—no guns!" Holland yelled. "Nobody needs to get hurt."

Both men looked as if they disagreed.

Gabe held his gun in a way that made Holland think he had probably slept in the cradle with one. And Adam looked alarmingly comfortable with his as well.

"I don't know what he's told you," Adam said. "But you can't believe a word."

Gabe made a sound too angry to be called a laugh. "You could have at least worn different clothes when you tried to seduce this one."

Seduce.

Holland froze.

Did this mean Adam was the one who had been *dating* her sister?

Adam vehemently shook his head. "You can't listen to him, Holland. I came here to protect you."

"He's lying," Gabe shot back.

"I swear I'm telling you the truth. I work with your sister, January. She is my partner. She sent me here to watch out for you."

"You can't believe him," Gabe said. "He lied to January and now he's lying to you. I'm the one your sister sent."

Holland wanted to tell both of them to stop. Her head was spinning again, telling her to climb out of this rabbit hole, to get back to a life of champagne problems, to leave *both* of these men behind.

"Holland." Adam softened his voice, as if he knew she was on the verge of breaking or running or both. "I swear, I'm telling you the truth," he said. He looked at her as if his entire life depended on her, as if all that mattered was what she was thinking, as if he'd take a bullet if she'd just believe him. And for a split second she wanted to believe him.

Then everything seemed to happen at once.

Holland's eyes were still on Adam's pleading face when she heard the gunshot.

It sounded like the world ending. The earth splitting. Mountains shattering.

Then broad hands were grabbing hold of her arms, dragging her toward the door.

Gabe. He was dragging her.

She could see his lips moving but she couldn't make out what he was saying. Her ears were ringing. The room was turning into one of those unfocused pictures where everything was blurry except for one thing. And the one thing in focus was Adam, slumped on the floor in the middle of the room.

"No!" Holland screamed, and the world suddenly snapped back into focus. She could feel the cold from the door behind her warring against the heat of Gabe's murderous hands as he tried to drag her away. "Let me go!"

"We have to get out of here," Gabe growled. Then he was picking Holland up.

"Put me down." She kicked her legs. "You didn't need to kill him!"

"Don't worry, that bastard is a lot harder to kill than you think. And—" Gabe took a shuddering breath as he pulled her closer, cradling her to him. "He shot first."

That's when she felt the wet on his chest. The blood. She hadn't seen Adam pull the trigger. She'd been too focused on his eyes, the same way she had been in the office, when just one look had made her flushed. He'd beguiled her again. Then, with a sick, sinking feeling, she wondered if it was the same thing he'd done to her sister.

Holland briefly stopped kicking. "Put me down. You shouldn't be carrying me."

"I'm not dying," Gabe grunted. But Holland could already feel his grip loosening. Carefully, she extracted herself.

Across from them, Adam was still slumped on the ground, eyes closed, golden head at an angle. But on second glance, he appeared to be breathing. He was shot, right near the heart, but somehow still alive.

"We need to go!" Gabe grabbed her hand and pulled her toward the door. "We don't want to be here when he wakes up."

CHAPTER FIFTEEN

The neighbors' houses were brighter than Holland remembered. A few front doors were open, and people were peeking outside anxiously, wondering where the gunshots had come from.

"Drive," Gabe ordered. His head was at an angle as he slumped in the passenger seat, gripping his ribs.

"Is this one of those cars you can talk to?" Holland asked.

He narrowed his eyes, or maybe they were only half-open to begin with. "Why do you need to talk to the car?"

"I need to take you to the hospital, but I don't know where it is." Her knuckles were white as she gripped the wheel. She started driving, but she had no idea where she was going. She just knew she needed to get out of there. Neighbors had moved from porches to sidewalks. At least one had taken a picture. She hoped it was too dark to capture her face, but if someone had, then she could possibly be wanted in connection with two murders.

"No hospitals." Gabe reached up and undid his tie with one hand. "You can stitch me up at my place."

"Oh, no—" Holland said. "I don't stitch people. I don't even stitch stitchable things very well."

"You'll be fine. Just think of it as stabbing me with a needle."

"But I don't want to stab you."

The corner of his mouth twitched. "You did earlier."

Holland couldn't argue with this.

"Relax, it's not that bad. I think it bounced off my rib," he said, but his voice was a little breathless. And Holland didn't think a bullet bouncing off anything sounded very good.

Gabe directed her to turn until they reached a main street. Traffic lights and neon fast food signs replaced the neighborhood lampposts. Holland felt as if she was driving too fast and too slow all at once. Every time a light turned red, she felt herself holding her breath until she could put her foot on the gas.

They passed a billboard with a shimmering ad for the Hollywood Roosevelt's Halloween Ball. The image kept blinking in and out. One second it showed the iconic *HOTEL ROOSEVELT* sign, then the words switched to *HAPPY HALLOWEEN.*

The holiday greeting glowed in neon Roosevelt red, and suddenly Holland was remembering earlier that day, when she'd seen the words stamped in the corner of a paper package. She'd thought it was just another esoteric book about the devil, but now Holland wondered if maybe the Professor had mailed her something else.

"We need to go to my house," she said.

"No, we don't," Gabe immediately replied.

But Holland was already heading toward the freeway that would take them back to Santa Monica.

"You're going the wrong way," he said.

"You just said you're not dying, and the Professor mailed me something that we might need. I just remembered when I saw that Happy Halloween sign—there was a Happy Halloween stamp on the package. Now I'm wondering if the Professor sent me her journal."

"Why would she do that?"

"I'm her favorite student. If she knew something bad was going to happen, she would send it to me to keep it safe. We need to go get it. Unless you have another lead for the Alchemical Heart?"

Gabe worked his jaw, as if he wanted to argue but couldn't. "Are there any other secrets or surprises you want to let me know about?"

"I wasn't keeping the package a secret," Holland said. "I genuinely forgot about it."

"Is there anything else you're forgetting?"

"Probably. A lot has happened today." A lot had actually happened in just the last few hours. Holland could still feel the dead leaves from the Professor's house on her feet, and the water from the sprinklers as she'd stood next to Jake's dead body. It felt like the sort of night that, even once it passed, would never fully wash away. And yet, she also felt as if she was already losing pieces of it.

She tried to make a mental checklist of what she did and didn't know.

She now knew for certain the Professor's myths were very real. Which meant the Watch Man's prediction was going to come true. Holland would die tomorrow, unless she found the Alchemical Heart. But she had no idea where to look, and after seeing the Professor's house, she was quite sure others were searching for it.

Gabe had said there was some sort of list of dates of when it was supposed to reappear. Holland had never heard of this list, but if it was true, then others would know that now was the time to search.

Like Adam Bishop.

Adam was clearly the person January was afraid of in her note, which made Holland suspect he was hired by the same person who had hired Jake.

She glanced toward the passenger seat, where she'd left the black folder she'd found in Jake's apartment. She wondered again if the art deco border was a coincidence, or if it was a clue that proved the devil was behind all this.

She thought once more about Adam warning her away from her thesis topic about the devil. Was he trying to keep her from finding out who he was working for? Or had he been trying to protect her?

Holland struck out the last thought. She couldn't keep trying to make Adam the good guy. He only looked like the good guy, with his eyes that effortlessly said *trust me*—which was probably why he'd been hired to seduce January.

"Do you think Adam is working for the devil?" she asked.

Gabe grimaced. Holland couldn't tell if he was just in pain, or if he was bothered by her question. "When you're talking about the devil, are you referring to the biblical devil?"

"What other devil would I be talking about?"

Gabe didn't respond.

Holland shot a quick look to the passenger seat. He was now fully slumped against the door, and his eyes were closed. "Hey!" She shook his shoulder. "Don't fall asleep." Holland wasn't an expert on gunshot wounds, but she'd seen enough movies to know that if someone fell asleep after being shot, they usually didn't make it into the sequel.

She pressed harder on the gas.

Gabe opened his eyes. "I'm fine," he said, but his voice was even more breathless.

"We're almost there," Holland said. "Stay with me."

"I'm not going to die," he grunted. Now he sounded annoyed, which was better than breathless, but Holland's heart continued to race as she pulled onto her street.

Holland lived in Santa Monica, near Montana Avenue, in a Spanish-style house that immediately made people feel as if they should take off their shoes and then ask questions she didn't want to answer.

She knew that everyone who visited wondered exactly how she could afford it. She didn't like to lie, but she also never told anyone the truth about her parents. Instead, she made up stories. Stories that were so obviously false, they didn't count as lies.

It's all dirty money, she'd say sometimes. *I was a child bride, married to a mob boss. He was Catholic and didn't believe in divorce. I poisoned him to end it and now his body is buried out back under the veranda.*

She tried to finish with a look that said *I might bury your body, too, if you ask another question.* And usually people didn't ask more. Usually, people would laugh or play along, and then she would change the subject.

Gabe didn't ask anything at all as they pulled up in the driveway and

Holland killed the engine. He only said, "You should have parked down the street."

"I don't think you can walk that far."

He looked insulted. She wanted to remind him that he'd been shot. But he actually seemed fairly recovered as he stepped out of the car. If not for the way he clutched his side, Holland wouldn't have known anything was wrong.

He moved ahead of her down the drive and disappeared behind the back of the house, before meeting her on the porch. "It's all clear."

She wanted to tease him for being overdramatic. But then she pictured Jake, lying in a pool of blood, followed by the Professor's ransacked house, and suddenly she felt a little nervous about stepping inside her own house. "How many other people do you think are looking for the Alchemical Heart?"

"I don't care how many are looking. I just care *who* is looking. There are certain organizations you don't want the attention of."

Holland wanted to bring up her devil theory again, but under the glow of her porch light, she could see sweat glistening on Gabe's forehead, his face a little ashen. He was still standing upright, but he didn't seem as steady as he had when he'd first exited the car.

"Maybe you should take a seat." She pointed to her rocking chair, which she'd gotten because she'd been inspired by the Professor. Same with her doormat, which, like the Professor's, had an old movie quote, only Holland's was from *The Wizard of Oz* instead of *Casablanca*.

Bell Out of Order
Please Knock

Holland felt a pang in her chest as she read the words. She really hoped that wherever the Professor was, she was all right. She also really wished she could talk to her. But hopefully there would be some answers in the package that she had sent Holland.

"Keys," Gabe said, holding out his palm.

Holland pulled them out of her purse, but she didn't hand them over. His eyes were drooping again. "I really think you should take a seat."

"We're not staying. You're getting the package and then—" Gabe swayed.

"Oh no!" Holland darted to his side and wedged her shoulder under his arm. He was heavy. He felt like pure muscle. And he was hot. She could feel the heat through his shirt and jacket. He definitely wasn't fine. And yet he fought her at the door. He wouldn't take a step past the threshold. "What is it? Are you a vampire? Do you need me to invite you in?"

"No," he groaned, and Holland *almost* thought she saw a hint of a smile. "I just feel like I shouldn't go in there." He cut a look from the blood soaking his hand to the white oak floors and smooth white walls. "It's very *clean*."

"It's okay," Holland said. "If I don't live past tomorrow, your drops of blood will only add to the mystery of my death." She hoped for a hint of another smile or a scowl or any sign of life, but Gabe really wasn't looking well. "Let's just get you to the bathroom."

She helped him through the door. "Come on, it's not much farther."

"I think here is good." Gabe slumped against the stair railing, shoulders drooping, eyes closing.

"Don't pass out," she warned. "I'm going to get medication and stiches and washcloths and—" She didn't know why she was babbling. She darted to the closest bathroom.

She grabbed towels and Band-Aids and hydrogen peroxide, and then she remembered that January had given her a first aid kit the size of a suitcase. Holland had never used it. She had never needed more than a Band-Aid. She remembered jokingly asking if her sister had thought the apocalypse was coming. *You never know when disaster will strike,* January had deadpanned in return. Holland had thought she was joking. But now, as Holland pulled out the enormous kit, she wondered if her sister had expected something like this to happen. Clearly there were things about her sister's life that January wasn't telling her.

Holland jolted at the sound of movement coming from the front of the house. The spot where she'd left Gabe . . . and the Professor's package.

CHAPTER SIXTEEN

Holland's heart started racing again. Or maybe it had never stopped.

She bolted out of the bathroom and skidded to a halt.

Gabe was still there, sitting on the steps. He'd moved the package behind him, while he sat in front of it, one hand clutching his wound, the other his gun.

Holland took a ragged breath.

"What's wrong with you?" he asked. His mouth screwed into a frown as he looked at her. "Did you think I was going to leave with this?" He nodded toward the package.

She wanted to tell him no, but there had been so many other lies tonight, she didn't want to tell even a tiny one. "I thought about it."

"You still don't trust me?"

"I don't know," Holland said honestly. Earlier in the night, it would have been an easy *no*. It still felt like it should have been—given what she'd learned about Jake and Adam, it seemed wise not to trust anyone, particularly any man she found attractive, until he went through a rigorous lie detector test or confessed all his sins under the influence of a truth serum. But Gabe had taken a bullet, he'd protected the package, he hadn't left her.

And she didn't want him to leave.

She wasn't sure if that was trust, but it was something. It was enough to make her feel just a little nervous as she stepped toward him.

Gabe moved to the right, closer to the railing, so that she could sit beside him on the stairs. He was still wearing his cobalt-blue suit coat, and from the way it fit him, it was clearly expensive. It felt that way, too, fabric smooth under her fingertips as she reached up to help him take it off.

"You shouldn't," he said.

Her fingers froze. "I shouldn't what?"

"You shouldn't trust me. I'm not a good person."

"Have I given you the impression that I think you're good?" Holland tried to say it like someone who still wanted to stab him, but then she made the mistake of looking at him. Really looking at him. This might have been the first time she'd done so under the light, and she was right, Gabe's eyes were dark, and he had a scar on his right cheek, just below his eye. It was exactly like the one Holland had pictured in the car.

She told herself it wasn't a stretch to imagine that a man like Gabe might have a scar on his face. But there was something about the scar that made her feel as if she'd seen it before, not just imagined it. For a second, she had a flash of his face, leaning close, eyes pained and red as they looked into hers.

Then she saw his actual eyes narrowing, as he caught her staring.

Holland quickly looked away and focused on helping him with the jacket. The shirt underneath looked as if it had once been pure white, but now it was covered in blood. So much blood. One of his broad hands was over the wound, and she had no idea what would happen when he moved it.

"What do we do next? Or what do I do now?" she asked. She hated to admit it, but she was starting to feel a little faint just looking at the blood. "Do I take off your shirt and then have you move your hand from the wound? Or should you move your hand and then we take off your shirt? Is there an order to this?"

Gabe looked at her darkly. She felt as if he'd expected a little more, like maybe he'd expected her to be January, who wouldn't have been flustered by blood, or by Gabe as he peeled her hand away. "I'll take care of my shirt. You work on getting a needle and thread."

Holland's fingers shook as she opened the kit. Everything inside was neatly and disturbingly labeled with things like *When you don't want to go to the hospital* and *In case of poisoning.*

And suddenly Holland felt certain that her sister had known something like this would happen. She grabbed the *When you don't want to go to the hospital* pouch and quickly tore it open.

There were more pouches inside, with gloves, cloths for antiseptic cleaning and surgical numbing, terrifying little pliers, and scissors and needles and thread that made her think of fishing wire. Only she knew it wasn't fishing wire. It was stitching wire.

She needed to distract herself. "I'm guessing my sister doesn't really collect rare books?"

"That's a question you need to ask her, not me."

"Can you give me a hint? Is she an assassin? Are you two in a kidnapping league?"

"We don't work together." Gabe said this as if it was important.

"But you told me—" Holland actually couldn't remember what he'd told her in the car, either because of the trauma from the ride or because of the blood before her now. All she could recall was that Gabe and January hadn't dated.

"I work freelance. I'm good at acquiring difficult-to-find things. Now," Gabe said sharply, clearly wanting to put an end to any future questions, "grab one of those antiseptic cloths to clean the wound."

Holland did as instructed.

Gabe lifted his hand from the wound and there was so much blood and flesh and—

She had to close her eyes. She wasn't January. She couldn't do this. She wanted to do it, but her eyes wouldn't open.

"Hey," Gabe said. "Sweetheart, look at me."

"I don't know if I can."

"Don't look at my wound," he said, surprisingly gentle. "Look at *me.*"

She heard Gabe set down the gun, and then she felt his hand on hers. "You can relax." His hand felt warm as he guided her fingers toward the wound. "It's not my time to die."

"You don't know that."

"Yes. I do." His voice became even softer. "I know it, the same way you know the time you're going to die."

Holland's eyes cracked open. "You talked to the Watch Man?"

Gabe guided her hand to set down the antiseptic cloth. "It's not my time tonight."

Holland flashed back to the way he'd driven the car, as if accidents were things that happened to other people. "That's why you were driving like a maniac earlier."

"No, that's just how I drive," he replied. And she swore she saw the edge of his mouth inch up. He patiently instructed Holland to put on gloves, then use the wipe to numb the flesh around his gaping wound.

She still didn't want to look at where the bullet had ripped through him, but after what Gabe had just told her about the Watch Man, she didn't feel quite so nervous. Now she was just terribly curious. She wanted to ask what his time was, but that felt like too intimate a question. Then again, Gabe was sitting in her house, shirtless, as she carefully stitched up his bare skin.

"What time did he give you?" she blurted.

"All that matters is, it's not tonight."

Holland sewed another stitch. She thought the wound looked better already. Some of the color had returned to Gabe's face. But there was now something tragic in his eyes. "Did the Watch Man tell you something you can do to get more time?" she asked.

"Why? You worried about me?" He said it as if he possibly possessed a sense of humor. But the corners of his mouth moved down, as if being concerned for him was a very bad idea.

"I'm just curious, since right now I feel like my whole life depends on doing what the Watch Man told me."

"You want to know if there's another way to get more time?"

"Is there?"

"Not that I know of. But—" Gabe drew out the word slowly, as if debating whether he should say what he was thinking. "Your situation might not be entirely hopeless." He looked over his shoulder, at the brown paper package from the Professor.

Holland probably should have opened it as soon as Gabe was stable. She definitely should have been rushing to open it now. But for a second all she could do was stare.

"What are you waiting for?" he asked.

CHAPTER SEVENTEEN

Holland couldn't tell Gabe why she hesitated.

She had already taken off the gloves and used another cloth to clean her hands, but she took another moment to wipe her palms on her skirt before picking up the package. Her skin prickled as she touched it.

If it wasn't the Professor's journal, then Holland had no other leads on the Alchemical Heart.

Carefully, she unwrapped the stiff brown paper.

With bone-deep relief, Holland recognized the worn red leather cover. The Professor's journal was thick and beautiful—or it was beautiful to her just then—full of pages that had wrinkled and spread apart from years of use.

"This is it," she said.

The front cover was plain, but Holland could feel something scored onto the back. She flipped it over. There was a large symbol covering the book, freshly carved. Holland wasn't a symbol expert, but last quarter, she'd taken a course called Common & Uncommon Symbols in Folklore. The class had been as dry as stale toast, but Holland had been interested enough in the subject that she'd done a lot of studying on her own.

Holland could tell that this symbol was actually composed of at least five other symbols—a burning heart, filled in with a labyrinth, which wrapped around an antiquity eye that appeared to have two symbols coming out of it. On top of the eye was the symbol for tin, and below it was the symbol for sulfur.

"This middle part is the same symbol that you and January have tattooed on your wrists," Holland said.

When January had first gotten the tattoo, she'd claimed to have done it on a whim, after her breakup. She had said she had no idea what the combination of symbols meant, but she'd thought they looked interesting. She'd lied.

Holland reached up and touched the matching symbol around her neck, but for the first time, it didn't feel special. It made her feel like she'd been placated.

"I want to know about the tattoos. What do they really mean?" Holland asked.

"Doesn't matter right now," Gabe said. Then he pointed at the larger image on the journal. "This is the symbol for the Alchemical Heart."

Hours ago, he'd talked about the Alchemical Heart as if it was just a myth. But it was clear now that Gabe believed in this *myth* more than he was letting on, or more than he wanted to admit to himself. He ran a hand across his jaw. "How would she have known to send this to you?"

"I don't know," Holland said. "But there are a lot of things I don't know right now." She wondered what her sister knew about the Alchemical Heart. And what other secrets January was keeping.

Then she opened the journal. The pages were covered in the Professor's cursive. Holland scanned the notes about familiar urban myths and legends: the devil's business cards, the After Midnight Menu, the Watch Man.

Holland continued flipping pages, until the myths turned unfamiliar. There was a new one, which Holland had never heard before, about a hotel called the Regal.

Then, near the end of the journal, she found it.

Class #6
The Chained Library

Most of the Professor's notes were exactly what Holland remembered from the class. But then near the bottom was a fresh line of ink.

All that remained was a slip of parchment with a series of numbers on it.

The Professor had then written a list of numbers. They looked like dates—months and years. The numbers went back for centuries. The last date, 10.2025, was this month, which aligned with what Gabe had said about the sudden frenzied search for the Alchemical Heart. But it was the number before that Holland found even more arresting: 10.2010.

Fifteen years ago, one of my clients leased a safety deposit box, Mr. Vargas had said.

Holland had thought he was a con man. But now his words felt more like a clue in one of her father's old treasure hunts. If she was piecing things together correctly, then she knew why someone might send people after her and her sister. They believed that fifteen years ago, her father had found the Alchemical Heart. And he had hidden it for his daughters.

"Did you find something?" asked Gabe.

"I think you were right—"

A heavy knock pounded against the front door, cutting Holland off. Gabe picked up his gun.

Holland jumped to her feet—still holding the journal—and looked out the window flanking the door. "Oh no," she muttered.

Chance Garcia stood on the porch, hands in his pockets, concern etched across his perfect movie star face.

"What the hell is he doing here?" Gabe asked.

"He's my friend."

Gabe looked immediately skeptical. "*Friends* don't just stop by at a quarter to midnight."

"Is it really that late?"

Gabe nodded, as if this proved his point.

"We're just friends," Holland repeated.

"Then get rid of him," Gabe warned. "Or I will." He held up his gun.

"Put that away. He's not involved in any of this."

"Then why is he here?"

"Probably because I was on the phone with him when I found Jake. I hung up to call the police, and then, a little bit after that, *someone* tossed my phone out the window." Holland gave Gabe a tart look. "My guess is that Chance has tried to call me for the last couple of hours and been terrified that I haven't answered."

"Fine," Gabe muttered. "Just make sure whatever conversation you have is quick—and *keeps* him out of this." He tucked the gun in the back of his pants. "Oh, and you might also want to cover that up." He pointed toward her pale pink blouse, which was spattered with his blood.

Holland quickly opened the hall closet and grabbed a long trench coat. She was going to look ridiculous, but she couldn't let Chance see the blood. She wished he hadn't come here. But part of her also loved that he had. He cared. He was her friend. Her good friend. Which was why she needed to get rid of him.

With a deep breath, Holland cracked her front door open, just enough to dip her head out.

The relief on Chance's face nearly broke her heart.

"Hey!" she said. "What's going on?" But her voice might have been a little too cheerful. Chance's relief turned sideways, into something that looked more like frustration.

"What the hell happened to you? I've been trying to call for hours." He took a step toward the door, but Holland knew she couldn't open it wider. She wanted to, but then she thought about Gabe and his gun and she narrowed the door instead of opening it.

Chance's frown deepened.

"I'm sorry—" She didn't want to lie. But she also knew there wasn't anything truthful she could say that would make this situation better.

"Holly, I'm worried about you. You told me someone died and then you disappeared."

"I know—I said that. But—"

"Babe, who is it?" The deep sound of Gabe's voice was followed by his arms, wrapping around her waist from behind. He pulled her close to his bare chest. Then, in a voice made of pure exclamation points, "No way—you're Chance Garcia! Babe—you didn't tell me you knew this guy!"

Hurt cut across Chance's face.

Gabe tightened his arms, in a way that didn't feel necessary.

"We've been friends for years," she said, and she tried to put as much feeling into her voice as possible. But Chance seemed fixated on Gabe's naked chest pressed against her back. He also appeared to be eyeing her trench coat with a new level of disdain.

"Babe, I can't believe you never told me you know Chance Garcia!"

"That would make two of us," Chance said. "She's never mentioned you, either."

"Well, Holly and I are pretty new." Gabe leaned down and pressed a kiss to her cheek. His lips were warm and soft and he let them linger. "I've been trying to keep her all to myself. But, dude! You should totally come in! I have so many questions about that unaired episode of *The Magic Attic*."

Chance's face turned ashen. For a second, he didn't even look like himself.

"I try not to get into conspiracies," Gabe said, as if oblivious. But Holland knew he wasn't. She wanted to pull away, but Gabe's grip felt like a warning and a reminder of what he'd just said minutes ago about not being a good guy. "Man, there are some wild theories out there," he went on. "I'd love to get your take on them."

"Maybe another time." Chance started backing away. His eyes met Holland's for a painful second. Questions, disappointment, and hurt all flashed in his gaze.

Holland tried to think of something to say.

Gabe tightened his arms and rested his chin on her shoulder. Then she felt his lips move closer to her ear. "Don't even think about chasing him," he whispered.

CHAPTER EIGHTEEN

Gabe kicked the door shut as Chance reached the sidewalk. "I don't like that guy," he muttered.

"You didn't have to hurt his feelings." Holland ripped herself free of Gabe's arms.

He looked utterly unapologetic. "He's not your friend."

"Yes, he is—or he was," Holland said.

Gabe shook his head. "You can't trust him. Trust me."

"Didn't you just tell me *not* to trust you, because you're not a good person?"

"Exactly. I'm not a good person, and I can tell you that there's something off about that guy."

"Chance has been my friend for years," Holland argued.

"Not your friend." Gabe turned his dark eyes back to the journal. "What were you saying about a list of dates?"

"Nothing really. Only that you were right. There's a list of numbers in here, and the final number is for this month and year." Holland shut the journal, as if there was nothing more to say.

"Let me see it," Gabe said.

"See what?"

"The journal."

Holland's fingers tightened around it. She knew she was being petty. But the stunt with Chance confirmed that she really didn't know Gabe well, and she didn't feel like sharing more with him just then. Actually, she wasn't even sure if she needed him anymore. If she was right, and her father had hidden the Alchemical Heart in his safety deposit box, then all Holland needed to do was open the box tomorrow morning.

"Why are you acting cagey?" Gabe asked. "Is this because of your little boyfriend?" He took an intentional step forward.

Holland took one back. "Stop trying to intimidate me. And if you want me to be less *cagey*, I need you to do the same. I need answers about my sister." Holland nodded toward Gabe's exposed wrist. A little bit ago, he'd said the meaning behind the tattoo didn't matter, but Holland didn't believe him.

Holland knew January loved her. She also knew that sometimes her sister's form of love was very different from Holland's. January saw the world as a much harsher place than Holland did and felt as if she needed to protect her from it.

Holland wanted to believe that was why her sister was keeping secrets. January probably thought she was doing the right thing. And maybe she was. Maybe January's secrets were the reason Holland was able to see the world in the bright Technicolor way that she did. But Holland liked to think that even if she knew harsh truths, she could still hold on to her hope and her belief that the world was full of magic—the wondrous, treasure-hunt kind of magic—and she could find it if she just reached her hand out far enough to grab it.

"I just want to know how much my sister has been hiding from me," Holland went on. "Does she know about all these myths and legends the same way you seem to? How did she get involved in all this?"

Gabe stared down at Holland the way she imagined a wolf might eye a fluffy white bunny or a fire might glare at a marshmallow, as if there was no contest. "I'm not answering your questions."

"Why not?"

"I don't believe in a lot of things, but I believe in loyalty. January's secrets are hers; they aren't mine to share."

On another occasion Gabe's *loyalty* might have been commendable, but this just felt like an excuse to leave Holland in the dark. She turned away and marched down the hall.

"Where are you going?" Gabe asked.

Holland kept marching.

Gabe grabbed her arm and spun her around, a spark of frustration finally cracking his stony facade. "You can't just run off like this."

"I'm not running off. This is my house. And if you're not going to tell me anything about my sister, I'm going to figure it out for myself." Holland pulled free as Gabe said some nonsense about needing to leave because it wasn't safe.

"You're welcome to come with me if you want," she said as she stepped inside the guest room.

January's favorite color was blue, and so Holland had piled the bed with blue pillows, bought a blue gingham carpet for the floor, and even filled in the floating shelves with only pale blue books.

January's job required her to travel a lot, and whenever she was in LA she came to stay with Holland. January actually visited often enough to leave a number of clothes here, along with a backpack.

Gabe stepped into the room just as Holland opened the closet and pulled out the backpack. Hair ties, ticket stubs, spare change, and pieces of mail cascaded out. For all January's intelligence, she'd never learned to use a trash can.

Gabe leaned against the doorway. He'd put his shirt and his coat back on, and was now eyeing Holland curiously as she started to dig through January's miscellanea. "What do you think you're going to find in there?"

"More than you're willing to tell me." Holland riffled through a few more items, until she came to two thick emerald-green envelopes. They were the sort of fancy envelopes that might have carried wedding invitations, except that they were in the shape of business correspondence. One had January's name and address. The other had Holland's. January's letter was already open.

"I don't think you should touch those." Gabe shoved away from the doorframe as Holland started to rip open the letter addressed to her.

"Why not?" she asked.

Gabe was now just a foot away. He looked like he wanted to rip the letter from her hands, but he also looked afraid to touch it. "That's from a place you don't want to mess with," he said, as Holland unfolded a cream-colored piece of paper.

First Bank of Centennial City shimmered across the top in green ink.

And Holland instantly knew who this letter was from. She could hear Mr. Vargas's voice saying, *Did you not receive my letters?*

Why had her sister kept this a secret?

She might have asked Gabe, but he'd already made clear his stance on January's secrets, and he was still staring at the letter as if it were a lit stick of dynamite.

"Why don't you like this bank?" Holland asked.

Gabe pulled at the back of his neck, looking supremely uncomfortable. "It's evil."

At that moment, the room grew lighter. A car with too-bright headlights was driving down the street. It stopped in front of her driveway, completely blocking Gabe's car.

He suddenly reached down and grabbed Holland's hand. "We need to go."

CHAPTER NINETEEN

Holland barely had time to glance out the front window before Gabe was dragging her from the room. "Wait—"

"We don't have time to wait!"

"If you want me to run, I'll be faster in shoes." Holland's pulse pounded as she tugged free of Gabe's hand.

Car doors slammed outside.

Holland threw on January's backpack first, imagining it still held answers to secrets. Then she shoved her feet into a pair of January's sneakers. The right one hurt, as if there was something wedged underneath the sole.

"We need to go now." Gabe grabbed her hand again, stopping her from taking off the shoe.

"Who is out there?" Holland asked. And then the world went black. The house. The streetlights. The car that had just blocked their exit. All were suddenly dark.

"Keep moving," Gabe urged.

"But the lights."

"That's not what we need to worry about. We need to go out the back."

He seemed unbothered by the darkness as he propelled her forward. And this time, he wouldn't let go of her hand. She tripped more than once, but his grip stayed firm.

In the backyard, there was only a simple wooden gate between them and whoever was out there. Holland could hear their muffled voices and the sound of footsteps approaching the front of the house. "Who's here?" she whispered.

Gabe ignored her, scanning the fences surrounding the yard. His movements were sharp, tense. "Any of your neighbors have dogs?"

"No." As soon as she said the word, Gabe was helping her hop the back fence and muttering something about hoping the neighbors didn't have a pool.

There was no pool. But there was a lot of rock. It bit into the soles of Holland's feet, and she became very aware of whatever it was January had shoved into her shoe. But there wasn't time to stop. Gabe still hadn't said who he thought was chasing them, but Holland imagined it must have been someone else who was after the Alchemical Heart.

"Come on," Gabe said. "We need a car." He kept hold of her hand as they raced down the side of her neighbor's house, until they reached a street just as black as hers. It felt as if someone had switched off the whole world. Although Holland swore she could hear a swarm of cars, just around the block.

"We have to keep moving." Gabe pulled her farther down the street.

As Holland's eyes adjusted, she could see just beyond the outlines of the houses. "There—" She pointed down the street, where someone had parked an old VW Bug.

Gabe gave her a look. It was difficult to fully see it in the dark. But she could tell there was definitely a look from the harsh way he turned his head and said, "I don't know if you understand the concept of a getaway car."

"I was trying to think of a car we could hot-wire."

Gabe made a choking sound that might have been a laugh. "We're not hot-wiring a car."

A light flickered, two houses down. It was a single soft yellow light in front of a garage where someone had parked a sleek sports car.

"That's the one," Gabe said softly. His steps finally slowed as they approached it. His fingers reached toward it, not quite touching, but he looked as if he wanted to pet it.

Holland had never understood the fascination men had with cars. In her ideal world, everyone would ride bicycles, beach cruisers preferably, with baskets and glossy coats of colorful paint. Instead of honking horns, people would ring little bike bells, they'd wave hellos instead of flipping people off, and the world would be an all-around happier place. At least for her.

Holland couldn't picture Gabe riding a bike. She also couldn't picture him happy. Although he looked as if he was hovering near something like joy now.

"I don't think you can steal this one," said Holland. She might not have known much about cars, but she knew this model was new enough that you needed a key or—

Gabe opened the door with one simple touch of his fingers. In that same second, the engine purred to life. "You were saying?"

Holland gaped at him. "How did you do that?"

"Cars like me." Gabe slipped into the driver's seat.

The radio was already on, pouring out a rock ballad that was actually perfect for a getaway, and as Holland got into the car, she couldn't help thinking the movie of her life had just turned into an action flick. *An action flick with magic.*

"Did you just use magic?" she asked.

She waited for his gravelly laugh, or for him to tell her she'd just imagined it. But she knew she wasn't imagining it. Another person might have assumed that Gabe had some sort of advanced technology hidden in his pocket. But not Holland.

Holland had always believed in magic. As a child, she knew there was a difference between fantasy and reality. But she had also always wondered if there was more fantasy in reality than people let on. How could there be so many stories about magic if magic didn't exist? This was one of the other reasons she'd been drawn to the Professor's class. The Professor's myths felt like a bridge between the ordinary world and a magical world where someone could snap his fingers and all the lights would wink out.

"What else can you do?" Holland asked. From the look on his face, she could already tell he didn't like her asking questions, but she couldn't contain her excitement. "Did you also use magic to make the neighborhood go dark? Do you even need your hands to drive this car?"

She watched Gabe press his foot on the gas pedal. But now she imagined it was probably because he enjoyed driving stolen cars like a maniac, not because he actually needed to.

"First, we don't use the word *magic*," he said gruffly. "Second, it's rude to ask people about their ability."

"Why?"

"You just don't. If you use the word *magic*, people will know that you're not a part of this world."

"And by world, you mean the world of the Professor's myths?"

Gabe frowned. "The myths don't belong to your Professor, but yes . . ." He trailed off as his eyes went to the rearview mirror. "Strange."

"What's strange?"

"No one is following us."

Holland looked behind her. The streetlights had turned back on. The October night was glowing once again. Holland thought she saw a person in the driveway they'd just left. But whoever she saw wasn't racing after them. They were standing there, watching them drive away.

Gabe took a sharp turn, and then it was only the two of them, the blast of the air conditioning, and the angry rock ballad pouring out of the speakers. "It doesn't make any sense," he muttered. "It's almost as if they let us get away." He abruptly turned to Holland. His hands weren't even on the wheel. He'd given up the pretense of being a normal person like her. Although now he was looking at her as if she was the one hiding a secret. "What aren't you telling me? I don't know who that was, but anyone chasing after you thinking you have the Alchemical Heart wouldn't just stop."

"Maybe they were chasing after you," Holland said. Again, she waited for him to dismiss her with a laugh, or a one-liner ending in *sweetheart*.

But Gabe didn't say another word for the rest of their drive.

Gabe remained quiet as he pulled the stolen car into a darkened drive-way. Holland could smell the ocean as she opened the door. They must have been practically on the coast, although she wasn't exactly sure where. The night was foggy enough to curl her hair as she followed Gabe down a curved walkway that magically lit up after every step he took.

If she'd taken the time to imagine where Gabe might bring her, she probably would have pictured a sleek high-rise to match his expensive suit, but this was the furthest thing from it.

It was a small, picket-fenced beach house, with a rope swing hanging from an island oak tree that looked older than she was.

"Is this your place?" she asked.

"It is for tonight."

The porch light flickered on, lighting up a doormat with waves and the words *mi casa es su casa*. Holland wondered if it had ever occurred to the owners that intruders might take the welcome literally.

The door had one of those electronic keypads, but Gabe didn't bother with a combination. The lock clicked open as soon as he touched the han-dle. Holland made a note to herself that if she lived through the night, she was never getting one of those electric handles. Although she had a feeling that even regular locks wouldn't keep Gabe out.

"After you." Gabe waved a magnanimous hand toward the entry. But he was once again looking at Holland as if she was holding on to a secret made of gunpowder. Something big and explosive, with the power to destroy them both.

The beach house was now flush with warm yellow light, illuminating a room Holland would have bet was advertised as perfect for social media pics. The wall behind the couch was entirely covered in fake green foliage, except for a white neon sign in the center that read, in cursive, *I love Los Angeles!*

Gabe clearly didn't care for the sign, because it was the only light he'd left off.

On the coffee table, a pink plastic record player sat next to a pile of neon coasters resembling old floppy disks. The pillows on the orange velvet sofa were all embroidered with sayings that wouldn't belong at a grandmother's house. And across from the windows that looked out onto the Pacific was an enormous picture of Dolly Parton, in the style of Andy Warhol.

It all made Holland think, once again, about her dreams of living inside a movie with a pop music soundtrack. She suddenly felt as if those dreams could have led her here, but under very different circumstances, and definitely not with Gabe.

He frowned at one of the sofa's inappropriately embroidered pillows and tossed it aside, before deciding he didn't actually want to take a seat. He looked exquisitely out of place, standing in this bright oversaturated room in his dark tailored suit and his blood-soaked shirt.

"You're the one who picked this place," Holland said.

"I should have looked at the pictures," he grumbled.

"I like it," Holland said.

"Good, because this could be where you're going to die if we don't find out what makes you so special." Gabe's dark eyes started to look her over, as if trying to figure it out himself, but after only a second, he turned away. "Before today, I'd never even heard your name. I knew January had a twin, but she rarely talked about you. Now, it seems as if everyone believes you're the key to finding the Alchemical Heart, and I want to know why. What aren't you telling me?"

Holland took a deep breath and finally confessed. "A lot."

CHAPTER TWENTY

The expression on Gabe's face was nearly impossible to read. One small corner of his mouth moved in a way that could have just as easily been his form of extreme surprise or a satisfied *I knew it.*

Holland took a seat on the orange velvet couch, then she waited for Gabe to do the same before saying, "Today, a banker visited my house."

Gabe narrowed his dark eyes. "A banker from where?"

"The First Bank of Centennial City."

The color drained from Gabe's face. "That's the Bank." He said the word with emphasis on the letter *B.* "What did they want?"

"The banker said that someone left me a safety deposit box fifteen years ago, and that I had to open it by tomorrow or the contents would be destroyed. At first, I thought it was a scam, but then I couldn't help myself, and I called for an appointment."

Gabe looked at her as if she'd just confessed to drinking a bottle of poison. "Don't tell me you think this mystery safety deposit box contains the Alchemical Heart."

That was exactly what Holland thought. She could tell Gabe thought she was being naive, but she wasn't ready to tell him about the connection to her father just yet.

"What's the harm in just looking at this box? If it doesn't have the Alchemical Heart, then all we've done is waste fifteen minutes."

"It's not that simple."

"Then explain it to me."

Gabe rubbed a hand along the dark stubble lining his jaw for a long, uncomfortable minute that made her regret choosing to sit on the sofa instead of the kitchen table. This close to him, she could feel tension and anger and some other unnameable but very uncomfortable emotion pouring off him.

Finally, he said, "This isn't a regular bank. When the Sacred Order of the Parallel Dawn split up, it fractured into three separate groups. One faction felt that the magic created by the Alchemical Heart needed to be destroyed."

Holland nodded.

"One of the other factions felt the opposite. They wanted to continue to use the Alchemical Heart to create magic—"

"Wait—" Holland interrupted. "I thought you said not to use the word *magic*?"

"People have abilities," he said, annoyed. "Objects have magic."

"So . . . I *can* use the word *magic*?"

"*Only* when you talk about an object. But just . . . don't."

"Oh, my gosh—you're a snob!"

Gabe immediately looked offended, but then his snobby expression returned, which only proved her point.

"You're a magic snob! You're a part of this magical world, and you don't want me saying the word *magic* because you're afraid it will make you seem less serious and scary."

He scowled. "Do you want me to finish telling you about the Bank, or do you want to argue about magic?"

For the record, Gabe was the one who kept saying *magic*. But Holland thought it was probably not wise to point that out. "Please, continue," she said sweetly.

Gabe's mouth shifted into a crooked line, as if he wasn't quite sure what expression to make. Murders, car chases, and ransacked homes were all just part of his average day, but teasing had surprised him. Holland watched his mouth twist uncertainly for a few more seconds before, finally, he said, "The third faction claimed that it didn't think the Alchemical Heart should be destroyed, but they also didn't think it should be used. They said they wanted to protect the world and the Alchemical Heart by keeping it out of anyone's hands. This faction came to be known as the Bank."

"That doesn't sound so bad," Holland said.

"I'm not done. Back when the Bank first split from the Sacred Order, it began a campaign to erase all mentions of the Alchemical Heart and the Sacred Order of the Parallel Dawn from history. But it didn't stop there. The Bank is the reason no one who's not a part of this world ever remembers hearing about the Alchemical Heart. They erase memories, and they're ruthless about it."

Holland also didn't see how this was necessarily evil, but it seemed Gabe still wasn't done.

"During World War II, the Bank conscripted a number of powerful objects from people. They claimed it was in service of the war, but the objects were never given back—and many of the families they stole from were in open opposition to the Bank's practices. They did the same with abilities. You're not supposed to be able to steal an ability from another person, but the Bank has managed to take abilities from entire families, and now they loan those abilities out to those in their employ, as an incentive to get people to work for them." Gabe curled his mouth as if he found this distasteful, and Holland had to admit she did as well.

"The Bank claims their goal is to maintain order and keep people safe, but what they really want is to control, manipulate, and possess all the power in the world. That's why they want the Alchemical Heart, and if you go in there tomorrow, I promise you that before you leave, they'll take whatever is in that box, and then they'll take your memories. Not just of this conversation—they'll erase everything you learned from your precious Professor, everything you learned about your sister tonight, they—" Gabe's eyes were on hers, and for a second Holland imagined he was going to say they'd take every memory of him as well, but what he said next was far worse. "Just to be *safe*, they might even take the last several years of your life. You'll become one of those people who end up in Griffith Park with no memory of how they got there or who they are."

Goosebumps sprang up on Holland's arms. The Professor had a class about this. Every year, she told her students that there was any-where from one to several dozen unexplainable cases of amnesia re-ported at the Old LA Zoo, and the Professor claimed that these were all people who had stumbled upon the myths and legends she taught in her class. Then she warned her students this was why they could never repeat the stories she shared.

Holland had always been skeptical of this myth. It felt a little bit like manipulation. But Gabe didn't sound as if he was trying to manipulate her, he sounded as if he was just telling her the cold hard facts. And Holland believed him.

It made Holland wonder if maybe this was what had happened to the Professor, if she had gotten too close to too many truths and the Bank had erased her memories. Maybe this was why she'd sent Holland her journal—so someone would remember.

Gabe started to shove up from the sofa, as if the conversation was over.

"Wait—" said Holland. "What if the box actually does hold the Al-chemical Heart?"

"You just don't give up, do you?"

"Not when my life depends on it." Although Holland would have wanted to open her father's box even if her life didn't depend on it.

"Give me one good reason you think that box might hold the Al-chemical Heart," Gabe said.

Holland took a deep breath. She had always told herself that when she finally fell in love, she'd know because *this* would be the secret she would share. It was the one thing she never told anyone. And it was the one thing she desperately *wanted* to tell someone. She just hadn't expected that someone to be Gabe, a reluctant bodyguard who may or may not have kidnapped her earlier that night—she still went back and forth with how she felt about that one.

But she reminded herself that her sister trusted him, so she could as well.

She tried to keep her voice steady. "I wasn't being entirely honest with you when I told you about that list of dates in the Professor's journal. I noticed that the second-to-last date in there was fifteen years ago this month, which was when my father opened the safety deposit box at the Bank."

"That doesn't mean he put the Alchemical Heart in there."

"What if I told you my father was also part of one of the Professor's myths?"

This seemed to capture Gabe's attention. His head cocked to the side as he asked, "Who is your father?"

Holland took another deep breath. "Benjamin Tierney."

"As in the director who—" Gabe broke off.

But Holland knew what he'd been about to say. He'd been about to say something about Ben's wife murdering him, which is what most people said when Ben Tierney and Isla Saint came up.

And suddenly Holland regretted telling him anything. She never should have said her father's name. She—

"Hey, don't—" Gabe gripped her shoulder, his hands steady in a way that made her realize just how unsteady she felt. "You haven't fallen apart yet tonight. Don't do it now." He looked at her as if he wanted to say more, as if maybe he even wanted to say he was sorry, but Holland imagined that while Gabe was adept at abducting damsels in distress, he wasn't used to comforting them.

"It's all right," Holland said. "I'm not going to fall apart. I'm very familiar with my parents' story."

She started to pull away, but Gabe held her there a second longer, before very quietly saying, "I didn't know. Your sister never told me."

"We don't tell anyone," Holland said. "I only told you because I didn't think you'd let me go to the Bank otherwise."

"I'm still not sure about letting you go." Gabe removed his hand from her shoulder. "But as much as I hate to admit it—you might be on to something." His expression suggested he might regret what he was about to say next. "There were rumors about Ben Tierney being in possession of the Alchemical Heart."

"So you think I'm right?" Holland asked cautiously.

"I didn't say that." Gabe rubbed his knuckles across his jaw. "It was just a rumor. That's why I told you the Alchemical Heart was a myth, because all the *recent* stories aren't even real stories. They're just whispers, bits of gossip that people like to repeat."

"Just because it's gossip doesn't mean it's not true. My father opened the box fifteen years ago. So the timing matches the date in the journal."

"That could just be a coincidence," Gabe argued.

"One thing can be a coincidence, but when you have multiple things that all add up, it's a story," Holland said.

"And you think this story ends with your father putting the most valuable object in the world inside a safety deposit box?"

Holland wanted to say yes. Her gut kept telling her the answer was yes. But she didn't feel as if her gut was enough to win an argument with Gabe.

Holland pulled out the Professor's journal.

"What are you looking for?" Gabe asked.

"The Professor taught a class on the Bank," Holland said. It was the one class she could never seem to remember, but she felt as if it presented a different picture of the Bank than Gabe did, and she imagined the Professor had written things about it in her journal.

"The Bank is good at propaganda," Gabe muttered.

Ignoring his glare, Holland continued to flip pages. "Here it is. The Professor wrote that the Bank's vaults are the safest and most secure in the world—no one has ever stolen anything from the Bank, including the Bank. The Bank enforces all the laws of their world. One of the reasons they are able to keep this power is because they abide by all the rules. The Bank's branches hold the greatest number of magical objects in the entire world, and one of the reasons people are willing to store their most valuable magic objects there is because they know they won't be touched. As long as they have an appointment." She paused. "Is this true?"

Gabe worked his jaw unhappily, which made her feel as if the answer was yes. "What else does she say?"

"One of the Bank's most well-known rules is that they offer protection to anyone with an appointment. If you have an appointment, no one, not even the Bank, can touch you during that window of time."

Holland looked up at Gabe hopefully. If this was true, then it made even more sense that her father would have put the Alchemical Heart in one of the Bank's boxes.

Gabe paced the tiny room. He looked as if he was debating sending her into an evil bank to retrieve a mythical treasure that might not actually be there or . . .

There actually wasn't another option available, which he seemed to realize.

"You're not going to have a problem getting into the Bank," he finally gritted out. "If you have an appointment, then they want you in—they want you to open your father's box. The tricky part is going to be getting you out. As soon as your appointment is over and you're off the property, they'll try to detain you."

"So you're going to let me go?"

"I don't think I can stop you," he said, which sounded like about as nice of a compliment as Gabe could give.

Holland tried to say as much, but suddenly she was having a difficult time breathing. The light had faded and the room had gone fuzzy. Her head was spinning a little, and when she was able to speak again, words came out that she didn't mean to say. "What if my father's box doesn't have the Alchemical Heart and the Bank detains me?"

"I won't let that happen. You get in, I'll make sure you get out," Gabe said. But suddenly he no longer looked like Gabe. He looked just like Adam Bishop. Golden hair, golden skin, devil-may-care expression on his beautiful face.

Holland blinked, but when she opened her eyes, she was still looking at Adam.

Adam was in the beach house, right in front of her, real enough to touch, wearing the same ripped jeans and plaid shirt as before, only now the shirt was open and she could see a bandage wrapping around his shoulder.

"Trust me, Bright Eyes," he said, and he sounded like Adam, too. "I'm not going to let anyone hold on to you but me." His mouth slowly tipped into a smirk as he wrapped his arms around her waist.

Holland tried to pull free, but she felt helpless as he tugged her closer. All she could do was shut her eyes again. Tighter this time.

"Holland—" This time the voice sounded like Gabe. He took hold of her shoulder, just as she felt something wet drip from her nose.

CHAPTER TWENTY-ONE

Holland opened her eyes.

Adam was gone.

Gabe was back, and the beach house was suddenly too bright, as if someone had turned all the lights on at once. The wall of fake greenery looked lurid, the couch was a brasher shade of orange than before, and there was *a lot* of bright red blood on her hand.

Was this how she died? Was something happening with her brain that only the Alchemical Heart could fix?

Gabe carefully dabbed at her nose with a small yellow towel. She hadn't seen him go and grab it, but she also hadn't seen him during the minute she'd been imagining Adam.

"You all right?" Gabe asked.

Nope. Definitely not all right. Not even close.

The microwave clock read 2:17. Suddenly she was exhausted to her bones.

All she wanted was to sleep, and to hear someone say it was all going to be all right by the time the credits rolled, and maybe she wanted a hug. She actually really wanted a hug. If she'd been with anyone else, she might have asked for one, but Gabe seemed as if he might be allergic to hugs. "I think I'm just tired."

Gabe looked at her skeptically. "Do you always bleed when you're tired?"

"I don't know that I've ever been this tired," she said. And she decided to believe that rather than confess that this was the third time in twenty-four hours her nose had bled and she'd seen things that weren't there. Maybe it wasn't the best decision she'd ever made. But as Aunt Beth always liked to say, *Only mistakes happen after two o'clock in the morning.* "I'm going to go . . . clean up."

The bathroom Holland went into was covered in wallpaper printed with giant lemons. The floor was tiled in black-and-white checkers, and right in the middle of it was a large bath mat shaped like two red cherries. The bright little carpet looked clean and soft, and Holland immediately plopped down on it.

First, she took off January's backpack. Then she finally removed her shoe and tipped it over. The sole immediately dislodged, and a key attached to a red plastic key chain with the words *Motor Hotel* fell out into her hand.

There was a quick bolt of static electricity, but other than that the key was unremarkable. It looked like something from a '60s motel. This was not what Holland had expected. She might have thought it was a useless tchotchke, but then why had January hidden it in her shoe?

Holland remembered then that the Professor had mentioned a hotel in her journal. She quickly pulled the notebook from her backpack and flipped until she found the right page.

The Regal

Perhaps the greatest myth of all, or at least the grandest. The Regal is the embodiment of why people spend their lives searching for magic.

Must be a registered key holder, or on the official guest list of a registered key holder.

Guests of registered key holders may stay up to 24 Regal hours.

Key holders may stay as long as they wish, and some of them do just that.

It's rumored that a number of mysterious disappearances are actually people who checked into the Regal and never checked out.

Behavioral and dress codes are strictly enforced.

No naked animals (not sure if this is a joke).

It's said to exist outside of time. One hour in the Regal is one minute in the real world, making it the perfect place for those who never want to grow old, or those who wish to hide.

Holland wondered if this was a key to the Regal. But grand hotels didn't have plastic key chains. When her father used to create treasure hunts for her as a child, he would always let her know when she'd found all the clues. He'd gently tell her, *You already have everything you need. You just have to see it.* Then she would know that she didn't need to keep searching for clues, she just needed to piece together what she had. But she didn't have her father to tell her that now.

That was what she really wanted—for her father, or her sister, or someone else who loved her to tell her she had everything she needed, that she was going to be okay, that she wasn't all alone.

Continuing to search for more answers might have quelled some of her curiosity, but it wasn't going to give her what she really wanted. A shower started in another bathroom. Holland could hear the pipes vibrating through the thin walls. Gabe must have been taking a shower, and suddenly she was desperate for one, too.

The water was cold by the time she stepped in, but it still felt good to clean off all the grime. Once she was dry, she changed into a clean tank top and a thin pair of shorts from the backpack.

After dressing, Holland opened the door and stepped into the at-tached bedroom. The light in the room was soft and low, pouring out from a chandelier made of wooden beads. There were no neon signs, just plastic vines of flowers on the wall behind the bed, and Gabe stand-ing there without a shirt on.

His dark hair was damp, his bandaged chest was a bronzed shade of brown, and all he wore were black boxers that sat dangerously low on his hips. Holland told herself not to stare, but he was so close, standing right in front of her, with barely any clothes on, and barely any space between them.

He needed to move if she was going to walk past him to the door. And she was going to walk past him.

Holland didn't want to sleep with Gabe. Not that way or the other way. Except she sort of did. She just knew if she did, it would be another one of those after-two-in-the-morning mistakes.

Holland needed to leave the room and sleep in a bed *alone*. Even if this was her last night alive, which it wasn't. She couldn't think like that.

Water dripped down her back, soaking through her white tank top, as she took a step toward the door.

Gabe reached out. His hand landed on the dip in her waist. Butterflies fluttered inside her. She hadn't expected him to touch her there. The hint of surprise on his face made her think he hadn't expected it, either. That he had been reaching for something else, but his fingers had landed on her waist instead.

"Where are you going?" he asked.

"I need to go to bed," she said.

"There's a bed in here." His hand slid around her back, pressing against her damp shirt.

"Oh, no—" Holland wriggled free, bare feet nearly slipping on the wood as she took a step back. "You're also in here and—"

"I don't know why you're arguing." He took another step until she was once again too close to him and his bare chest. "We both know I'm sleeping in whatever bed you're sleeping in."

Her stomach dipped. And then he was pulling her onto the bed.

One second she was standing, and the next they were lying in bed. Together. His arms around her. "I'm not letting you out of my sight," he murmured.

Holland should have told him he didn't need to hold her this close to see her. She didn't need to be wrapped up in his arms, which were so much stronger than she'd expected. But the truth was that the weight of Gabe's arms felt nice. Maybe a little more than nice, maybe it made her feel as if she wasn't so alone.

As Gabe drifted to sleep, one of his hands slipped under her shirt just enough that his warm fingers were pressed to her bare stomach, and instead of pulling away, Holland leaned deeper in.

CHAPTER TWENTY-TWO

t didn't feel like morning.

It felt like a late summer afternoon, when the light was a grainy sort of bright, and the day was so warm that everything had turned a little hazy.

Holland was awake, but she couldn't quite open her eyes. They were heavy with sleep and leftover dreams. For a second, she couldn't remember where she was. The room smelled like the ocean, and there was another person entwined with her.

She panicked, briefly flailing, and the arms around her tightened.

"Babe, relax, you're safe." His hand rubbed a circle over her stomach.

Then she felt his lips on her shoulder, her neck, her ear.

This was a bad idea.

This was a really bad idea, for too many reasons to list, reasons that would only make her more nervous, because she would only do this with him if she knew she really was going to die today. And she didn't want to die today.

"We can't do this." She wiggled out of his arms and turned on her side to face him, which was definitely a mistake.

Adam looked beautiful in the morning. He was softer in the grainy light, with his hair mussed and his eyes still hooded from sleep. "Good morning, Bright Eyes." He put a hand on her hip. It was confident and warm and—

A drop of blood fell from his nose, followed by another, and another.

"Adam—" Holland reached for him, but he didn't move. He didn't even flinch as more blood poured onto the bed. His eyes were still open, but they had gone glassy.

"Adam!" Holland screamed his name as she shook his shoulder, but the only thing that moved was the blood. "Adam! Adam—"

"Holland—" he said, but his mouth wasn't moving. He was still frozen and bleeding.

"Adam!" She continued to shake him.

"Holland!" his voice cried, louder this time. Then she felt a hand on her shoulder. "Holland, wake up! Wake up!"

For a second, her eyes were still shut, refusing to open. Trapped in that broken space between dreams.

"It's all right," Gabe coaxed. Not Adam. Adam was just a dream. Gabe was real. "I've got you. I'm here."

Her eyes finally blinked open. Gabe was sitting up in the bed. One hand held her shoulder, the other held a pillowcase, soaked with her blood.

She tasted it then: blood on her lips. "What's wrong with me?" she asked.

"I don't know. You—" Gabe hesitated, jaw briefly clenching. "You were screaming Adam's name."

Holland felt a wave of mortification, followed by alarm. She didn't want to tell Gabe she'd had a very realistic dream that she was in bed with Adam. Especially not right now, when Gabe had a look on his face that said he'd very much like another chance to shoot Adam. Instead, she said, "I was probably just reliving yesterday. And I should probably go clean up."

Holland rose out of the bed on wobbly legs and hurried to the bathroom. After washing her face, she opened January's backpack again. Underneath her sister's miscellanea, Holland found a surprising number of clothes along with a very complete bag of toiletries. Holland pulled out an emerald-green silk dress with cap sleeves, a plunging neckline, and a wrap waist. It looked dressy for a visit to a bank, but Holland had a feeling the Bank was fancier than the average savings and loan.

Next, she tried on her sister's heels. They were black patent leather and higher than she would have liked. But at least they were a little chunky, with cute retro buttons on the sides that went well with the green dress.

They would not be great for running, but Holland hoped she wouldn't need to run. There was a small black purse in her sister's backpack as well. Holland pulled it out and put a few personal items inside, including her sister's plastic Motor Hotel key. She felt another burst of static when she touched the key and, once again, wondered what it was for.

Gabe knocked loudly on the bathroom door. "You almost ready?"

There was a different scent wafting through the beach house when Holland opened the door. Butter. Syrup. Cinnamon. Bacon. Coffee. Had Gabe cooked her breakfast?

The kitchen was just off the living room. Like the rest of the house, the little nook was primed for photos. The cabinets were a freshly painted mid-century shade of green, the appliances were glossy vintage cream, and retro vinyl diner chairs—with thick cream stripes down the center—surrounded the table.

Holland stepped closer, taking in the mountain of cardboard take-out containers. If she was reading the scrawl correctly, then Gabe had ordered pumpkin pancakes, pumpkin French toast, pumpkin sausages, pumpkin waffles, and her favorite pumpkin chocolate chip muffins. All of a sudden, she remembered it was Halloween. Had he ordered all this for her?

The back of her shoulders prickled with a feeling of being watched. She spun around to find Gabe leaning in the doorway.

He was dressed in a pinstripe blue suit she was certain he wasn't wearing last night. She would have remembered how brilliant it made his eyes look. Or maybe she was just painfully aware of the way he was looking at her, gliding up her bare legs before taking in the short silky dress.

Then he was striding toward the table, as if checking her out had been an accident. She wondered if he thought sleeping in the bed with her had been a mistake as well. Instead of feeling more comfortable around him, she felt as if everything was a little more awkward.

Holland had a fleeting thought that it would be nice if certain relationships came with care instructions like clothing labels:

For emergency use only.

Avoid close contact.

Do not put in bed together.

Gabe's eyes narrowed. "You look like you're worrying."

"What's there to worry about?" Holland said flippantly. "Besides not making it out of the Bank, not finding the Alchemical Heart, having another bleeding episode. Wait—what happens if I start bleeding at the Bank?"

"Don't start bleeding there."

"But—"

"You only have twenty minutes," he cut in.

"Actually, it's just fifteen."

"Did they tell you to get there five minutes early?"

"Yes."

"Then you have twenty minutes." He handed her a white ceramic watch. "Put this on. It's accurate to the millisecond. You'll need every single moment you have to get in and out with the Alchemical Heart."

"But what if it isn't in the box?"

"I will still get you out."

"How?"

Gabe looked offended she was even asking. Then he reached in his pocket and pulled out a disposable phone. "This has my number." He placed it in her hand.

"Do you just carry multiple burner phones around with you?"

Ignoring her question, Gabe said, "I'm the only contact. Call me as soon as you have the Alchemical Heart or you need to get out of the Bank."

"Wait," Holland said, realizing they actually hadn't talked about this last night. "Can't you go in with me?"

"I don't think that's a good idea."

"Why not?"

"Your appointment only protects you, sweetheart. Speaking of that appointment—" Gabe eyed her backpack. "You're not going to want to take that in. The Bank is going to look for ways to waste your time, to make it more difficult for you to escape. If you carry in a backpack, they're going to check every item inside to make sure it's not imbued with any magic."

"It's just a backpack of clothes," she said, which wasn't entirely true, but she felt reluctant to part with it, since it also now contained the Professor's journal.

"You don't have to leave it here. You can leave it with me while you're inside."

"What about the phone you gave me?"

"They won't care about that, it's clearly a piece of junk. Come on—we should go."

"Hold on—speaking of the phone. Have you heard anything from my sister yet?"

Gabe shook his head.

Holland felt a small pang of worry.

"Don't worry, I'm sure we'll hear something soon."

Holland also knew her sister was in another country, but it still made her uneasy. "Can you at least give me her number for my phone?"

"You really think your sister is going to reply to an unknown number that claims to be you?"

He had a point, but Holland said, "I'd like to try all the same."

Gabe pulled out his phone and rattled off a number.

Holland quickly typed a message.

Hey! It's me, Holland—your friend
Gabe tossed my phone out the
window so I'm texting from a new
one. And

She mulled over just how much more to say. Holland had so many questions, but a text didn't feel like the place to ask them. Finally, she settled on I'm going into the Bank this morning.

"Come on," Gabe repeated. "We need to go."

"Just one more second." Holland turned back to the table and grabbed an iced coffee and the entire bag of pumpkin chocolate chip muffins.

Gabe stood in the doorway without touching a thing.

"Aren't you hungry?" she asked.

He shook his head. "Don't really like pumpkin."

"Then why did you order all this?"

He shrugged. "You seemed like someone who likes to celebrate holidays." He walked away quickly, as if saying or doing something nice might cause him to break out in hives.

Holland missed the weight of her sister's backpack as soon as she put it in the trunk.

"It will be in there when you get back," said Gabe.

But suddenly all Holland could think was that when people said things like this in movies, they never actually made it back.

"Are you nervous?" Gabe asked.

"Why would I be nervous?" Holland said. "I'm just going into an evil bank to retrieve an object that may or may not be there, and I'm just now realizing that I don't even know what it looks like."

"*No one* knows what it looks like. Some people suspect it can change form."

"Not helping," Holland said.

Gabe frowned, and then he reached into the pocket of his suit coat and pulled out an old bronze coin.

"What's that?" Holland asked.

"Just something I picked up," he said, in a way that made clear it was definitely more than *just something*. "Now I need you to put out your hand."

"I feel like I need a little more to go on," Holland said.

Gabe sighed. "I'm going to give you a quick lesson in sensing magical objects, just in case you don't really understand what's in your father's box. Now put out your hand."

This time Holland obeyed.

"When I set this in your palm, I want you to tell me if you feel anything or sense anything when you touch it. The tricky thing about magic is that it doesn't always feel the same. Sometimes it makes goosebumps rise up on your arms, other times it might make the world around you go quiet for a second. It does things that people notice all the time, but they don't really notice *why* unless they're paying attention. So"—Gabe paused, and his dark eyes locked onto hers—"I need you to pay attention."

Holland nodded, but she felt inexplicably nervous. Gooseflesh broke out across her arms, but he hadn't even set the coin down, so clearly it wasn't from that. Then Gabe pressed the coin into her palm, and she felt it. A sharp, icy breeze cut through the warm morning air. It was only for a moment. Then Holland felt the sun shining on her again.

"I think I felt it." Holland smiled. "I felt a change in the air."

Gabe nodded once and reached back for the coin.

Holland tightened her fingers around it. "Not so fast," she said. "I want to know what it does."

Gabe looked at her seriously. "If I step into a bar, as long as I have this coin, I never have to pay for drinks."

"Are you joking?"

"I'm not really known for my sense of humor, sweetheart." But now Gabe was grinning. It might have been the first time she'd seen him properly smile, and it was a really good smile. Holland might have felt just a little bit dazzled, and Gabe seemed to notice. She expected his smile to immediately fade, but instead he reached out for her fingers and slowly peeled them back from the coin. "When you get out of the Bank with the Alchemical Heart, drinks are on me tonight."

Are the Professor's classes really canceled, or is this just another one of her tests?

Most of your classmates believe it's a test—you all know the Professor likes her games. A few of your friends are tired of playing, but you're not ready to give up. Not yet.

You think the Professor must have left clues about the next class; you just need to find them.

You go over your notes. *The Devil, the Bank, the Regal, the After Midnight Menu, the salacious deaths of Isla Saint and Benjamin J. Tierney.*

You feel as if any of the stories could hold a clue, but Benjamin J. Tierney is the name that keeps jumping out at you. He might have died almost fifteen years ago, but people are still obsessed with him. He was famous for nesting stories within stories and hiding personal Easter eggs. And you find yourself wondering if there's something hidden in *his* story.

You become a little obsessed with watching old interviews and films and looking up his Wonderpage.

Price of Magic Trilogy

Article Talk   Read   View   Edit History   Tools

The unfinished **Price of Magic** trilogy (a JME production) was the last
project Benjamin J. Tierney worked on before his death.

Summary of Films [edit]

Price of Magic centers around Sophia Wescott (played by Michelle Peña), a
small-town librarian with a gift for necromancy. At the start of the film, it's
unclear why Sophia and her husband Red (played by Sam Young) moved
to the middle of nowhere, leaving behind all their friends and family and
their beautiful cliffside house in Seaspray, California. The film alternates
between the past and the present, slowly revealing to viewers the secret
behind why Red and Sophia moved across the country.

Red, a firefighter, died one year ago, in what should have been an easy fire
to put out. Sophia used her gift of necromancy to bring him back to life,
but in doing so, she started an apocalyptic blaze that tore across the entire
state. Vowing never to use her magic again, Sophia moved with Red to
Secret Ravine, Louisiana, where their quiet new life is quickly interrupted
by a disturbing string of child murders.

Together, Sophia and Red discover a magical cult is behind these vicious
murders, and there is only one way Sophia can stop them and bring all
the murdered children back to life: by sacrificing the power that has been
keeping her dead husband alive.

Symphony of Death

In the second film, determined to get her powers back, Sophia teams up
with a psychic who's wanted for murder. By the end of the film, Sophia
succeeds in clearing the psychic of murder charges by finding the real

killer. She also brings her dead husband back to life again, but this time the cost is her own life.

Untitled Third Film

There is no summary for this film.

Benjamin J. Tierney's final screenplay has never been found. Some suspect he never actually wrote it. There are also rumors that the screenplay does indeed exist, that it's cursed—just like his second trilogy—and the world is better off never finding it.

Last updated: Oct 30, 2025

You've read this page before, but you don't remember any mention of his missing screenplay being cursed. You notice the page was updated yesterday, and you wonder if maybe it was the Professor. If this is the clue—

Black lines streak down the screen of your computer.

"What the—" You swear as you try to move your cursor. You attempt to close the browser, but the only thing moving on the computer is the black lines. They are wavy on the screen, making your laptop look like it's sick. You press *Esc* over and over. You have a paper you can't afford to lose, and this computer is practically brand—

The entire screen goes gray and fuzzy. For a second you think you see two words: *Game Over*. Then the screen turns black. Pitch-black. Dead black.

"No!" You press the power button.

Nothing happens.

You press again.

Nothing happens.

You plug in the laptop, thinking maybe it's just your battery. You give it a full ten minutes, then you press the power button again. But your computer never comes back to life. You think about the words *Game Over*. You don't know if this is the Professor's game, but you're done. You're so done.

You just bought this computer. You have a paper due tomorrow. You like the Professor's stories, but you wish you'd taken Science from Superheroes instead.

CHAPTER TWENTY-THREE

The clock on the car's dashboard reads 9:01 a.m. One hour from now, Holland would either be out of the bank or . . . she didn't want to finish that thought. Her brief excitement over Gabe's magic lesson had faded. So had his mayfly smile. Which made her think he hadn't been serious about the drinks. Not that it mattered. What mattered was getting in and out of the Bank alive.

The drive to Centennial City went faster than any drive in the history of Los Angeles. There was no traffic. No stops at all. Only one red light, next to a neon billboard of the newest Vic VanVleet film. Holland felt a pang of regret at the sight of Chance's smiling face.

Then there were no more billboards, just beautiful trees and birds and matte-black lampposts that looked as if they'd been imported from the early twentieth century.

They were driving through a neighborhood with yards so large she couldn't even see the houses, just rows of trees bursting with gorgeous colors Holland rarely saw in the city. It actually looked like fall.

There were colors she hadn't seen on cars since possibly ever: shimmering greens with cream tops, burning oranges with racing stripes over the hood, sparkling reds with hints of glitter, vibrant ocean blues with lightning bolts on the side, deep plum purples, and retro mints.

It all should have seemed garish, but it just looked more vibrantly alive than any other street she'd seen in LA. It didn't seem at all like the sort of place that would house the headquarters of an evil organization. It seemed like somewhere to picnic or to visit fancy open houses on a Saturday. Although Holland had a feeling that the people who lived here never moved.

"Are you sure there's a bank here?" she asked Gabe.

Then she saw it, about one hundred yards away. It took up an entire block. An absurdly tall, jade-green jewel of a building with a dazzling gold art deco pattern cutting across its endless floors of windows. It was so stunning and so high she didn't know how she hadn't seen it before.

Magic.

She could feel it then, the same way she could feel a change in the air whenever she drew close to the ocean. What she was feeling she couldn't say. It didn't have a scent. But it felt like what she had experienced with the coin.

The Bank looked bolder and brighter and even taller the longer she stared. It now seemed impossible that she had never seen this building before. That it hadn't ever been in a movie or on a postcard. Holland wanted to ask what kind of magic could hide a building like this from the world, but Gabe was stopping the car in front of a house with needlepoint-perfect hedges, and suddenly she was too nervous to speak. She wasn't even sure she still knew how to breathe. Her head was getting light. All she could take were sips of air.

The Bank was on the next block. One crosswalk away. She hoped the Alchemical Heart was in there waiting for her. But now that she was so close, it seemed impossible. And even if it was in there, it seemed like it would be impossible to get it out.

"There's one more thing you should know," Gabe said.

"I think I already know enough." Normally, Holland loved information. She loved facts and stories, but she felt that if she learned anything else right now, it might be too much. She was already in a new world full of new rules she didn't know. Rules she might break by accident.

"Relax," Gabe said. "This will all be over soon. Just make sure when you go inside you stay away from the Manager."

"Why? Who's the Manager?"

"I don't know. They keep it a secret. But I've heard the Manager can read minds." Gabe hesitated. "If you meet them, make sure you don't think of me. If they find out I'm here, waiting for you, then I might not be able to get you out."

Holland suddenly had a thousand questions. But there were only minutes left until her appointment. Seconds were moving faster than seconds were supposed to move, and all of it was feeling like too much. The magic and Gabe's mysteries and the overwhelming feeling that she really didn't know what she was getting herself into. "I don't know if I can do this."

"Hey—" Gabe killed the car and looked her right in the eyes. "Once you're leaving the vault, call me, and I'll be there as soon as you step outside."

"What if they grab me first?"

He leaned in closer. "I won't let that happen."

"But—"

He wrapped one hand around the back of her neck and pressed his lips to hers. His mouth was soft but a little rough, as if he kept wanting to pull away, as if he knew this kiss was a mistake. The tips of his fingers slid into her hair as he took her lower lip between his teeth and gently bit. Then he was letting her go, but he was looking at her as if he wanted to take her back.

Holland started to lean in again, but he pulled away. She almost thought she saw a flash of regret in his eyes, but it was gone so fast, she wondered if it had actually been there.

"I'll be here when you get out," he said.

CHAPTER TWENTY-FOUR

Holland gave herself one minute to think about the kiss. To wonder why Gabe had kissed her and why he had looked regretful and why she was feeling nervous about a kiss when her life literally depended on what would happen inside the Bank.

A kiss didn't matter. Except that kissing always mattered.

And that had been a very good kiss.

Holland let herself think about the kiss once more. She admitted to herself that she wanted it to happen again. Maybe she wanted more than a kiss.

Then she stepped inside.

The Bank looked like the sort of place where you weren't supposed to touch anything.

Do not touch the pristine glass doors.

Do not touch the antique knobs.

Do not touch the marble desks where bankers sat behind ivory typewriters with shiny brass keys.

Click-clack-click.

Click-clack-click.

Click—

For a second everyone stopped their typing. It was only for one instant, just long enough for the quiet to reach the geometric sunset covering the arched ceiling. Then the typing started again.

But Holland swore that underneath the clean clack of the typing were quiet little whispers. She couldn't make out any words, but the hair on her arms was standing up and her heart was racing in the way a heart races when it knows its person is being talked about.

"Good morning, Miss St. James," said a pretty banker wearing a cowboy hat, cowboy boots, a belt with two fake plastic pistols, and a shiny silver star that read, *Just call me Sheriff.*

The whispering stopped as soon as she spoke.

Now people were pretending not to watch as Holland attempted to puzzle out why this banker was dressed up like the female version of Wyatt Earp.

Then she remembered it was Halloween. She had forgotten for a second. She supposed the kiss had muddled her brain. But she was still surprised to see this banker dressed in costume. All the shininess and the do-not-touch-this-ness fit with what she had expected of an evil bank. The costumes did not. As she looked around at the bankers who were all trying not to stare, she noticed an abnormal number of cowboy hats and cowboy boots and leather vests with fringe.

"It's Wild West Friday," the banker explained. "We always pick a theme for Halloween." The banker started walking toward the back, steps so light her heels didn't make a sound against the intricate gold-and-emerald chevron tiles. "I'm Padme, by the way. I'll be your escort to the Manager's office, as I believe this is your first visit."

"It is—but wait," Holland said. "Why am I going to see the Manager? I'm here to open a safety deposit box."

"I know. But the Manager wishes to see you first," Padme said pleasantly, the way a banker who worked for a normal bank might signal to a not-so-normal customer that they've been given a special audience. But this didn't feel special. All Holland could think about was Gabe's warning.

Unless the Manager was Manuel Vargas. That was who she'd asked for the appointment with. Maybe there was something else he wanted to tell her. "Is the Manager Mr. Vargas?" Holland asked.

Padme looked puzzled. "I don't know Mr. Vargas. But if he's part of the Bank, I'm sure the Manager knows him."

"If it's all right," Holland said, "I would prefer to see the Manager after I've opened my box."

Padme continued to smile warmly. "I'm afraid that won't be possible." She stopped in front of an old-fashioned brass elevator, the sort with an elaborate metal gate and a fancy dial above, which currently indicated it was still three floors up. Then she looked down at her watch. "Technically, your appointment doesn't begin for another two minutes. I don't have to take you anywhere just yet. And trust me, Miss St. James, you will want to talk to the Manager before you open that box."

The elevator dinged. Padme slid back the gate.

Holland imagined she could stand there for another two minutes and then demand to be taken to the box, but Padme was looking at her as if that would be a grave mistake. And Holland wasn't sure waiting would actually do anything except waste two minutes.

She stepped inside the elevator.

"Wise choice." Padme closed the gate and pressed a round brass button with the number twenty-three. The elevator replied with a chime. The doors closed, and Holland's heart leaped into her throat as they began to rise.

A cover of "Season of the Witch" played from the elevator speakers. Padme gently clicked the heels of her boots to the music. Working for an evil bank was just another day to her.

The elevator rose a few more floors before Padme slowly turned to Holland. "I was trying to contain my excitement earlier, but I'm a big fan of your sister's." She said it in a way that Holland had never heard anyone speak of January before, as if she was a minor celebrity or a hometown superhero. And Holland was suddenly very confused.

"How do you know my sister?"

"Well, I don't actually know her well," Padme said. "She doesn't technically work at this branch, so I've only met her a couple of times. But

she's so good at her job, everyone knows who January St. James is."
Padme smiled brightly, as if Holland should be extremely proud.

But all Holland felt was something churning in her stomach. There
was no way January could work here. The Bank was evil.

Padme continued blithely. "I also wanted to say how terribly sorry I
am about your sister's partner, Adam." She clutched her heart. "I felt
so awful when I heard about the shooting." Padme said something else
about how everyone at the Bank was manifesting a full recovery for
Adam and hoping the shooter would get caught, then it sounded as if
she started talking about January again. But Holland could barely process any of it. Because all she could hear were the words Adam had said
yesterday: *I swear I'm telling you the truth. I work with your sister, January.
She is my partner. She sent me here to watch out for you.*

Holland hadn't believed him. She'd believed Gabe. But what if she'd
been wrong?

No. Adam was lying. Not Gabe. Gabe had given Holland his phone
to call January yesterday. And he'd given her January's number this
morning. But had he really? Holland didn't know what number she'd
called yesterday, only that she'd reached her sister's voicemail, which
was an easy enough thing to fake. Even the number he'd given Holland
today could have been the wrong number, and Holland wouldn't have
known.

Holland quickly checked her phone. There was still no reply from
January.

Maybe Gabe was right, and January would never reply to an unknown
number. Or maybe he'd only said that so it wouldn't seem suspicious
when she didn't respond.

"Are you all right?" Padme asked. "Do you need some water?"

Holland shook her head. What she needed was more time to process
all this.

The elevator stopped with another chime. Padme pulled the metal
gate open, and then she took hold of Holland's hand. Her brown fingers
were warm and soft. "Don't worry." She squeezed. "I'm sure that Adam

is already better." With that, Padme said goodbye and took the elevator back down to the lobby.

Holland checked her watch again—she had exactly fifteen minutes left in her appointment, which meant she had fifteen minutes to figure out who she trusted. And just then she didn't feel like she could trust anyone.

She wanted to believe there was a world where Adam could be January's partner and Gabe could be a good guy. But she couldn't see a way that worked. One man had been sent to protect her, and the other man was lying to her.

Holland's head was pounding as she walked toward the lone door at the end of the hall. She should probably knock, but she couldn't waste any more time. With a nervous "Hello," she turned the knob.

The first thing she noticed was all the glass. An entire wall of green stained glass cast the office in glittering emerald light. It looked like *The Wizard of Oz* and *The Great Gatsby* had both dropped from a bookshelf and spilled out words that had then turned into art deco shimmer. The drapes were velvet, the lights were suspended gold-and-glass globes, the carpet was a lush pattern of diamonds and stylized florals, and standing in the center of it, leaning against a great ebony desk, was the Professor.

CHAPTER TWENTY-FIVE

The Professor was wearing high-waisted forest-green trousers and a creamy silk blouse with a large elegant bow at the collar. Her earrings were pearls, and there was an ornate diamond and mother-of-pearl comb pulling back one side of her silver hair.

Standing there in the misty green light, she looked more glamorous than she ever had in class. She looked like the rumors Holland had heard before meeting her. Film star chic, larger than life, and clearly not who Holland had always believed she was.

"What are you doing here?" Holland asked. The answer seemed rather obvious, but she was hoping for an explanation that would stop the feeling that her heart was on the verge of being broken.

Holland had been so afraid that something awful had happened to the Professor, and now she felt utterly foolish. If she was reading this situation right, the Professor had never been in danger—she was the one pulling the strings. "Who are you really?"

"You know who I am," the Professor said softly.

"No. I don't. Until minutes ago, I thought you were my mentor. I thought I could trust you."

"Why don't we both take a seat?" said the Professor. "I'll order tea and tell you everything you want to know."

Holland wanted to know a lot. But she wasn't sure she could trust a single word the Professor said, and she now had only fourteen minutes left. "I'd rather just be taken to my father's safety deposit box. Please."

The Professor frowned. "You must be worried about the time, my dear." She took a large jade hourglass from her desk. "This glass will pause time until all the sand runs through." She tipped over the hourglass and set it back down. "Go ahead, take a look at your watch."

Holland did. The second hand had stopped, frozen at ten seconds past. "How do I know you're actually stopping time and not just all the clocks?"

The Professor wrinkled her nose, as if a cheap trick like that would be beneath her. "Come here." She strode to the wall of green glass windows.

Holland didn't move.

The Professor huffed. "Don't be so dramatic. I'm not going to toss you outside, my dear, there are far more elegant ways to kill someone than defenestration. And the last thing I want is for you to die." She reached behind a lush velvet curtain and pressed a button. The glass immediately turned clear. "I want you to take a look outside."

Holland took a few cautious steps forward, until she could peer out.

The world had never looked so still. The trees were frozen. The cars had stopped halfway through intersections. But it was the bird that convinced her. Midflight, unmoving, wings stretched out in the midst of a swirl of suspended fall leaves.

"It's a delightful little trick, isn't it?" The Professor looked quite pleased with herself, presiding over a world she had stopped with a twist of her wrist.

Holland couldn't deny that she was impressed. This was all the magic she'd been searching for, finally, here, right in front of her. And now the Professor was smiling at her as if Holland could have it, too.

"I've wanted to show you this and so many other things for ages." The Professor's voice brimmed with affection, as though Holland was her most prized pupil and this was a moment she truly had been waiting for. But did she really mean it, or was it just an act? Because clearly, from the moment Holland had met her, this woman had been acting.

"I can see you still have questions and doubts. But I assure you, I'm still the same person." The Professor walked closer to Holland so that both of them were standing in the center of the glittering office. "The stories I told you in 517 were all true. Nothing I taught in that class was a deception."

"You just left out the part about how you're one of the stories."

This made the Professor smile. "Unfortunately, that was necessary. I always omitted some of the pieces so that only the cleverest students would find their way into this world."

"Why would you do that? Why the charade?"

"Who doesn't love pretending to be someone else? And in this case, it was quite helpful. Until recently." The Professor pinched her mouth at this, but she didn't expand on what had happened with the University.

"I wanted to be the Professor because I wanted the best and the brightest to work for me. Being born into a family with abilities can make people lazy and, honestly, quite dull. But finding out magic exists and that you can have it if you work hard enough—this turns ordinary people into extraordinary treasures. People like you." The Professor's eyes lit with pride as they met Holland's. "When I first met you, my dear, you were a Storytelling major writing fan fiction about vampires. And look at you now—you've found your way into our world."

The Professor paused, and Holland could tell she was waiting for some sort of reaction. It was the same thing she always did in class, and year after year the students provided what she wanted. But all Holland could do now was check the hourglass.

A third of the golden sand had already slipped through. Holland didn't know how many minutes that translated to. But she guessed she had only about ten more until time started up again.

"You should be extraordinarily pleased with yourself," the Professor finally said. "Of course, I've always thought you were bright. I was actually going to offer you a job here when you graduated from undergrad."

"Then why didn't you?" Holland asked.

The Professor sighed. "It was actually because of your sister. January had already been recruited by another branch, and she said she would take the offer only if you were kept out of this world." The Professor's expression turned sour, as if she was still resentful about this.

The Holland of yesterday might have felt wounded as well. She might have wondered why her sister would have kept magic from her— knowing that Holland had been searching for magic her whole life—but all she could think now was that January must have been protecting her.

"And what exactly is it you think she's protecting you from?"

Holland jolted, remembering what Gabe had told her about the Manager reading minds.

The Professor smiled wryly. "I try not to use the ability except when absolutely necessary."

"Why do I find that hard to believe?"

"Because you don't want to believe anything I'm saying today. But I swear, everything I've told you since you've stepped into this room is the truth. I admit, I could be wrong about your sister. I actually didn't meet January until very recently. But, as far as I can see, she hasn't been watching out for you. All January has done is lie and keep you in the dark. That's why I called you up here today. I think it's all been utterly unfair to you. I know your sister won't like it, but I want to give you a job, here, working for me."

The Professor smiled her Mona Lisa smile, the one that promised secrets and stories and magic. Magic that was just out of reach, but *she* could show you how to find it, to grab it, to make it yours.

"That's exactly what I'm going to do," she said softly. "Come work for me and you'll finally have answers about the devil and your parents— because, yes, I know all about them, my dear, and I'm so very sorry— but I promise to continue to help you uncover the truth." She looked devastatingly sincere. It didn't erase all the betrayal Holland felt. But it chipped away at it, as she thought about all the books the Professor had sent her. There had been moments when Holland had been tempted to share the truth, and she imagined the Professor had sensed that during their many conversations.

"This will all be easier *when* you're working for the Bank. You'll have access to all our vast resources. And you'll have an ability." The Professor's eyes glittered, as if this was what she'd been most dying to say. "Usually new recruits only get minor ones, like the ability to always find a good parking spot. But I have something special in mind for you."

The Professor stepped back to her desk and patted a lovely golden box. Holland wondered if the ability was sitting inside. She didn't know how any of this really worked. But the Professor looked ready to tell her. She looked ready to give Holland the keys to the kingdom as soon as Holland said yes.

"What is this ability?" Holland asked.

"Oh, you'll love it," the Professor said. "It will literally change your life. I just need one little tiny favor first." She gave Holland another smile, a sly smile that made Holland think this favor was actually going to be quite far from tiny. "I know you're here to open a safety deposit box, and when you open it, I need you to give me whatever is inside of it."

Holland started to laugh. She couldn't help herself. "You actually had me hypnotized for a minute there."

"I meant everything I said."

"No, you didn't," Holland said, still laughing. "You said you wanted to help me and give me an ability. But you don't want to help me, and you don't want to give me anything. What you want is an exchange." Holland took another look at the hourglass. The sand seemed to be moving faster. "I'd like to leave now," she said. "Please tell me how to get to my father's box."

The Professor clenched her jaw. "I'll let you go when the sand runs out. Until then, I need you to hear me out. I know you're a good person, Holland. I don't think you want to hurt anyone. And I know you're smart, so I believe you already know what I suspect is in your father's box. If I'm right, letting that object fall into the wrong hands could be catastrophic. If you give the Alchemical Heart to me, I can assure you the Bank will keep it safe from anyone who wishes to do harm with it. Like your new friend, Gabriel Cabral."

Holland stiffened. She wondered how the Professor knew about Gabe, but then she remembered that she was a mind reader. "You don't have to worry," Holland said. "Gabe isn't my friend."

"Good, because Gabriel Cabral is a very dangerous man." The Professor let her words hang in the air as more precious sand slipped through the hourglass.

Holland already knew Gabe was dangerous—he'd killed her car, abducted her, lied about her sister, shot Adam—yet there was something about the way the Professor spoke that made Holland think Gabe was even more vicious than she had realized. He wasn't just someone to stay away from, he was someone to fear.

"I don't know how your path crossed his," said the Professor. "But I dread what might happen if the Alchemical Heart were to fall into Gabriel's hands. And I hate the idea of him using you and then killing you, just like he did with his wife."

CHAPTER TWENTY-SIX

No. Holland's first thought was that the Professor had to be wrong. Holland didn't want to believe anyone was a murderer, especially not the man she had spent last night with.

There was still a little sand left in the hourglass. If Holland left now, she would have a head start. And she wanted to leave. After talking to Padme, she had already decided she couldn't trust Gabe. She didn't need more reasons to stay away from him. But if the Professor was telling the truth, this wasn't just about not trusting Gabe. This meant Holland should never go near him again.

She knew the Professor had deceived her, but Holland actually didn't think she was lying about this. And Holland always did have a weakness for the Professor's stories.

"Tell me about Gabe's wife," said Holland.

"Gabriel Cabral wasn't born into a family with abilities," said the Professor. "When that happens, there are only two ways to get an ability. The most respectable way is to come and work for the Bank. The other way is to ingratiate oneself with someone with an ability in the hope that when they die, they'll leave you that ability. Gabriel Cabral chose the latter. He married a woman from a family with a lot of magic, and, the day after the wedding, he murdered her."

The Professor frowned, her mouth softening, her eyes turning down. She was once again the Professor Holland had known and loved, and she looked truly apologetic. "I'm sorry, my dear. I hate to be the bearer of such bad news, but unlike many of my stories, this is a very well-documented fact. If you don't believe me, you can look at the Bank's Most Wanted list." She waved toward a glass mail chute near her desk, as if she could simply ring for the list. But Holland didn't feel as if she needed proof.

Holland had known Gabe was dangerous from the second he'd rolled down his window in that parking lot. She'd trusted him because he'd shown her a piece of paper with her sister's handwriting. That wasn't actually the only reason. But looking back, all the other reasons felt flimsy now. Holland feared that maybe she had believed him simply because she wanted to. Maybe Cat was right after all and Holland truly was drawn not just to stories but to people who scared her.

Holland looked toward the hourglass, hoping it was finally time to go. There was still a little sand left in the top of the hourglass—but a crack was working its way down it. Suddenly, the glass shattered, and golden sand poured out onto the desk. A bird smacked against the window, hard enough to crack that glass, too.

"That wasn't supposed to happen," said the Professor. Slowly, almost mechanically, she ran a hand through her hair. Her fingers came back bloody.

"Professor, your hand!" cried Holland.

But the Professor didn't seem to hear her or notice the bleeding. She just repeated, "That wasn't supposed to happen. This hasn't happened before."

Then, like whiplash, the Professor suddenly looked at Holland with a placid smile and said, "You should get going, my dear. It seems your time is up."

Holland desperately wanted to point out the blood still on the Professor's fingers. She wanted to ask what had just happened. Was it the same as whatever kept happening to Holland?

But time had literally run out.

Holland started toward the door.

"Think carefully about the contents of your father's box," the Professor called, as if blood wasn't still dripping from her head onto her pristine floor. "I'm sure you're feeling a lot of pressure right now, but I believe you'll make the right decision."

The woman really was indomitable. Holland hated that she was no longer sure she could trust her, because a part of her still respected her.

The Professor winked.

Holland turned away before she could read any more of her thoughts. But there was one last thought she needed to share. Holland didn't know for certain what she was going to do after she opened her father's box, but she did know for certain she wouldn't be going back to Gabe.

"There's something you should know," Holland told the Professor. "Gabriel Cabral is sitting in a car a block away from here."

CHAPTER TWENTY-SEVEN

The elevator was quiet as Holland stepped inside. No Halloween music poured from the speakers. No banker stood beside her, clicking the heels of her cowboy boots.

And Holland was grateful. She was also nervous. Holland clutched the charm around her neck as she watched the second hand move around her watch. She only had twelve minutes left. It didn't feel like even close to enough time to get the Alchemical Heart and get out of the Bank, especially without Gabe to help her.

Holland felt a sick twist in her stomach at the thought of Gabe. She thought she'd feel better after turning Gabe in to the Professor. But all she felt was a pit in her stomach. She hated that she had kissed him and she had trusted him—she'd told him about her parents. It made her feel foolish. She also felt sad, which made her angry because she was supposed to feel terrified. But the problem with feelings is sometimes you don't get to choose them. Sometimes the best you can do is fight them.

The elevator stopped.

The doors opened.

Mercury glass sconces lit a small rectangular room that was decidedly older than the rest of the Bank. The floor was covered in diamond tiles of pink-and-green marble, scuffed and worn from years of use. Across from her was a small velvet sofa, green as the squares on the floor, and in front of it, on top of a round brass table, was a metal box.

Her father's box.

It was larger than she'd expected. In the movies, safety deposit boxes were always small narrow things, but this was the size of several of those put together.

This was it. The last thing her father had left her. Her heart clenched painfully in her chest.

Her watch ticked. But she couldn't bring herself to open the box quite yet.

Holland had been only ten when her father had died. The memories of him and her mother were starting to feel old and worn, like photos in albums she'd looked at too many times. They seemed more like snapshots of moments than actual memories.

Her dad sitting at Christmas breakfast with a Santa hat on. Her mom reading by her bed and using her most dramatic voices. Family movie nights in the backyard beneath the stars, with little bags of popcorn and films projected on great white sheets. Hanging lollipops on every branch of a tree in the backyard for a birthday.

Her parents might have been there for only a brief period of her life, but they had tried to fill it with wonder. And Holland had been trying to hold on to that wonder.

When researching her thesis, Holland had come across a quote. Right after James Dean died, Humphrey Bogart had said, "He'd never have been able to live up to his publicity." Holland thought about that a lot. Benjamin Tierney did so much in his life, but it was all overshadowed by how he died.

Holland liked to believe that had her father lived, he would have become so much more than all the tragic publicity. Over the years, Holland had watched every interview she could find of him, and her father was smart and magnetic and kind, and she hated that he had been taken from her.

Finally, she lifted the lid of the box.

Inside was a slim leather satchel, the kind you might slip a laptop into. Holland's hands turned clammy as she pressed her palm to the leather and tried to feel for magic the way Gabe had taught her. Nothing sparked or tingled. She didn't feel a prickling of her skin or a change in the air. It was just an ordinary leather satchel.

She told herself that didn't matter. The Alchemical Heart could still be inside.

Nervously, she opened the satchel and pulled out a plain manila folder. Once again, Holland didn't feel anything magical when she touched it. It was just paper.

Her heart started to sink.

She'd been so convinced the Alchemical Heart was going to be in the box, she hadn't even thought about what she would do if it wasn't.

Dejectedly, she opened the manila folder, and everything immediately changed. Her heart started racing at the sight of her father's familiar handwriting, scrawled across the front above three neatly typed lines:

```
ALCHEMY OF SECRETS
A Price of Magic film
Written by Benjamin J. Tierney
```

It was her father's missing screenplay.

CHAPTER TWENTY-EIGHT

Holland had thought that she would never read more words written by her dad.

Everyone said this screenplay didn't even exist, and people had spent years searching for it. Why had her dad hidden it here?

Holland looked at her watch.

Six minutes left.

It looked as if there were only a handful of pages, and yet there wasn't enough time to read them all.

But she couldn't leave the vault without at least looking at a few pages. This might be her last day alive, and in that moment, there was nothing she wanted to do more than read her father's final words.

EXT. A GRAVEYARD. SUNSET

A hand (the hand of Red Westcott) sets a bouquet of flowers in front of a grave covered in spring-green grass. The tombstone reads:

    Sophia Westcott   *My neighbor*
    Beloved Wife. Beautiful Soul.   *next door?*
    This is only temporary.

There is a moment of perfect silence, except for the
sound of a breeze rustling leaves on a sycamore tree.
Then . . .

Red plunges his fist into his wife's grave and pulls out
a handful of dirt.

He fills a jar with the dirt. A blue Ball jar. But
instead of the word *Ball*, it reads:

> Alchemy
> Of
> Secrets

Red continues filling the jar with angry fistful after
fistful of dirt, until the jar is full . . .

Match cut to

INT. A BOWLING ALLEY. EVENING.

Red slams the jar full of dirt down on a table. The jar
now says the word *Ball* instead of the title of the film.

In the background, balls are rolling, pins are falling.
When someone gets a gutter ball, a neon sign inside of
a heart lights up with the words *Not Your Lucky Day*.
Think Cassius Marcellus Coolidge meets Spanish colonial
revival. The neon sign is on as Red walks in. He
approaches a vinyl table with a group of stylish older
women in matching bowling shirts. The word *Hollybells* is
monogrammed on the backs of their pink-and-green shirts.

Five of the women are sipping sodas from vintage glass
bottles with striped straws. The sixth is stitching a
yellow house on a needlepoint pillowcase.

                    RED WESTCOTT
          How do I bring her back?

                    ALMA HERNANDEZ
          I told you not to come back
          here, boy.

                    RED WESTCOTT
          Tell me how to bring her back
          and I'll never darken your
          door again.

Alma sips her cola and eyes him like a bowling pin she'd
like to strike down. The lights in the bowling alley go
dark, switching to black light as the neon sign flickers
between *Lucky Day* and *Not Your Lucky Day*.

                    ALMA HERNANDEZ
          You need to see the Watch Man.

In the background Frank Sinatra begins to play.

                    RED WESTCOTT
          I'm already familiar with my
          time of death.

                    ALMA HERNANDEZ
          The Watch Man can tell you
          more than just when you'll

die. If you want to bring my
daughter back from the dead,
you'll need the *Source*, and to
get the *Source*, you'll need
the Watch Man to tell you
where to look.

                RED WESTCOTT
How do I find the Watch Man?

                ALMA HERNANDEZ
That's for you to figure out.
I'm telling you how to bring
my daughter back. But I don't
think it's a good idea. The
dead are meant to stay dead.
When they come back, there are
always consequences. Haven't
enough people already died
because of your undying love?
Do the right thing. Leave
what's better left untouched
in the past, think about the
future, and move on.

Holland could picture every word in brilliant, saturated colors, filling a wide movie screen as she read. Benjamin J. Tierney's stories might have been grim subject-wise, but visually his films were always lush and vivid and full of light.

In one of Holland's favorite interviews, he'd said, "When you tell a dark story, it's important to make sure the people watching never lose hope. You need to give them something bright to hold on to, even if it's just a color on a screen, reminding them that there is still light in the world. The dark night might get its time every day, but the sun will always rise and put it out."

As Holland read about the sunset and the grave, she wondered if her father knew he was going to die in a handful of months. Then, when she read the scene in the bowling alley, she knew almost instantly why her father had hidden these pages.

He approaches a vinyl table with a group of stylish older women in matching bowling shirts. The word *Hollybells* is monogrammed on the backs of their pink-and-green shirts.

These pages were a clue for her. Another treasure hunt. And she wondered if it ended with finding the Alchemical Heart. Why else would her father have gone to such great lengths to hide these pages?

Holland wanted to cry, or call her sister, or cry and call her sister. It was too much emotion for her to think clearly, on a day that was already emotional.

Holland had told herself she'd only read a couple of pages, but she couldn't stop. She was a child on a treasure hunt, a little girl who hadn't lost her dad, a young woman who felt hope returning. This was her father's final gift to her, and it felt like the most beautiful and bittersweet thing she'd ever held.

There was a curious handwritten note penciled onto the screenplay. But what really drew Holland's attention was Alma's mention of the Watch Man.

Holland had seen the Price of Magic movies at least fifty times. The Watch Man was never mentioned. This was clearly a clue.

What if her father was telling her to find—

The vault was suddenly plunged into darkness.

No lights. No power.

Gabe.

Holland wondered if the Bank was coming for him—or if they had him—and he was using his ability to turn off all the power.

Holland tried not to feel guilty, but for a second all she could picture was Gabe at her house, bleeding on her steps in the middle of the night, then patiently guiding her to stitch him up. And she definitely felt guilty. But she told herself that someone like Gabe probably didn't feel anything.

Steeling herself, Holland held tight to her father's screenplay pages and then carefully reached out to grab the satchel that the pages had been concealed in. When she'd come in from the elevator, she hadn't seen another door, but there had to be an emergency exit down here.

Blindly, she shoved the pages in her father's satchel and slung the strap across her body.

She moved carefully but quickly, arms stretched out, until she hit a wall. She could feel the wallpaper under her fingers. Then—a hairline crack. She traced the crack. It went all the way to the ground. This had to be the door.

Holland pushed as hard as she could, nearly stumbling when it gave easily.

There must have been a window somewhere above, because she could see the gently gilded outline of a staircase. She wasn't far from the exit. She had no idea what she'd do when she got out, but for now she just had to focus on escaping. As she neared the top of the steps, she heard the chaotic voices of bankers on the other side of the walls. Holland stood near the exit door, listening until the voices quieted.

She listened for another handful of seconds. If no one else walked by, this could be her chance. She had one shot at escape, or this treasure hunt would be over before it began.

Her pulse spiked as she turned the doorknob.

The door opened next to a pair of very leafy potted plants in an alcove of the lobby. They were enough to conceal her for a minute, but not for long. With so many windows in the lobby, she couldn't really tell the lights were out. All it would take was one cowboy to look her way.

Holland could see the front doors, about twenty feet away. She debated whether she should just run for it. She had ninety seconds left.

Then she saw it. Discarded just a few feet away was a wide-brimmed cowboy hat. Holland grabbed it, threw it on, and bolted for the door.

She might have moved a little too fast, but she didn't look around, she didn't check behind her. She could see the street and the sun. And then she was there, she'd made it out with one minute to spare.

Holland kept running down the street, in the opposite direction from where Gabe had parked. At least she hoped it was the opposite direction.

"Holland!" A cherry-red car that looked straight out of the 1940s pulled up beside her. "Get in now—"

The door opened, and Holland saw Eileen in the leather driver's seat. She was dressed like Calamity Jane in fringe and leather, with two fake pistols tucked into a belt with a large brass buckle.

"Am I the only person in my life who doesn't have a secret identity?" Holland asked, gaping at her friend.

"I'd say I'd explain everything, but there's no time." Eileen quickly motioned her toward the passenger seat. "Get in. Now."

Holland cut a glance to the clock on Eileen's dashboard. 10:01. Holland's appointment was officially over. The protection of the Bank was gone. "How do I know I can trust you?" she asked.

"Because if I did what I'd been asked, I wouldn't have left my cowgirl hat by the emergency exit and . . . I'm your friend." Eileen threw down the word *friend* the way a gambler might place all her chips in the center of the table.

"I want to believe you," Holland said. When she looked at Eileen, she saw her friend. But apparently Eileen was a part of this world, where it seemed everyone was deceiving her.

"Even if you don't believe me," Eileen said, "at the very least be practical. We both know those heels are adorable, but you're not going to get very far in them."

The fringe on Eileen's cowboy jacket shook as she drove. Holland had always thought of Eileen as her most straitlaced friend, but she was a bit of a maniac now, treating stop signs like suggestions. It made Holland think of someone else who'd been hiding a big secret. Although she really didn't want to keep thinking about him. And, if Holland was being truthful, Eileen having a secret identity wasn't entirely surprising.

Eileen had always been the friend Holland had said she'd call if she ever needed to hide a dead body, and she supposed this explained why.

"You know," Holland said, "you just missed an excellent opportunity to say, *Come with me if you want to live.*"

Eileen rolled her eyes. "I'm not a deadly robot."

"But you do work for the Bank?"

Eileen pursed her lips before saying, tightly, "An NDA prevents me from answering that."

Holland tried another tactic. "Do you work for the Professor?"

Eileen worked her mouth again as if fighting to answer. There must have been some magic in whatever NDA she signed.

The car sped faster the more frustrated she became. "I was offered a job right out of college. The—" She broke off, screwed her mouth into a pained expression, and, after what looked like a significant effort, said, "It was an offer that was really difficult to say no to."

"The Professor offered you an ability," Holland supplied.

Eileen nodded.

"Can you tell me what it is?"

Eileen shook her head then she gave Holland a look that made her think her friend had been swindled. "It's not as impressive as you might think."

Holland thought back to what the Professor had said in her office. "Do you have the ability to always find a really good parking spot?"

Eileen's eyes widened. "How did you guess that?" she asked, then she looked down at Holland's wrist. Her eyes lingered for a second and she frowned, as if she hadn't found what she'd been looking for.

All of a sudden, Holland understood what the tattoos represented. "Were you looking for an ancient eye with the symbol for sulfur and the symbol for tin?"

Eileen frowned, as if she wasn't supposed to answer that question. Then she turned her wrist, which was normally covered in a watch or a sleeve, to reveal a tattoo exactly like January's, Gabe's, and Adam's, except Eileen's was an inky shade of green.

Holland must have been right. The tattoos meant that a person had an ability. "Why—"

Holland's phone beeped with a text. For a second, she wondered if it was January, and if she'd made a terrible mistake about Gabe. But the text was not from her sister.

What have you done?

Suddenly, Holland did feel scared. There were just four words, but the fact that Gabe had sent them meant the Bank hadn't apprehended him. And that he knew she had turned him in.

Holland anxiously looked out the window to see if Gabe was following them. There was nothing, just road and trees and . . .

A billboard appeared on the side of the road. One moment it wasn't there, and then it just was.

The billboard pictured a couple riding in a convertible with the top down. He looked like Cary Grant. She looked like Grace Kelly, large sunglasses covering her eyes, Tiffany-blue scarf blowing in the wind as they rode toward a mansion.

During warmer months of the year, the Hollywood Forever Cemetery projected classic films on the side of one of their mausoleums after sunset. Holland wondered if maybe this billboard was an old ad for that, if perhaps this summer they'd shown *To Catch a Thief*.

But the writing on the billboard read:

THE REGAL HOTEL
Next Turn
.5 miles

"Oh. My. God." Eileen's voice jumped to a fevered pitch that Holland had never heard before. "You have a key."

Eileen's gaze volleyed excitedly from Holland to Cary and Grace and then back to Holland.

"What are you talking about?" Holland asked.

"That's a billboard for the Regal. You can't see it unless you have a key."

Holland was about to say she didn't, but then she hesitated. She opened her purse and pulled out her sister's plastic Motor Hotel key chain. Her fingers sparked once again as she touched it. Then, right before her eyes, the key transformed into a gleaming gold skeleton key attached to a shimmering gold oval with two words etched into it: *The Regal.*

CHAPTER TWENTY-NINE

The next street was Hitchcock Way.

Eileen didn't even hesitate before turning. Everything changed as she did.

It had been morning, but now it looked like the golden hour. The sky was all buttery glowing clouds and streams of melting colors. Palm trees with Technicolor-green fronds lined a curving road paved in the reddest bricks Holland had ever seen. Everything was perfect. Birds soared and bright butterflies floated above the palms.

"It's magnificent." Eileen glowed with awe as she drove up a hill. A Gilded Age mansion at least ten stories tall came into view. "You have no idea how long I've been wanting to come here."

"What makes this place so special?" Holland asked. Although, just from the magic of the key, she could already tell this hotel was out of the ordinary.

She knew the Professor had written about it in her journal, but it had been so late and Holland had been so tired when she read it that all she could recall was something about animals being required to wear clothing, which might have actually been a joke.

"The family who built this place is known for having abilities involving time and its manipulation," said Eileen. "So every hour inside the Regal is only a minute *outside*. Right now, since we are on the Regal property, time has slowed to a crawl everywhere else. You could spend a month here, and only twelve hours would pass for the rest of the world."

This was just what Holland needed. *Time.* She also liked the idea that a person couldn't enter without a key, which hopefully meant Gabe couldn't follow her.

Eileen briefly took her eyes off the road and looked directly at Holland. "How did you get your hands on a key?"

Holland didn't want to lie, not after so many people had been dishonest with her. But her sister had hidden the key, made it a secret. And Holland still wasn't entirely sure how much she could trust Eileen.

Holland wanted to believe Eileen was a good friend. But Eileen was also an employee of the Bank, run by the Professor, who knew that Holland was the sort of sappy sentimentalist likely to trust her friends.

"I wish I could tell you," Holland said, "but the key isn't actually mine."

This only made Eileen appear more intrigued. "Did you steal it? Is that why the Bank wanted to detain you?"

"You don't know why they wanted to detain me?"

"I only know that this morning, everyone seemed to be talking about you." Eileen looked at Holland as if trying to figure out why.

They now were getting close enough to see the wide curving driveway lined in immaculate hedges and buzzing with crisp valets and perky bellhops, all dressed in cardinal-red coats with polished brass buttons that matched the gold stripes on their pants.

There are places that look like magic, and places that feel like magic, but the Regal *was* magic. Holland could feel it from the tips of her fingers down to her toes. This was big magic. Rabbit hole magic. The other side of the wardrobe magic. The world Holland had always felt deep down in her bones had to exist magic.

"Can you stop the car and drop me off just up there?" Holland asked. "Where the road briefly bends and the valets won't see?"

"You can't be serious." Eileen's smile vanished.

"Trust me, you're better off not knowing."

Eileen looked at Holland as if she couldn't believe she'd just used such a trite line. Eileen hated triteness with the same disdain she had for people who spoke on speakerphone in public.

"It's for your own good," Holland said.

Eileen shook her head. "You're getting worse."

"You'll thank me later."

"No, I won't."

"I'd tell you, but I'd have to kill you."

Eileen cringed. "I can't believe you said that." Then she was pulling over to the side of the road. "Get out. That's it, I'm sick of you and your overused lines." But then she looked at Holland as if she really didn't want to let her go and do this alone.

No one could be sincere like Eileen. Just like no one could be warm like Cat or charismatic like Chance. Holland loved her friends, which was another reason she couldn't let any of them get properly involved in this.

"I'm sorry I can't tell you everything," said Holland, "but here's what I can say. I opened a safety deposit box at the Bank today. The Manager and a number of other people all thought it contained something valuable that they wanted, but it didn't. It was just something sentimental." Holland placed one hand over her satchel. "If you really want to help me, you can go back to the Bank and tell them that."

Eileen met Holland's gaze. "I'm in a very junior position. But I'll try my best."

"Thank you." Holland opened the car door and stepped outside. She wanted to give Eileen a better goodbye, but as soon as her feet touched the ground, Holland sensed the magic. It was in the birdsong. For one moment, every bird in the sky hit the same bright note. It sounded like a chime, welcoming her as Eileen and her cherry-red car disappeared.

The Regal possessed the kind of glamour that existed only in black-and-white movies.

As Holland approached the rotunda, full of bustling valets and candy-apple-shiny cars, even the air felt different. Cleaner. Crisper. The kind of air that reminded her how good it was to breathe—to live.

The guests who entered ahead of her were all beautiful, of course, dressed in suits and furs and strings of pearls she knew were real. This was the sort of place where she believed everything was real. And yet it felt entirely unreal as she reached the velvet carpet leading up to the gilded entrance.

A girl in a smart red cap and polka-dot dress worked a glass popcorn machine, filling the air with a slightly sweeter version of the nostalgic scent as she handed out cheery red-and-white-striped boxes of it to arriving guests.

"Hello, Miss St. James," said an older attendant, who reached for the Regal's double doors with hands gloved in pristine white. "Welcome ba—" A frown line formed between his brows. "You're not January." He said it like an accusation. She wanted to ask how he could tell; no one could ever tell her and January apart.

But the attendant looked ready to throw her out of the hotel before she'd even entered. She half expected him to yell, "Impostor twin!"

Holland wondered if that was why he was at the door—if he had an ability to detect guests who didn't belong.

"I'm January's sister, Holland," she said quickly. "I have her key." She frantically extracted the key from her purse and dangled it in front of him.

The attendant no longer looked ready to throw her out, but judging by his unpleasant expression, she'd clearly broken some other rule she wasn't aware of. Then, with a smile Holland didn't trust, he said, "You'll need to visit the check-in desk. It's just beyond the entrance to the left." He pointed in that direction as he finally opened the doors. "Enjoy your stay."

Perky piano music and animated voices greeted Holland as she stepped inside. She'd always loved the lobby of the Hollywood Roosevelt, but this was something else entirely. It was all cocktails she didn't know the names of and people she felt she should know the names of. Everyone looked pretty or powerful or so unexpectedly peculiar that she wanted to talk to them.

This felt like the reason she'd come back to Los Angeles. Not to chase after myths about the devil, but to find magic. Like this.

Even the check-in desk looked like a work of art. A mosaic of ivory and brass covered the front, forming a gleaming art deco image of the Regal's exterior. Behind the desk was a low series of wooden mailboxes containing neatly rolled newspapers, smartly wrapped packages, and a few coveted keys. Above the mailboxes was a row of enamel clocks, all labeled with different place names: Sydney, Tokyo, London, New York, Los Angeles, the Regal.

The only clock that appeared to be ticking was the Regal's. It said the time was 5:47 p.m., which didn't make sense. According to Holland's watch, it was 10:23 a.m.; even if it was a different time zone, the minutes should have aligned. Then she remembered what Eileen had said about time working differently here: *Every hour inside the Regal is only a minute outside.* Which meant Holland suddenly had more time.

Unless . . . it was also Halloween inside the Regal, which would mean she had less time.

Anxiously, Holland approached the check-in desk.

There was a line, and Holland genuinely couldn't tell if the people in it were wearing costumes or were just extremely eccentric. The woman just before her wore a fur across her shoulders and held a champagne coupe in one hand and a lit cigarette in the other. Then there was a man with an excellent silver mustache speaking rapid French into a silver rotary phone with a long curly cord that extended back behind the check-in desk. In front of him was a couple with a pet monkey dressed in a little top hat and a striped vest. They appeared to be either quite important or quite a bit of trouble: Three staff members were currently helping them.

Holland couldn't hear what anyone in line was saying, but they all appeared to be growing more frantic. The strap of the satchel carrying her father's screenplay dug into her shoulder, suddenly heavier. Even though the outside world had slowed, the minutes inside the Regal seemed to be ticking by too fast.

Finally, another staff member in a more managerial outfit stepped up to the desk. Holland hoped he was there to help the next person and move the line along. But then he whispered into the ear of another staff member, and soon both of them were looking directly at Holland.

CHAPTER THIRTY

U sually, Holland hated to assume the worst. But with all that had happened in the last twenty-four hours, she felt as if she must.

Quickly, she stepped out of line and into the fray of the lobby. Parrots flew overhead, soaring between the potted palms, only unlike at the Roosevelt, these palms were lush and alive. Everything smelled faintly of citrus. And then she saw that, indeed, there was a beautiful orange tree in the center of the lobby. Someone with white gloves plucked an orange, then cut expert slices to garnish drinks for a pair of smiling guests.

It was lovely, and bright, and unfortunately far too open a place for Holland to hide. She wasn't sure if any of the staff from the check-in desk were following her, but she didn't waste time looking.

She scurried past the orange tree.

Holland heard a thud, followed by another, and then there was a noise so loud a series of gasps broke out.

Holland couldn't help turning. It was only for a second, but that was all she needed to see that every single orange had dropped from the tree and broken on the ground.

"We're so sorry." A hotel worker was already apologizing to nearby guests. Holland didn't know what was happening, but she started running. There was an old-fashioned elevator up ahead, similar to the one in the Bank. The dial said the lift was currently seven floors up and climbing, slowly. Holland barely saw the dial move. And, she realized, she didn't actually know her sister's room number. There was no indication on the key.

Maybe there was a gift shop she could hide in? Beyond the lobby was a little alcove. Holland saw a pair of black lacquered doors garnished with a simple chalk sign: *The Black and White*. Holland had no idea what the words meant, but she ducked inside.

Immediately, the world shifted from the Regal's Technicolor palette to the enigmatic shimmer of silver screen. It felt like the scene before the opening credits; the moment when you know something is about to happen, something that will show you exactly what sort of story you are in for.

Holland couldn't help slowly turning, taking in this new type of magic. Puffs of smoke floated overhead as people sat in tall booths and had animated conversations over black-and-white drinks garnished with speared trios of little onions.

On the far side, across from Holland, a bartender in a black bow tie and white rolled-up sleeves worked behind a full bar. He tossed a cocktail shaker into the air, earning a long line of claps and cheers.

Across from the bar, couples spun and twirled on a checkered dance floor, flooded with the music of a lively band and a singer in a jazzy sequin dress. She was holding one of those old-fashioned microphones, the large rectangular ones, and singing a perky Edith Piaf song.

Holland knew she needed to keep moving, but it was hard not to be mesmerized by all the black-and-white wonder. No one was on a phone or taking pictures. People were chatting and laughing and dancing and kissing.

It felt like a hundred stories were unfolding around her, all at once.

Next to the stage was a pair of long velvet curtains with a narrow sign above them containing two words: *The Abracadabra*. Holland had always liked the word *abracadabra*. She wondered if this could be a good place to duck into and read her father's screenplay pages. She started to step that way, but she paused at the sound of a familiar voice.

Her eyes cut back to the bar and instantly she saw him, sitting next to a woman with the bone structure of a starlet. Adam Bishop.

Her heart did an unexpected flip.

Adam looked absolutely flawless in the silver-screen light. And yet Holland had the strangest feeling that her heart wasn't flipping just because Adam looked good in his dark slacks, his velvet jacket, and his white collared shirt, insouciantly half-unbuttoned. His jacket sleeves were messily rolled up, and his tie was hanging loosely around his neck. He looked careless and harmless, and Holland couldn't help thinking that she missed him.

It made no sense. She hadn't known Adam before yesterday, and yet she suddenly felt as if she did. She knew him from somewhere. Somewhere before tonight, or last night, or yesterday afternoon. She couldn't remember how. She couldn't remember anything about Adam Bishop that she hadn't heard within the last twenty-four hours. But she felt it in the prickling across her skin, the rising of her heartbeat, the way he drew her attention like a magnet. *She had known him before.* And it wasn't because he was her sister's partner. He was someone . . . someone to her that she couldn't remember.

Suddenly she wanted him to look at her, to see her, to notice her. She was feeling far too aware of everything about him. He didn't look as if he'd been shot last night. In fact, he looked as if he'd never been shot.

She thought once again about how time moved differently here. If Adam had been brought to the Regal after his injuries, then days, possibly weeks, had passed for him, while it had been merely hours for her.

He was now grinning intoxicated wide, his entire attention on the stunning woman beside him. She was dressed in a gown with '40s-style cap sleeves, a plunging neck lined in fine crystals, and a pair of ruched gloves.

It seemed he'd forgotten all about Holland and the promise he'd made to January, which was fine. Holland didn't need Adam to notice her. She was probably feeling this way about him because of the strange visions she'd been having. She tried to shake it off, nearly bumping into a server who was ferrying a tray of frothing drinks covered in glass cloches. Then another server passed, carrying drinks garnished with popcorn, which seemed to be a popular snack at this hotel.

"Dance with me." The words, barely audible above the din of the bar, were followed by an uninvited hand on the small of Holland's back.

"I'm sorry, I'm not really in the mood."

"And I'm not really asking."

The hand at her back moved possessively to her waist, confident fingers turning her until she was face-to-face with Adam.

Her heart kicked up nervously.

Adam smelled like citrus and vodka, and this close, Holland could see it wasn't just his tie that looked loose and undone. Everything about Adam Bishop looked perfectly negligent and disreputable in that charming way only really attractive men could pull off.

"You're drunk," Holland blurted.

He grinned with an unfairly perfect smile. "It's good to see you, too. I'm glad that mercenary didn't kill you. And yes, I'm just swell. I didn't almost die. Thank you so much for asking." His hazy eyes sharpened, some of the intoxication slipping away and revealing a hint of something like anger.

Then he was spinning her around in the middle of the dance floor as he drawled, "I'd offer to buy you a drink, but I believe you actually owe me, for all that taking-a-bullet-for-you business." Adam waved down a server before Holland could object.

She started to say, "I'm really sorry about the shooting. I made a terrible mistake and—"

"Hello, sir, what may I get for you?" The server cut in with a deferential nod toward Adam.

"Hi, yes, the lady would like to buy us some drinks. She'll have a Shirley Temple with extra cherries." He looked at Holland and winked. "And I'll take a sidecar."

CHAPTER THIRTY-ONE

For a moment it felt like a flashbulb second. Time stopped. Entirely. The bar looked like a still photograph. The background was a blur of grays and whites. Holland could see figures but not faces, except for Adam Bishop's.

He was fallen-angel beautiful with his golden hair and devilish smirk. He was also drunk and cavalier. Adam was not the calculated villain Holland had always pictured, but that didn't mean he wasn't a villain. In the book of Revelation, the devil was referred to as the great deceiver. What if Adam had deceived everyone—January, the Bank, Holland?

"You're looking at me as if I've done something wrong," he murmured.

"I just really hate Shirley Temples," Holland said, because suddenly she didn't know what to say. Should she ask if he was the devil? Would he tell her the truth? What then if he admitted it?

"The Shirley Temple was supposed to be a joke." A sheepish smile played across Adam's lips, and for a second, he looked so innocent. He looked like the sort of boy next door who would sneak in through your window and steal a few kisses, not make a deal for your soul.

"Good evening, folks," cried the singer on the stage. "Before I get into my next song, I just want to remind you all about tonight's special. Bartender Bernard is visiting from one of our sister hotels in Charleston, where he's famous for making the perfect sidecar. I hope you all enjoy!"

The music started up again and Holland breathed a sigh of relief. "You ordered the sidecar because it was the special?"

A half smirk. "And it has a great name."

"Have you ordered one before?"

Adam narrowed his hazy eyes. "Why all the questions?"

"No reason." She started to pull away. Even if Adam wasn't the devil, she couldn't stay here with him. She needed to get somewhere safe to study her father's screenplay pages. "I should let you get back to your—"

She caught a sudden flash of red out of the corner of her eye. Men wearing red ties, four of them, had entered the bar. The rest of their suits were still black and white, but somehow their ties were brilliant red.

The air in the bar immediately shifted.

The music on the stage stuttered.

The chatter of voices hushed.

The singer accidentally sang the wrong line of lyrics.

Adam was the only person in the room who didn't seem to care. He pulled Holland back into a dance, giving her no choice but to wrap her arms around his neck, and when he spoke again his voice was almost playful. "I need you to tell me, did you somehow sneak in here without a key?"

"No—I have a key."

"How did you get it?"

"It's January's."

His eyes narrowed by a fraction. "Did she give it to you?"

"No, I found it."

Adam gave her a look that made Holland think she'd given him the wrong answer, but there wasn't time to explain. The red ties were at the edge of the dance floor now. People quickly scurried out of their way. Holland felt like she needed to run.

"Stay with me." Adam held her a little closer. "If you don't, those thugs will escort you from the Regal and prohibit you from ever returning."

"And you think you can stop them?"

Adam scoffed, offended. Then he turned to the red ties and flashed the most confident smile Holland had ever seen.

The red ties stopped moving.

"Good evening, Mr. Bishop," said the broadest red tie in the group. He was at least twice as wide as Adam, yet Holland swore there was a distinct tremor in his voice. The three others flanking him didn't say a word, just stood there, rigid.

Adam made a vaguely annoyed sigh. "Did you need something?" He let the hand on the small of Holland's back dip lower and lower.

A blush crept up her cheeks.

"Please forgive the intrusion," said the red tie who'd spoken before. "Unfortunately, the young woman you're dancing with is not a key holder or a registered guest."

"Then put her on my guest list," Adam said lazily.

"But—" one of the other red ties piped up.

"You heard what he said," the first red tie cut in. "Forgive us once again for the intrusion, sir. Can I have some complimentary drinks sent to your table?"

Adam ordered two drinks, which weren't sidecars or Shirley Temples. Then he waved a dismissive hand, and the red ties left as quickly as they'd come.

On the stage, the music returned to its regular tempo. Everyone was back to dancing and chattering, as if nothing had happened. But Holland felt shaken. She unwrapped her arms from Adam's neck. "Thank you for your help. But I think I can manage on my own from here."

Adam grabbed her hand and reeled her back before she could step away. "I don't think you understand how this works. You're my guest, which means if you want to stay in this hotel, you need to stay with *me* for the next twenty-four hours."

"Why twenty-four hours?"

"It's hotel policy. Official key holders can stay as long as they want, but guests are only allowed to stay twenty-four *Regal* hours. So, until then, I say either we get drunk at this bar, or"—Adam looked her straight in the eye, and every hint of charm and carelessness vanished—"you tell me what happened after I got shot and why you look as if you're running for your life right now."

Holland froze. She was tempted to tell him something along the lines of what she'd said to Eileen. She'd only met Adam yesterday; trusting him didn't make any sense. But her sister trusted him. Her sister had sent him.

Holland had a lot of questions about a lot of things, but she knew all the way down to her bones that her sister loved her. Whatever secrets she'd been keeping, it was for a good reason, and if she'd sent Adam Bishop to keep Holland safe, that was for a good reason, too.

"I'll tell you what happened," Holland said. "But I don't think we should talk here."

CHAPTER THIRTY-TWO

The color returned as soon as Holland stepped into the elevator with Adam. There were just two buttons.

Main floor
Penthouse

Holland wondered what kind of money or power a person must have to own the key to a penthouse in a place like this.

A bell chimed.

The door opened.

And the enormous space on the other side answered her question.

More.

Adam had more power and more money than she could have imagined. She'd sensed it in the bar. From the way people responded to him, it was clear he was more than someone who worked for the Bank, which made her wonder why he even worked for the Bank.

Across from her, a row of perfect windows looked out onto the most extraordinary skyline she'd ever seen. Adam didn't even glance at it. He dropped his key in a bowl by the elevator, before shucking off his velvet jacket and tossing it onto a taxidermy fox.

Now that he was back to color, she could see his slacks were black and his jacket was a striking red velvet. In fact, the entire penthouse was a striking shade of something, all deep aquamarine, rich emerald-green, shimmering obsidian-black, lines of brilliant gold, and touches of creamy alabaster. Holland wondered if this was actually Adam's preferred decor, or if the hotel rooms only came in bold, rich colors.

It was the sort of place you weren't supposed to wander around and touch things, but that was exactly what Holland wanted to do. She half expected to find fancy art on the walls—the kind that had been stolen from museums years ago—but what she found was even better. There was a row of some of the rarest movie posters she'd ever seen. A *Metropolis* poster in German, *King Kong* from 1933, *Frankenstein* from 1931, *The Black Cat* from 1934, and her favorite, a *Casablanca* poster from a 1947 release in France.

Her father had mentioned the rare *Metropolis* poster in one of his old interviews, and Holland had fallen down a rabbit hole lined with old film posters after that.

She wanted to ask Adam about the collection, but her attention snagged on a framed black-and-white picture sitting on top of the mini-bar. It showed two men with arms around each other's shoulders. One of them was Adam, wearing the kind of pure-happiness wide smile that could sometimes look goofy in pictures but looked incredible on him. He was dressed much like he was just now, in a white shirt with an undone bow tie around his neck, and next to him was a guy in a white dinner jacket who looked exactly like the man Holland had seen at the Roosevelt.

Her skin prickled as she remembered the familiar way he'd looked at her, and she couldn't help picking up the picture. "Who is this?"

Adam's smile immediately vanished. "That's my older brother, Mason." He looked at the photo almost as if he'd forgotten it was there, the sort of thing he'd passed by every day without really seeing it, but now that he remembered it, he wished he hadn't.

Clearly, it wasn't something Holland should ask more about. But it felt like too strange a coincidence for her to just set the picture down as if it was nothing. "Do you know if he knows my sister?"

"No," Adam said, almost protectively. "Why?"

"I saw him yesterday."

Adam stiffened. "Where?"

"At the Hollywood Roosevelt."

"Did you talk to him?"

"No. He was on the mezzanine, and I was in the lobby. I just re-member because he looked at me as if he knew me—like really knew me—which didn't make sense until you said he was your brother, and I thought maybe he mistook me for January."

"My brother just has an effect on people." Adam glanced again at the photograph. His eyes were still a little unfocused, but they seemed to sharpen as he spoke. "When I was a kid, I idolized him. He was the center of the universe wherever he went. Mason always said the right thing and did the right thing. I thought he was the kind of good I would never be." Adam went quiet in a way that made her feel as if there was a *but* followed by another sentence he didn't want to say.

"What happened?" Holland asked.

"It's a long story, one that's not particularly flattering for either of us. But it ends with me no longer idolizing him." Adam took the picture from Holland, and placed it face down on the minibar. "So," he said, in a new tone that made it clear he was done with the subject. "Tell me what you think about this place." He dropped onto the sofa. It was a deep aquamarine velvet, shaped like a horseshoe, and it seemed to say, *I'm bigger and bolder and fancier than your practical beige couch.*

"Um, it's very nice."

Adam made a wounded face. "*Nice* is such a disappointing word. But, honestly, it is a little much for me. I don't spend a lot of time at the Regal."

Holland eyed him skeptically.

"You don't believe me?"

"I don't know. You seemed to be having a good time at the bar down-stairs."

"I can have a good time anywhere." Adam lounged back and threw his arms wide across the cushions. "After I was shot, the Bank brought me here to heal, and I've spent a lot of time at that bar. That's when I heard the rumors that *you* were the girl with the Alchemical Heart."

"I'm sorry to disappoint you, but you were misinformed. I don't have it."

"Good." Adam's drunken playboy grin returned. "We can have some fun now."

Holland frowned.

It seemed to her that everyone wanted the Alchemical Heart. Why didn't Adam? Her eyes wandered around the lavish penthouse once more. This place must have taken up at least half of the Regal's top floor, if not all of it, and he hadn't even deigned to look out the window. He clearly had the money, and he probably had all the shiny toys, but he really didn't seem to care about it.

"Don't get me wrong," Adam said. "I'm not indifferent to the power of the Alchemical Heart, but searching for that thing is a good way to die, and I really like being alive. I also really enjoy not being shot."

"Is that why you didn't come looking for me after you recovered?"

Adam cocked his head to the side. "Are you hurt that I didn't ride to your rescue on a white horse?"

Hurt was not the word Holland would have used, but she did suddenly feel worried. Her hands went to the charm around her neck.

She had just assumed that Adam had brought her up here to help her, and that once she told him about her treasure hunt, he would fully be on board. But now she realized Adam's idea of help might only go as far as getting her drunk in this hotel room. For a fraction of a second, she missed Gabe, but only for a second. She refused to think about him longer than that.

"I'm not hurt," she finally said.

"Are you mad? Because you look kind of pissed." Adam reached toward the coffee table, then frowned when he seemed to realize there weren't any drinks. He shoved up from the sofa and started toward the minibar. "You want a drink?"

"I want to find the Alchemical Heart."

Adam shook his head. "That's a good way to get killed, and your sister asked me to keep you alive."

"In that case, you need to help me find it," said Holland. "The Watch Man called me yesterday."

Adam froze. "What did he say?"

"He told me I'd die at 11:59 on Halloween night, unless I find the Alchemical Heart."

Adam slowly ran a hand over his jaw and cursed under his breath. "So, let me get this straight. You're going to die tomorrow and you still don't want a drink?"

Holland picked up a pillow from the sofa and threw it at him. "I'm being serious."

"So am I," Adam said, but he'd stepped away from the minibar and now looked as if he was trying to sober up. "What do you need from me?"

"I thought you just said looking for the Alchemical Heart was a good way to die."

"I did, but if I let anything happen to you, then your sister will kill me." After everything Holland had learned about January in the past twenty-four hours, she had a feeling Adam was being more literal than figurative, and she loved her sister dearly for it.

"If you're really willing to help me," Holland said, "then we need to find the Watch Man."

Adam looked at her, bemused. "Why?"

Holland considered telling him about her father's screenplay. Adam's lack of interest in the Alchemical Heart made her feel better about trusting him. But she also felt as if she couldn't share her father's last words with *anyone*.

"Would you believe me if I said I have a hunch?"

"Not even a little."

"What if I said I don't know where the Alchemical Heart is, but I have a clue from a very reliable source that we need to go see the Watch Man?"

"Better. But if I'm going to risk my life to get mixed up in this, I need a little more than that." His gaze cut to her satchel.

Holland wondered if perhaps he was more sober than she thought. Or maybe this was just him turning off playboy Adam from the bar and turning on the Adam her sister had sent to watch out for her.

"I can't give you more right now," Holland said. "I'm trusting you because my sister trusts you, but I'm going to need *a little more* than that, if you want to know everything."

Adam smirked. "How about I take you to the Watch Man, and we can renegotiate after that?"

"So you know where he lives?"

Adam looked instantly insulted. "I know where to find everyone. Why do you think your sister asked me to watch out for you?"

"That's what I keep asking myself."

This earned her an actual grin, the kind that made his hazel eyes light up. "This world you're in now is not very welcoming to outsiders. I know I'm not the most responsible person, but I can get you through any door you need." He said it the way someone else might have accepted a dare, as if he couldn't wait to show her how good at this he was, as if the idea of her dying was just a challenge, not an actual threat.

Holland didn't know if she found his cockiness unnerving or reassuring. Maybe a little bit of both. There was something about Adam Bishop, some unnameable quality that made Holland feel as if either he was going to be her unlikely drunken savior or he was going to be the end of her.

CHAPTER THIRTY-THREE

I'm going to go change," Adam said. "Feel free to snoop, or steal things from the minibar while I'm gone."

Holland's stomach growled as soon as Adam left the room. She hated to turn down an opportunity to snoop, but all this running for her life had made her hungry. She also found herself quite curious as to what sort of minibar a place like this possessed. To her surprise, it was modest, the size of an old record player cabinet. She was about to open it when she noticed a peculiar sort of button on the wall beside it.

The button was in the middle of a small golden frame, situated below the words *Press for Champagne*. Holland was of course about to press it, but then she noticed a notched dial beneath the frame. Her fingers tingled as she gave it a turn.

Press for Sidecar now appeared in the frame around the button. Clearly, the hotel was pushing this special. And yet, she felt just a little inkling of worry. So many of the other people in her life were not who they seemed.

She gave the notched dial one more turn. *Press for Popcorn* now appeared. Her stomach growled again, and she pushed the button. She wasn't entirely sure what she expected to happen, but nothing resembling popcorn appeared. She looked toward the elevator, wondering if someone from the hotel would deliver it. Then she heard a popping sound coming from inside the cabinet. She turned back and finally opened the minibar doors.

Holland didn't notice if her fingers tingled, if there were sparks, or if the air around her changed for a second, but she did know this was magic. It wasn't the simple magic of timeless things, or big rabbit-hole magic. It was something in between.

The cabinet smelled like butter and sugar and that first moment when you step into a theater. Inside it was a small stage lined in red velvet curtains, and in between the curtains were three tall pink-and-white-striped boxes. Holland watched in wonder as they filled, until the popcorn overflowed onto the candy bars positioned in front of the stage.

None of the candies were familiar. They all came in ultra-bright labels with shiny foil wrappers that said things like *Taste a Ray of Sunshine* and *Bite into Nostalgia*.

The popcorn appeared to come in three flavors: butter, caramel, and cheddar. Holland took the caramel box. Then she couldn't help herself and grabbed one of the candy bars, too—*The Best Memory You've Forgotten*.

"What did you find in there?"

Holland spun around at the sound of Adam's voice, spilling some of the caramel corn onto his perfect floors.

He looked like that old Lana Del Rey song come to life, dressed in blue jeans and a soft white shirt. He must have taken a shower, because he smelled clean and botanical, and his golden hair was damp at the tips. A drop of water fell onto his forehead as his eyes moved from the candy bar she held in one hand to the box of popcorn in the other. He grinned, clearly entertained. "How did you get popcorn?"

"The button." Holland motioned toward the wall, but now the words over the button were *Press for Whiskey*. "That's strange."

"It changes depending on who's using it," said Adam.

She was about to ask him to turn the dial, to see what else came up for him. But after stealing a handful of her popcorn, he started toward the elevator, and Holland didn't want to stop him.

It was time to visit the Watch Man.

"Today is going to be a scorcher, friends. Most of Los Angeles is scheduled to hit triple digits by noon, making today the hottest Halloween in Southern California history. This should be good news to everyone who's excited about wearing their slutty Halloween costumes. I'm expecting to see lots of skin tonight. But friends, please be careful. I don't know what's going around—maybe it's just the heat—but in other record-breaking news—"

Adam switched the radio station to one playing music. Holland wondered if he thought the music might relax her. She'd wanted to find the Watch Man right away, but now that they had left the Regal, seconds were skipping over each other and rapidly turning into minutes.

The clock on the dash read 11:16. They'd already been driving for a half an hour. Noon was rapidly approaching, half the day was almost gone.

Adam put a hand on her leg. She was certain it was just to calm her, and to her surprise, it did. She continued to feel as if she'd known him much longer than one day. He had let her drive his car, since he wasn't entirely sober. He made a surprisingly good passenger, not commenting on her driving or worrying about the way she handled his fancy car, which made her suspect he owned more than one.

"Up here," he said softly.

The Beverly Hills Hotel was one of the first hotels Holland and her friends had visited after hearing the Professor's sidecar myth. It was the type of place where the pink and green colors never faded, the neon never blinked, and if you spent an afternoon by the pool, it was easy to believe your life would always feel like the glossy cover of a magazine.

Holland had immediately known this was not a place where people made deals with the devil. This was where you took selfies by the glowing *Beverly Hills Hotel* sign and pictures of your drinks, which she herself had done before (they were really too pretty not to).

After stepping out of the car and entering the lobby, she whispered to Adam, "I'm surprised the Watch Man lives here."

"Why?" he asked.

"It just seems so alive."

"That's probably why he picked it. If your job was telling people when they're going to die, wouldn't you want to live somewhere full of life?"

Adam opened a large glass door that led outside to a maze of green foliage and petal-pink flowers. The sky above was cornflower blue and just as hot as the DJ on the radio had said. Within a few steps, Holland's skin was glistening, and some of the plants looked as if they were . . . *melting*?

She reached out and touched a shiny green leaf. It wasn't made of plastic, but it left a shiny green stain on her fingers. "Look at this," Holland said.

Adam wrinkled his forehead. "Maybe they used the wrong pesticide."

"Is this hotel . . . magic?" she asked.

Adam shook his head. "There are a few other hotels like the Regal, but none of them are anywhere near Los Angeles. This is just ordinary we've-ruined-the-world stuff."

Holland noticed a few more melting plants on the way to the Watch Man's bungalow. Stems were bending like rubber, and more than one flower dripped bright drops of pink onto the brick pathway. Holland was aware she wasn't very familiar with the magical world yet, but whatever was happening here seemed like magic.

She wondered if Adam was lying to her, or if he simply was unbothered. He was starting to sober up, but he continued to move through the world with a careless grace, as if nothing could ever touch him. Holland, on the other hand, felt more anxious with every step. She wondered if somehow the world around her was reflecting her anxiety.

She swore she saw steam rising off the bricks that led to Bungalow 22. The building was painted one of the Beverly Hills Hotel's signature shades of pink and was shaded by a lush collection of tropical plants.

Adam knocked on the door. "I hope this is the right one."

A second later, an older gentleman answered. He wore a long brocade smoking jacket and a curious expression. "Are the two of you lost?"

"I hope not," Adam said. "We're here to see the Watch Man."

The curiosity fled from his expression, and so did the kindness in his eyes. "I'm afraid he doesn't welcome unsolicited guests."

"Tell him Mason Bishop's younger brother is here."

The older man's face went a little gray.

"It's all right. Let them in, my love," said a voice behind him.

"Seems it's your lucky day." He put on an imitation of a smile and slowly opened the door.

Holland had never been inside one of these bungalows, but she knew several of them were inspired by the hotel's more famous guests. Number 1 was Marilyn Monroe's, number 5 was Elizabeth Taylor's, and this one was clearly Frank Sinatra's.

It was a mid-century modern masterpiece, complete with an elegant black grand piano, a vintage record player spinning out the song "Witchcraft," and tall pillars and golden walls. Holland wasn't certain what the pillars and golden walls had to do with Mr. Sinatra, but they added even more flair to the already impressive space.

"I feel as if the pillars are a little much," Adam murmured.

"I don't know," Holland said. "I think they're kind of fun." She also didn't think it was a good idea to insult the home of a man who told people when they were going to die. But Adam didn't seem to be of the same mind. He looked disturbed by the number of houseplants—Holland had to admit, the living room felt a bit like a jungle. Scattered across it were more living houseplants than you'd expect inside a hotel, and at least twenty-five rotary phones.

Another gentleman, the same age as the man who'd opened the door, was talking on one of the phones. "I suggest you take more walks with your partner, make time to watch the sunset, and stop eating those poison cookies. Good day." He set the phone down carefully before slowly approaching Adam and Holland.

He appraised Adam with slitted eyes, which only seemed to amuse Adam. But the man smiled widely when he saw Holland. "I was hoping I'd have the pleasure to meet you some day. And I'm flattered you'd pay me a visit on a day with such limited time." He took her hand and shook it between both of his.

This must have been the Watch Man. But his voice didn't sound like the one Holland had heard on the phone. She distinctly remembered that voice having a mid-Atlantic accent, but this one sounded very typical Californian. Slow, easy, relaxed. "What happened to your accent?"

He smiled wider. "It's purely affected. I found it helps with the calls. The accent also gives me a separation between work and life."

"So being the Watch Man is your job?"

He wobbled his head. "It's a complicated story. I'd be happy to tell it to you. Believe it or not, Ernest and I don't get too many visitors. But with your limited time, Miss St. James, I'm supposing you're here for a different tale."

Holland actually had no idea what she was supposed to be there for, but she felt a once-familiar rush, that pitter-patter of excitement she used to feel on one of her father's treasure hunts, the burst of joy that came with chasing a clue and discovering she was right. Her father's hint to find the Watch Man had seemed rather obvious, but she still felt a swell of satisfaction to have it seemingly confirmed by him.

The Watch Man guided Holland and Adam toward a private patio at the back of the bungalow. It was larger than most backyards in California, with a wooden fence covered in tropical flowers, a stone fireplace, and two seating areas with iron-green tables and bright white cushioned chairs. Holland couldn't see a fountain, but she could hear the gentle sound of water as the Watch Man directed them to sit in the love seat opposite him. "Let's have some tea."

On the table between them were three teapots: a black one with a purple flower, a white one with pale orange flowers, and a teal one with a pink flower that matched the hotel's colors.

"You were expecting us," Holland said.

The Watch Man smiled knowingly. Then he turned his head toward Adam, who had just picked up the white teapot. "Oh no, Mr. Bishop, that's for Miss St. James. I gave you the black tea." The Watch Man genteelly leaned across the table to pour Adam a cup of tea. And it was truly black. Dark as ink and piping hot. "Trust me, young man, you'll enjoy it."

The Watch Man kept his keen gaze on Adam until, finally, Adam brought the cup to his lips. He blew away the steam and took a long intentional sip, clearly not wanting to offend the man who tells people when they will die.

"It's delicious." Adam said it as if he didn't truly mean it, but the Watch Man smiled all the same before turning to Holland.

It was her turn now. She poured herself a cup, took a cautious sip, which was actually quite refreshing, and she said as much.

"You're very kind." The Watch Man poured himself a cup. "Now, let's move on to the reason I assume you came here. Let's talk about your father."

loved your father's films," the Watch Man began. A tabby cat with gold-and-white fur came over and rubbed itself against his legs. He petted its head and said, "I even named my cat Red. Because of *The Price of Magic.*"

Holland smiled. She couldn't count the number of times people had referenced her father's films in front of her. But this was the first time someone had ever done it knowing who Ben Tierney was to her. It was something Holland had imagined but never experienced, and it made her feel like a happy puddle, as if part of her had melted in the sun. Then she remembered Adam was sitting right next to her.

She nervously turned his way. His eyes were already on her. He looked unsurprised, but not unmoved. *He already knew.*

Adam's eyes had lost their smile, and his mouth had tipped down at the corners in a way that seemed to say so much more than *sorry*. Holland wondered when January had told him. She wondered *why* January had told him. Although neither of those things mattered half as much as the fact that January had trusted Adam enough to tell him. That one fact felt like everything Holland needed to know.

"Such a tragedy that Ben never finished the third film," the Watch Man continued. "He once told me he loved writing about characters like Red because he needed to believe that an ordinary man with nothing but mettle and grit could come up against the most extraordinary forces of our world—the unexplainable, the unbelievable, the grossly unfair—and prevail."

He looked at Holland meaningfully, and she felt a bittersweet something twist inside of her. She wasn't sure if this quote was a breadcrumb her father had intentionally left, or if it was just something he'd said because that's who he was. Either way, she was glad to hear it.

"So, you actually knew my dad?"

"*Knew* might be taking it a little far. I had the honor of a brief meeting with Ben before his tragic passing. He had a heart, and he was one of those rare people who only became better at using it throughout his life. But I'm getting ahead of myself." The Watch Man paused to take a sip of tea, and he must have been waiting for Holland and Adam to do the same because he didn't continue until they did. "Your father came from one of the old families."

"I'm not sure I understand what you mean by that," Holland said.

"There are two types of people in this world: those who are born into it, like your friend Mr. Bishop, and those who find it at some point during their lives and then spend the rest of their lives trying to fit into it." The Watch Man took another slow sip of tea. Again, he sat and smiled until Adam and Holland did the same. Still, Holland couldn't relax. Sitting in a garden sipping tea was a luxury she didn't have time for. She wished the Watch Man could go a little faster.

"Your father was the first type," the Watch Man continued. "And not only was he born into a family with magic, but he was born into a family that has possessed magic for centuries."

This was news to Holland, and yet somehow she wasn't entirely shocked. Perhaps because she had always believed in magic. She wondered if her father had planned to tell her someday, or if he'd designed his treasure hunts so she would find out on her own.

"In your father's family, it was tradition that the children would always call me on their eighteenth birthday. Given that the Tierneys were a practical, old-magic family, they believed there was no point in bequeathing an inheritance to a child who would die before the age of forty."

"Couldn't the children just lie about their time of death?" Holland asked.

Another pause for more drinking of tea, before the Watch Man said, "Not in the Tierney family. They were famed for their ability to tell truth from lies. Of course, when your father learned he would die so young, they decided not to share this ability with him."

"So you're saying his parents disowned him because he was going to die young?" Holland had always known her father had been estranged from his family, she'd just never known why. The aunt and uncle who raised her weren't actually blood relatives—they'd been old friends of her parents, and they had left LA right after her parents had died.

She was tempted to ask if her grandparents were still alive, but she wasn't sure she cared to know a family who had disowned her dad because he was going to die young.

"Before you judge your father's family too harshly, you should know it's quite common to consider age of death when deciding who will inherit power," said the Watch Man. "If your grandparents had passed on their abilities to your father, those abilities would have been taken by the Bank when he'd died, not passed on to you, since there are rules about receiving power before you come of age. Your father's family also knew he wasn't going to complete the task I gave him to have a longer life. It was an impossible task—quite like yours. But unlike you, I cautioned your father not to do it."

"What was the task?" Holland asked.

"I told your father that if he wanted more time, he would need to find the Alchemical Heart and give it to one of the devils."

"What do you mean *one* of the devils?" Holland asked, alarmed. This was not a story she'd heard before. In all the research she'd done, there was only ever one devil. She shot a look at Adam, to see if he had any thoughts on this, but he appeared relaxed as ever, lounging back casually in his seat.

She nudged him with her leg, but he didn't move. Was he sound asleep?

"Finally," the Watch Man said on an exhale. "I was afraid I had made the tea too weak."

"You did this to him?" Holland looked at Adam's teacup in horror.

"There is no time to explain." The Watch Man shot a quick glance down at his watch. "We have only a few minutes before Mr. Bishop wakes."

"But why did you put him to sleep?" Holland looked at the carefully orchestrated scene before her—Adam asleep, the Watch Man suddenly on high alert, three pots of tea laid out with a prescient level of precision. "How did you know I was coming today?"

"Your father told me," he answered sharply.

"But you told me his family didn't give him an ability."

"They didn't."

"But then—"

"Your questions will have to wait, Miss St. James." The Watch Man reached under his cushion and pulled out a long brown document envelope. "Your father gave me this before he died. He had decided to take my advice: He said the power of the Alchemical Heart was too much for anyone to possess, and he couldn't give it to either of the devils."

"Wait," Holland interrupted again, "please—what do you mean by *either of the devils?*"

Quietly, he said, "There are two men who make up the devil. Two brothers." The Watch Man's eyes went back toward Adam, and this time, Holland had a sinking feeling that he wasn't making sure Adam was asleep.

"Are you saying—"

"No—" the Watch Man cut in. "I've not said anything." But once again, his gaze rested on Adam, and Holland knew exactly what he wasn't saying.

Lying beside her, eyes gently closed, golden hair strewn across his forehead, Adam definitely didn't look like a devil. Maybe she'd thought so when she first met him, but now he just seemed like a reckless young man with a beautiful face. "Are you certain?" Holland asked the Watch Man. "I saw him get shot. I saw him bleed."

"I did not say he was God." The Watch Man pressed his lips into a frustrated line. "Now, would you like to waste more time debating this or shall I tell you what your father said?"

Holland quieted, although her thoughts about Adam still felt extremely loud. How well did January actually know her partner?

But January had told Adam about their parents. Holland had never trusted anyone enough to share that secret. The only reason she'd told Gabe was because her life literally depended on him. Now she felt her life depended on whether she could trust Adam, and whatever the Watch Man was about to tell her next.

"After saying the Alchemical Heart was too powerful for any man to possess, your father asked me to hold on to the envelope I just gave you, until a day came when one of his daughters paid me a visit."

Holland glanced at the envelope in her hand. It was similar in weight and size to the folder that had been in the safety deposit box. She had been so excited about the start of this treasure hunt, but now she felt a different sort of gravity that brought her down to earth as she imagined her father bringing this to the Watch Man before he died. This wasn't just his last treasure hunt; this was his dying wish for her. She couldn't let him down.

And yet, she still didn't understand how her father had known the exact minute when she and Adam would come. Unless her father had been in possession of the Alchemical Heart. And the Alchemical Heart had given him the ability to see into the future—just like it had given abilities to the people who had come across it in the Chained Library.

Holland's fingers tightened protectively around the envelope. "My father had the ability to see the future, didn't he?"

The Watch Man sighed. "Visions of the future can be deceptive. I don't know what your father saw, but I know that whenever someone asks me the time, I always see multiple outcomes. The future's course does not become fixed until it turns into the past. And, for what it's worth—" The tabby cat purred. The Watch Man checked his watch. "We're almost out of time. Hurry, Miss St. James, put that envelope in your bag and do not show it to anyone. Hurry," he repeated. "Miss St. James, put that envelope in your bag and do not show it to anyone."

Holland looked at him, confused. Beads of sweat had formed a damp line across his brow. Or was it blood? Several of the drops looked darker than the others. "Are you all right?"

"Hurry, Miss St. James, put that envelope in your bag and do not show it to anyone." A bead of the unnervingly red sweat fell from his face and then he froze. His mouth, his eyes, his hands hovering above the table—nothing moved. Even the bead of red sweat didn't drop to the table. It remained suspended in the air.

Holland's chest went so tight, for a second it felt hard to breathe, and she thought perhaps she might freeze, too. She frantically grabbed the Watch Man's hand and tried to shake it, but nothing happened. This felt terrifyingly similar to what had happened at the Bank with the Professor, but this was lasting even longer.

Then the cat purred, and finally time seemed to start again. The drop of sweat fell onto the table.

"Hurry, put that envelope in your bag and do not show it to anyone," the Watch Man said again, as if he'd never said it before.

Holland quickly shoved the envelope in her satchel, next to the pages of her father's screenplay. "Sir, I think you're bleeding." She pointed toward his forehead.

The Watch Man dabbed it with a napkin, just as Adam blinked his eyes open with a slightly bewildered expression.

"I'm afraid that's all I have for you," said the Watch Man, as if he'd just finished answering a question. The blood on his forehead was already wiped away. Holland really wanted to ask about it, but she wasn't sure how she could without mentioning the words he'd just repeated. If she mentioned those words, Adam would know there was something in her bag. And yet, for a second, she debated it. Something was broken or breaking, and Holland had a terrible feeling it was somehow her fault.

Beside her, Adam wiped the sleep from his eyes. "How long was I out?"

"Not long," Holland said. "But I'm afraid we need to go." She turned

to the Watch Man. "Thank you so much for your time and for the tea."
She rose to her feet on legs that were suddenly shaking. She knew she
couldn't stay; she just hadn't yet figured out where to go. Back to the
Regal seemed like the obvious choice, but if she went there, she would
have to stay with Adam, and Holland was feeling less certain that trusting him was a good idea.

She thought about asking Adam if she could call her sister, but that
had only given Holland a false sense of security with Gabe. Perhaps it
was just better to leave Adam and go it alone from here, even if that idea
scared her.

CHAPTER THIRTY-FIVE

I t was 12:59 p.m.

There were eleven hours left.

As Holland and Adam left the Watch Man's bungalow, she noticed a number of people already in costumes. She saw a sexy Little Red Riding Hood holding hands with a wolf, and just before reentering the main hotel, she and Adam passed an angel smoking a cigarette and talking to a red-horned devil.

"So the Watch Man really didn't say anything useful while I was asleep?" Adam asked.

"No," Holland said, trying to keep her voice casual. "He just told me how much he loved my father's films."

Adam frowned, unconvinced. "If the Watch Man didn't have any information, then do you want to tell me why you thought coming here was a good idea?"

"It was just a hunch," Holland said.

Adam continued to watch her warily and accidentally bumped into a couple coming out of their room. "Sorry," he apologized. Then his eyes were back on Holland, sharp and accusatory. "Why are you lying?"

"I wasn't lying—" Before the words were out of her mouth, Adam took hold of her hand and pulled her through a door.

Suddenly, she was inside an elegant pink-and-green hotel suite with lots of light streaming through the windows and lingering hints of its previous occupant's perfume.

"What are you doing?" Holland squeaked.

Adam released her hand and strode across the suite as if it belonged to him.

"How did you even get us in here—" She broke off as she saw that Adam had taken her satchel right off her shoulder. Her chest tightened with panic. She lunged for the bag. "Give that back!"

"Give me the truth." Adam easily caught her wrists with both of his hands. He pressed them close together, holding her captive in the center of the suite.

Holland tugged against his grip. But Adam didn't budge. The only thing that moved was his mouth, as if he found her sad escape attempt amusing. "I'm not the one with a ticking clock, Bright Eyes."

Holland froze at the name. She'd heard him call her this before. But only in her visions. The thought returned to her that she had known him before. That Adam was someone to her that she couldn't remember.

His hands were warm against her skin. His grip was firm but no longer as tight as it could have been, and though his lips were still amused, his eyes held something else. He looked hurt, as if the idea of her lying to him pained him.

Holland had two puzzles to solve: the mystery of the Alchemical Heart and the mystery of Adam Bishop. And she felt certain she wasn't going to figure out the first until she figured out the second.

"All right," she admitted. "I lied. The Watch Man did tell me something while you were asleep." She paused. "He said you were the devil."

She waited for Adam to laugh, or to grin, or to say he was flattered. She waited for his beautiful eyes to show a hint of surprise. She waited and waited and waited.

He stood there for an eternity of seconds. Then finally, he said, "I'm not the devil."

"Then why did it take you so long to say that?"

He looked at her for another impossibly long second. His hands had been warm but suddenly they were very cold. "I swear to you, I'm not the devil, but once upon a time, I was."

Holland felt her legs going boneless.

And Adam let her go. He dropped her hands and backed away.

Holland heard people out in the hall, pushing noisy luggage and talking too loudly on their phones, living ordinary lives, as she felt another piece of stable ground crumble beneath her feet.

Across from her, Adam didn't say a word.

He looked at her as if he was afraid she would run. And as if he wanted her to run, as if he wanted to tell her to get as far away from him as possible. And for a brittle heartbeat, he felt more like someone who was haunted by the devil than the actual devil.

"Tell me the story," Holland said. Her legs were feeling steadier, and a part of her really wanted to run, but she knew she couldn't leave this room until she heard him out.

Adam ran a hand through his hair. "It's a long story and you don't have a lot of time."

"Then give me the CliffNotes version."

Adam wandered over to the minibar. He gave it a once-over, looking disappointed, before turning back to Holland and saying, "In this world, every family has a different way of deciding who will inherit. My father told my brother Mason and me that he would bequeath all his magic and abilities to whichever one of us could amass the greatest amount of power and influence. My brother had always been the golden boy, the good one. But everyone knows good isn't always what gets you to the top. I haven't been good, but all my life I've managed to come out all right."

Adam said the words *all right* the way someone else might say *barely getting by*, but Holland had a feeling that Adam's version of doing all right meant far more than just getting by.

"I wasn't sure what was going to happen, but then Mason told me he didn't want to compete with me. He wanted us both to have abilities, so he suggested we work together. And he had an idea of what we could do." Adam's smile made its way back, but it was bitter now.

"What was your brother's idea?" Holland asked, not sure she really wanted to know.

"He said that together, we could become the devil."

Dread pooled in Holland's stomach.

"You have to understand, I idolized my older brother, more than I ever did my father." Adam's voice was soft, pleading. Holland reminded herself that he had tricked her before—but he didn't look as if he was acting this time. He looked as if he was stripping parts of himself away. His voice was rougher, and every time his eyes met hers, the look in them was raw. "Mason promised no one would get hurt. He said we wouldn't really become the devil; we wouldn't become evil. We would just use his name to build an empire."

"How?" Holland asked.

"Everyone has heard of the devil," Adam said. "But most people couldn't tell you what he looks like, where he lives, or what his favorite drink is. So, Mason had this idea of creating a series of myths about the devil, myths that would lead to us."

"Like the devil's sidecar?"

"Exactly. But that wasn't the first story we came up with. We started with the story of Natalia West. I'd ask if you remember her, but I know you do, since you wrote about her in your thesis." For a second, he looked vaguely impressed. "My brother and I never made a deal with her, for the record. But we claimed that we did. We started a rumor that Natalia West's rise to fame was because she made a deal with the devil, and then we started another rumor that her mysterious death was because she didn't make good on her end of the bargain.

"When my brother first suggested it, I remember the way he smiled at me, like it was all just smoke and mirrors and fun. And I believed him. Mason said we weren't ever going to kill anyone." Adam looked down at his hands, and Holland had the impression he wished he was holding on to a drink. "Mason said if people believed the devil lived in Los Angeles and had the power to make people famous, then they would come to us. And they did.

"After starting rumors about the devil, my brother recruited people from families with lesser abilities to work for us. That's how we started collecting favors. Mason used the abilities of others to get people without abilities or magic through doors they couldn't open on their own, and once he got people through those doors, they all owed *the devil* favors."

"And what was your role in all this?" Holland asked, although that wasn't the only question she had; this whole story was making her head spin. In all her research on the devil, it had never occurred to her that it might just be a man—or *two men*—using the devil as a persona. When Adam had mentioned Natalia West, Holland had felt briefly triumphant that she'd figured out the truth, but now she felt as if she'd been tricked, just like everyone else.

"At first, I spread a lot of rumors and set up a lot of meetings. I'd go out around LA, meet girls who were pretty but not beautiful. Talk to men who were smart but lacked social skills, or excellent actors with unattractive faces. Then I would tell them I could change all that. We started by making deals with mostly actors at first. But then my brother wanted people who wielded even more power to owe us favors. He always wanted more. And he got it, until . . . our father found out."

"Wait—I thought you were doing this for your father?"

"We were. But he was not impressed. It was the first time I'd ever seen him disappointed in Mason. My father said we were no better than petty mobsters and that he was going to find another heir. The next morning, my father was dead, and Mason had *all* his abilities." Adam shook his head, as if he still couldn't believe it. "The worst part is, I didn't put it together right away. I thought we'd broken my father's heart and that was why he'd died. But it wasn't heartbreak. It was Mason."

"Are you sure?"

Adam nodded, anger replacing his pain. "My brother killed my father before he could find a new heir, knowing that by default all our dad's abilities would go to his oldest son. And that's when I tried to end it all.

I told my brother we needed to stop this. I never wanted to kill anyone. I never wanted to hurt anyone," Adam said, but the rough way he said the word *hurt* made Holland think that Adam had definitely hurt people.

Holland had the sudden thought that he was going to hurt her, too, if she stayed. This story was the reddest of red flags to ever wave, and yet Holland found she was feeling less inclined to leave. If Adam was telling the truth, then he wasn't her enemy—his brother was.

"Is this when you had your falling out?" she asked.

"No. Mason was happy to have the name of the devil all to himself. And I didn't have any of our father's magic, so I wasn't a threat. Not until I tried to take away Mason's abilities."

"What happened then?"

"It didn't go well." Adam's eyes shot to the hotel room, checking to make sure they were still alone. "You may have noticed in your research that no one has made any recent deals with the devil."

Holland actually hadn't noticed this. She'd been so fixated on the past, she hadn't been paying attention to the present. But Adam was right. Holland couldn't think of any recent celebrity deaths she'd attributed to the devil. And for all her visits to the Roosevelt, she had never seen his brother there until last night.

"My brother still has his abilities. But he's not able to use them—for now."

"Why can't he use them now?" Holland asked.

"It's nearly impossible to steal an ability from another person. The best I could do was something that would lock my brother's abilities away. But that all changes if he gets his hands on the Alchemical Heart."

"You think he's searching for it?"

"Yes. Even before I made it impossible for Mason to use his abilities, he wanted the Alchemical Heart. He's always wanted it. Why do you think so many of the people he made deals with couldn't pay him back?"

"Are you saying the only way to pay your brother back was to give him the Alchemical Heart?"

"For a lot of people, yes," Adam said, grim.

"But that's impossible." Holland felt sick. And then she thought about her dad and how the Watch Man had said the only way for Ben to live was to give one of the devils the Alchemical Heart. But even as she thought that, Holland couldn't imagine her father making such a foolish bargain.

"Did you and your brother make a deal with my parents?" she asked.

"No," Adam said immediately. "I never made a deal with your parents."

"What about your brother?"

Adam frowned.

"Is that a yes or a no?"

"I don't know," he said quietly. "Even before our relationship ended, my brother did a lot of things I wasn't aware of."

"So he could have done it," Holland said. "He could have been the real reason why my parents died."

"I can understand why you would want to believe that, but I meant what I told you yesterday. If you live through today, chasing the answer to this question will only get you killed tomorrow. My brother might not have access to all his abilities, but he's still incredibly dangerous."

Holland scowled. There was no universe where she was not going to hunt this answer down, but Adam clearly wasn't going to help her do it. "Does my sister know about all this?"

"I don't usually tell this story over drinks." Adam looked back down at his hands and then he held out her satchel like a peace offering. "If you want to run now, I wouldn't blame you."

Holland considered it. Walking away from Adam meant she wouldn't have to worry about trusting anyone. But it also meant she'd be alone. Holland didn't want to do this by herself, and if she succeeded in finding the Alchemical Heart, she could also help Adam stop his brother for good. And she really liked that idea.

Holland flashed back to seeing Mason at the Roosevelt, how he had clearly recognized her, and suddenly Holland wondered if she knew why. "I was dating someone," she told Adam. "Last night, he was murdered, and I found out he was only dating me because he'd been hired to look into my family. I found a gold-and-black folder in his apartment with detailed instructions about how to get close to me."

Adam ran a slow hand down his jaw. "Sounds like my brother. The gold and black have always been his calling card. And he doesn't have problems killing."

"I still have one question," Holland said.

"Only one?"

"I'd ask more, but like you said, we're on a ticking clock. How old are you?"

This earned her a surprised smile. "That's what you want to know?"

"The math on this story isn't mathing. Either you look incredibly good for your age, or you haven't aged in a very long time."

Adam's smile widened. "You think I look incredibly good?"

Holland fought the sudden urge to smack him. "You know you do."

He grinned for another second, before his expression turned serious. "Why don't we get back to the subject of keeping you alive?" Adam reached for the flap of Holland's satchel.

CHAPTER THIRTY-SIX

'm not supposed to show you what's in there," Holland said.

"Then you probably shouldn't let me open this," said Adam.

But she didn't stop him.

Adam had just confessed to being the devil once. But he wasn't the devil anymore. He was her sister's partner; January trusted him. Holland could trust him, too. And she really wanted to open the envelope from the Watch Man. Holland had no idea how many clues her father had hidden, and she didn't want to waste more time.

The posh hotel room they were currently in looked occupied, based on the open luggage and the toiletries strewn about the unmade bed and couch. She imagined the guests had probably gone to lunch but could be back at any moment.

"There's a document envelope," she said. "You should open that first and fast."

Adam pulled it out. "What is this?"

"I don't know. The Watch Man gave it to me while you were passed out."

"I knew that bastard knocked me out." Adam weighed the envelope in his hand, much the same way Holland had, and then he handed it over. "If it was given to you, you should open it."

Holland didn't need to be told twice. She quickly undid the clasp.

There were pages inside the envelope. Fewer pages than there had been in the safety deposit box, but Holland recognized them immediately.

EXT. HOTEL PATIO. DAY.

Tropical birds peer down as Red and the Watch Man sit on a patio that feels like Palm Springs in the 1960s. There are white wrought-iron chairs, umbrellas covered in teal stripes, neat grass between squares of white concrete, and, of course, plastic flamingos.

The Watch Man and Red are playing Scrabble. The tiles are white and teal, matching the decor. Red only has four tiles left: *OEMJ*.

> THE WATCH MAN
> It's your turn.

Red begrudgingly puts the *O* down, forming the words *to* and *go*.

> THE WATCH MAN
> I feel as if you're not really
> trying, Mr. Westcott.

> RED WESTCOTT
> I didn't come here to play
> games.

> THE WATCH MAN
> What is life but a game?
> Everyone you meet is an

opponent or an ally or
sometimes a clue.

The Watch Man places tiles on the board, forming the
word *REVERSE*.

                    RED WESTCOTT
What are you?

                    THE WATCH MAN
I think that's sixty-eight
points with the double-letter
score on the *V*.

                    RED WESTCOTT
You know that's not what I was
asking.

                    THE WATCH MAN
But perhaps I was still
answering. Your turn again,
Mr. Westcott. You have one
chance left to win.

Be certain you're going in the right direction before you dig in.

"I didn't think these existed." Adam continued to stare at the pages. His eyes were bright and wide, almost boyish in their excitement. He truly was a fan. "Do you know—" He looked up suddenly, as if he'd just remembered who he was talking to. "Wait—you don't seem surprised."

"This isn't the first set of pages I've received." Holland reached into the satchel and pulled out the rest of the screenplay.

Immediately, Adam was hypnotized again. When he reached the third page, he said, "This was why you wanted to see the Watch Man today? This was the reliable source you were talking about?"

"When I was little, my father was always creating treasure hunts. As soon as I saw these pages, I knew that he'd done it again."

"He was a genius," Adam said reverently. "You think these new pages will tell us where to look next?"

"I do."

Adam took the next set of pages and set them out across the sofa, shoving to the floor the clothes that had been left there. "I think that last line written in pencil is trying to tell us something about digging," he said. "Maybe we should go back to the bungalows and see if your father buried something there."

"There are usually multiple pieces to my dad's clues," Holland said. "If I'd been paying better attention to his first set of pages, I probably could have figured out on my own that I'd find the Watch Man at this hotel." Holland pointed to the screenplay, where the stage directions mentioned Frank Sinatra playing right after Red asked where to find the Watch Man.

"That seems like a little bit of a stretch?" Adam said.

"Not if I combine it with his first clue." Holland pointed to the second page. "Alma's bowling team is the Hollybells—that was my childhood nickname. The shirts it's embroidered on are green and pink, which everyone knows are the Beverly Hills Hotel's signature colors."

"So what do you think these new pages are saying?" Adam asked.

"I think the next clue has to do with the game they're playing. Look at Red's tiles." Holland pointed once more to the page. "This says he has four tiles at the start. He puts one down, forming the words *to* and *go*, leaving him with *EMJ*. Then, right after saying the word *clue*, the Watch Man puts down the word *reverse*."

A puzzled look from Adam.

"If you reverse the letters *EMJ*, it turns to into *JME*. Go to JME."

"Like the movie studio?" he asked.

"Not just any movie studio," Holland said. "Jericho Monroe Entertainment is the studio my father worked with. I think that's where we're supposed to go next. If my father buried something, I bet it's there."

Jericho Monroe Entertainment was the perfect place to hide something. The studio was so large, it had its own zip code. It also had a fire department, medical offices, and an athletic center that included a full basketball court, tennis court, and pickleball court.

"My friend Cat is an assistant for the head of the Storytelling Department. Just yesterday she said to give her a call if I wanted a costume for tonight's party."

"What party?" Adam looked slightly offended he wasn't invited.

"The Hollywood Roosevelt's Haunted Halloween Ball. My friends and I go every year. If we tell Cat we want costumes, she'll get us on the lot. I just don't know where to look once—"

Holland broke off as the door to the hotel room started to open.

CHAPTER THIRTY-SEVEN

W hat the hell?"

"Get out of our room!" Within seconds, a soundtrack of angry tourists' shouts filled the beautiful suite.

Holland started to panic.

Adam turned to her with a grin. "Don't worry, Bright Eyes. This is not how we get caught." Without another word, he strode confidently across the suite. "I think there's been a misunderstanding." His voice faded after that. Holland didn't hear what he said next, and she didn't see it, either—she was too busy collecting her father's pages—but within seconds the couple was laughing instead of shouting.

"We are so sorry," the woman said.

"Can we buy you two dinner?" asked the man.

"Oh, please, yes!" said the woman. "We'd love to take you to dinner." Then there was a full minute of chatter about the Polo Lounge. "It's the kind of food you want to take pictures of."

Holland had all the pages gathered now. She just needed the satchel and Adam—who was making the couple laugh again, possibly about food that you want to take pictures of. Holland tried not to be annoyed. Whatever he'd done had saved them. She just wasn't sure how he'd done it.

With another apology, the man took Adam's hand and shook it. Then the woman was hugging Adam. Did she have actual tears in her eyes? A second later they were both gone, and Adam looked immensely pleased with himself.

"What did you just do?" Holland asked.

He shrugged. "It's my charm."

She narrowed her eyes. "You're not that charming."

"Says the girl who just spilled all her secrets to me." Adam propped his shoulder against the door to keep it open.

Holland felt heat rise up her neck. "That's not why I spilled my secrets," she said. But as she watched him, standing underneath the golden afternoon light, leaning against the door in a way that somehow made him look even taller, she feared that his charm might have been a *little* bit of the reason.

"We need to go," she said abruptly, stepping into the hall. "You should know, I told you about the screenplay because I'm not familiar with this magical world and—" Holland broke off abruptly as she realized what had just happened with the couple. "I know what you did. Magic. You used magic on those poor people."

Adam didn't say she was wrong, but he also didn't look very pleased as they walked down the hall. Gabe had given her a hard time about using the word *magic*. But Adam didn't seem to have the same problem, possibly because he came from a family with magic. He didn't have anything to prove. Except. "Wait—" She whirled toward him. "You said you didn't have magic."

"No," Adam said flatly. "I said my brother got all our father's magic."

"But you *do* have an ability?" Holland asked. She'd seen the way people treated him. And if she'd learned one thing about this world, it was that abilities were everything.

"My ability is on loan from the Bank." Something like embarrassment colored his cheeks. But Holland only registered it for a second.

They were nearing the Beverly Hills Hotel's grand exit, and just on the other side of the glass, Holland spied a pair of cowboy hats. "Oh, no," she breathed.

"What's wrong?" Adam asked.

"It could be nothing. Look up ahead," she whispered. "There's a couple of people in cowboy costumes."

Adam gave her a questioningly look.

"I think they're from the Bank," Holland said. "Do you recognize them?"

"No, but I don't usually work at that branch." Adam slowed down and draped an arm across her shoulder, pulling her close. He was warm and very solid. She remembered the first time she'd seen his arms, she'd thought he worked out but not too much. But so close to him now, she suddenly felt wrong about that.

"What are you doing?" she whispered.

His fingers lazily stroked the side of her arm, sending little sparks across her skin. "Everyone is going to look at us if we run, but no one wants to look at a couple showing public displays of affection." He leaned down and pressed a slow kiss to the top of her head, and another one to her cheek.

They took a few more steps. They were nearly at the glass doors.

Holland's heart was racing, and Adam's lips were lowering. "Relax," he whispered. Then he kissed her. She expected it to be short and sweet, but this time his mouth lingered. He teased, licked, took her lower lip between his teeth, and teased some more. Holland felt her skin burning hotter as she kissed him back. He had said no one would want to look at them, but this felt like the sort of kiss you couldn't look away from.

It definitely felt like a kiss she couldn't pull away from. Even in the middle of the day, in front of a busy hotel, where people were staring. He bit once, a little hard, nearly bruising her lower lip, and then he pulled away. "I need you to follow my lead."

He kissed her again. Then he dropped his arm from her shoulder, took her hand, and led her toward the car the valet was pulling up. "This isn't yours," Holland said.

"It's about to be." Adam went over to the driver's side. Holland wanted to turn around to see if the cowboy hats were watching, but she couldn't take her eyes off Adam. She could never seem to take her eyes off Adam. And maybe what she really wanted to see was if he was as affected by that kiss as she had been.

She felt a sliver of guilt as she thought about kissing Gabe mere hours ago. Technically, he had kissed her. And letting Gabe kiss her had been a terrible mistake. She had nothing to feel guilty about. But all her emotions were living so close to the surface, it didn't take much to stir them.

The air felt warmer and the entire scene looked a little faded as she stood there, watching. Adam smiled at her from the other side of the car, and then, all at once, he wasn't Adam anymore. He was Gabe Cabral.

Holland's chest tightened with panic, her head felt light, and—

Drip.

Drip.

Drip.

"No!" Holland wiped blood away from her nose, red smearing on her fingertips. It was happening again. She was seeing something that wasn't actually there. Was it because she'd just been thinking about Gabe?

She knew Gabe wasn't actually stealing the car; Adam was. But she couldn't see Adam anymore, just Gabe. He was dressed more casually than when she'd seen him last, in dark jeans and a black shirt. "Babe, it's time to get in the car," he said affectionately.

She wanted to run, but her legs wouldn't move, she simply felt her body slide into the stolen car.

The leather seat felt hot beneath her. Her fingers reached out to turn up the air, while Gabe adjusted the radio. "Hate this song," he muttered. But the next station was playing it, too. He changed it again, but the same song was everywhere. "What the hell—"

Gabe turned the radio off, but the same damn song continued to pour out of the speakers.

Holland tried desperately to remember how she had made the other visions stop. She closed her eyes. She shook her head. But the music just kept playing. "Make it stop. Make it stop—"

"I'm trying," Adam said.

Holland recognized his voice with an intense sense of relief. She opened her eyes. Hot leather seats, weak air conditioning, the same song pouring out of the radio.

Adam looked worried as he gave her a handkerchief. She had a fleeting thought that his handkerchiefs made sense now that she knew he didn't age. She laughed a little then, the way a person sometimes laughs when it's the least appropriate response.

"You want to tell me what's going on?" he asked.

Holland finished dabbing her nose with the cloth and looked out her window to see they had left the grounds of the Beverly Hills Hotel. They were on the way to JME.

Holland reached up and changed the radio station. The same song played. She changed it again. Same song again. Just like in her vision.

"I think it's broken," Adam said.

"Did you change it before?" Holland asked. "When I was passed out."

"I wasn't really thinking about the radio," he said.

But she was still thinking about the broken radio. It made her wonder if somehow she was having visions of the future, but that didn't make sense because she would have seen Adam, not Gabe. Now that her initial wave of sadness was gone, thinking about Gabe made Holland feel a growing sense of terror, which was why she'd been ruthlessly attempting not to think about him.

"In your world, are nosebleeds a sign of anything?" she asked.

"Not that I know of," Adam said.

Holland tried to think of all the times she'd bled, in Adam's office, in the Roosevelt, in the beach house, and—her thoughts broke off as she looked down at what she was wearing. She still had on her sister's dress, but instead of heels she was wearing a pair of fashionable white sneakers.

Holland reached down to touch them, wondering if maybe her sister's shoes were magic, like her key. But there was no zip of electricity, no sudden quiet. They were ordinary shoes, and she had no idea where she'd gotten them.

"When did I change my shoes?"

Adam looked at her, puzzled. "You changed before we left the Beverly Hills Hotel, in case we needed to run. You borrowed sneakers from the guest room."

Holland was fairly certain that taking something without permission was actually stealing, but she was less concerned about her minor criminal activity than about the fact that she didn't remember this at all.

The same song that had been playing on repeat started over again on the radio, until Adam finally turned it off. "I hate that song."

Holland had a sense of déjà vu. But then she remembered Gabe had said nearly the exact same thing. Something else was going on, something that was starting to terrify her—first the visions and the blood, and now her memories were starting to vanish.

She was starting to fear what else she might lose before the end of the day.

CHAPTER THIRTY-EIGHT

Holland saw the iconic water tower first. Tall and silver, it popped against the blue of the sky, and painted across it in iconic block letters was *JME*.

Jericho Monroe Entertainment.

The first time Holland had come here, she was five. She and her sister were with their dad for *Kids Day!* All she had wanted was to see Princess Poppy and her pet pony Pistachio. Holland had even brought a rainbow wand, just like the one Poppy used on the show. January had wanted to see Sparkles the dog. She'd brought a box of treats and a leash, planning to use the treats to get the pup on the leash and then take it home.

Everyone had thought the two girls were so precious, with all their hopes and dreams and belief in fictional characters. Even now, all grown up, it was still hard for Holland not to believe, just a little.

The movie studio held a different type of magic than the Regal, but it was magic nonetheless. What is magic, if not something that makes you believe and feel and wonder?

Holland didn't know if she felt terrified or excited, or if all the buzzing in her head was some other unidentifiable emotion.

Adam stopped the car next to the security booth, and the security guard stepped out. He was dressed like the dad from the JME classic TV show *My Neighbor Next Door*.

"Happy Halloween," said Adam. "We're here to see our friend in the Storytelling Department."

"Name?" asked the guard.

"Charlotte Davis," Holland supplied.

"I'm not sure if she got the chance to call it in, but you should be able to reach out to her office to confirm." Adam spoke with a confident swagger that didn't leave any room for arguing. Holland wondered if he was using his magic, or if this was just him.

She thought of how easily he'd charmed her when they first met, and how perplexed he'd been when the charm had worn off. Not his magic, she decided.

Still, the security guard made a call without any arguing and then waved them through the gate with a friendly "You can park in the lot to the right. It's reserved for staff, but it's not that full today. Miss Davis will come out and meet you there."

"Thanks, man," said Adam.

And just like that, they were in.

Holland checked her watch as she stepped out of the car. It was later than she'd realized. 3:33. The sun was shining as if this was its last chance, not holding back any of its rays or heat. She could smell the asphalt melting.

The studio didn't look as if it had changed in the last few years. Holland walked toward her father's old parking spot, which now belonged to director Vic VanVleet. Vic's car was parked there now, a shiny mother-of-pearl electric with a vanity license plate that read VX3—the name of her production company.

"So where do we start looking?" asked Adam.

"My father's old bungalow. Number 17."

Adam looked skeptical. "You think there could still be a clue there, after all this time?"

"My father hasn't failed us yet."

"Hey guys!" Cat stepped into the parking lot, waving a sword with a jeweled heart on the hilt. She was dressed like Isabella Rose from one of

JME's most popular television shows, *Knife and Cross*. Which also happened to be Holland's favorite vampire show. And, yes, when Holland got particularly stressed, she sometimes still wrote fan fiction for it.

In the show, Isabella—the human love interest of the world's deadliest vampire and a vampire hunter, who had accidentally switched bodies—always wore gowns that were never quite appropriate for the time period but were absolutely gorgeous, like the one Cat was wearing now. It was all elegant black lace straps and layers of pale pink tulle that fell around her to make a gloriously full skirt.

"I love the costume," Holland said.

"Thank you! I've been so excited to wear it and I'm so excited you're here!" Cat gave Holland a tight hug before turning to Adam. "You must be Holland's plus one. I've heard so much about you!"

Cat thought Adam was Jake, and Holland wasn't going to correct her. Thankfully, Cat had only known Jake as Clark Kent—Holland never shared the actual names of guys she dated. It felt too much like prematurely saving someone's number in her phone.

Thankfully, in this case, it allowed Holland to introduce Adam by his real name.

"It's great to meet you," Adam said. "Thanks for getting us in here."

"Anytime," Cat said. "If you ever want to come back for a tour, I'm your girl. Well, I'm not your girl. Holland is clearly your girl, but I'm Holland's friend, which makes me your friend now!" Cat sounded flustered, and she was never flustered.

When Adam turned to look at one of the trams zipping by with a collection of tourists, Cat mouthed at Holland, *He's so hot!*

Holland tried not to smile, because she knew it would be a real smile. But she and Adam were just pretending. And Adam wasn't even doing much pretending anymore. Since their kiss at the Beverly Hills Hotel, he actually seemed to be making a conscious effort not to touch her.

"Oh, I almost forgot to tell you," Cat added out loud. "Chance is here, too."

Holland felt a sudden knot in her stomach. She couldn't run into him now, not after last night. If he saw her and she couldn't explain things, he really might never forgive her. "What's he doing here?" she asked.

"He's meeting with Vic VanVleet." Cat waved her fake sword in a little circle, because not only was Isabella Rose extraordinarily fashionable, she was also great with weapons. "I think she wants to do another film where he's the star."

"That's wonderful for Chance," said Holland. And it was wonderful for her, too, because she most likely wouldn't run into him.

"Don't tell him I said anything about it," said Cat. "I'm sure he'll want to tell you himself at the party tonight."

"Don't worry," Holland said. "I won't even mention we were here."

Cat gave her a grateful smile as she started to lead them across the parking lot. "Normally, I'd say we could walk, but this heat is absurd and the costume department is a trek, so I was thinking we could borrow a golf cart."

"Actually," said Holland, "I thought Adam and I could go over to the bungalows first. We were hoping to take a look at Ben Tierney's old bungalow."

Cat immediately looked uneasy. "I don't think that's a good idea."

"We just want to take a quick picture. I'm a film student," Adam lied smoothly. "Benjamin Tierney is the reason why, and I really want to see where he worked."

Cat worried her lip between her teeth.

"Please." Adam reached out and touched her arm.

Cat looked at him wide-eyed. The touch must have put her over the edge. She looked flustered before, but now she looked dazzled. She shook her head. Some of the dazzle left her eyes, but for a second her expression was a little vacant. "What were we just talking about?"

"You got a call from your boss," said Adam. "You need to head back to your office, so Holland and I were just saying we'd meet you at the costume department."

"Yes, right. That's a good idea." Cat pointed her sword to the right of the water tower. "See you in a bit," she said, but it lacked her signature enthusiasm. Her voice had a far-off quality.

And Holland now made the terrifying realization that she knew just how Adam's magic worked. It wasn't a magnified version of charm like she had thought. If she was right, Adam Bishop had the power to erase memories and write entirely new ones with merely the touch of his fingers.

CHAPTER THIRTY-NINE

Adam didn't look as if he'd done anything wrong—or done anything at all. Which was perhaps the scariest part.

"What did you do to my friend?" Holland demanded. "Did you just use your ability on her?"

Adam shoved his hands in his pockets. He didn't deny it, which meant the answer was yes.

"You didn't need to do that."

"Yes, I did," said Adam tightly.

"Cat's not part of your world. I don't want her hurt by any of this."

Adam worked his jaw. Until that moment, Holland realized, she'd never seen him angry, even in the Professor's office, right before Gabe had shot him. "You didn't seem to mind when I did it to the couple at the hotel."

Holland wanted to say she hadn't known he was using his ability, but she had—she just hadn't known what his ability was yet. She hadn't cared that he'd used magic, she just didn't like that *this* was his magic.

"Have you ever done that to me?" she asked. "Have you erased any of the conversations we've had?"

Adam burst out laughing. "If I had used my ability on you, you wouldn't be asking me that question. And you wouldn't have let your friend Gabe shoot me."

Holland felt another stab of guilt, but she couldn't quite let this go. Not with all the things that had been going wrong with her memories. "That still wasn't a no."

Adam sighed. "Anyone can say no, Holland, I just told you why you should believe my no." His eyes met hers and Holland saw a sliver of hurt. "I've never erased your memories or planted new ones. In my world, you have to have an ability, but I don't really like using mine, not unless it's necessary. And . . . I'd much rather get by on my charm." His mouth tilted into a familiar smirk. But Holland couldn't help noticing he still had his hands in his pockets.

He kept them there as they quietly walked the cobblestone path to the bungalows.

Everything at JME was picture perfect, and even with all Holland's fears and fraying nerves, she still fell under the studio's spell. The buildings were all from the golden era of Hollywood, when people still dressed up to go to the theater, and most moving pictures were under an hour and a half.

Movie posters were everywhere. Huge murals covered the exterior walls of buildings, so large that people could see them from certain freeways. Holland saw one that read *Knife and Cross—Season VII coming soon!* On the poster, the television show's namesake characters were facing each other as a fire raged behind them.

Then, of course, there were all the framed posters for classic films, hung in the ivy that covered most of the buildings.

Holland snuck a look at Adam. The movie posters in his penthouse had made her think he was a film fan, but he didn't seem as enchanted as she was. Of course, his hands were also still in his pockets, so maybe he was just uncomfortable.

"Did you know," she said to Adam, "that in the mid-90s a studio exec wanted JME to feel like an old East Coast college campus, so he had them plant all that ivy?"

Adam shook his head, as a squirrel darted out of said ivy and scurried across the path, reminding Holland of another story.

"I was also told that another studio, which I won't name, has allegedly trained their squirrels to come up to visitors and beg for treats."

This one earned her a smile and inspired her to keep going.

"Unfortunately, the squirrels here are not as friendly," she continued. "And there's supposedly an entire kingdom of feral cats that come out at night. Gardeners leave them treats because they keep out all the rats and mice."

"How do you know all this?" asked Adam.

"Cat told me." Holland was always asking her questions about work. Ben Tierney didn't come up much in Cat's stories, but every time he did, Holland felt like a piece of him was still alive somewhere.

They reached Bungalow 17.

Everything smelled like oranges, and for a second Holland was five again and her father was letting her and January pick oranges from a tiny grove.

The grove was still there, but it was no longer tiny. The trees in front of the bungalow had aged, just like Holland. They were full and knotty and beautiful, and in front of them was a faded hand-painted sign:

Free oranges
—Farmer Ben

It hurt, how much she missed him in that moment. She wanted to take one of her dad's oranges and keep it forever, even though she knew oranges didn't last forever.

She started to reach for one, when she noticed the production company name on the bungalow: VX3.

Holland dropped her hand, took a few steps closer, and looked through the window.

This bungalow was Vic VanVleet's now, and she was inside, talking to Chance Garcia.

CHAPTER FORTY

W hat do you want to do?" Adam asked, his voice low.

She checked her watch. 3:57.

"I don't think we have many options," she said. They could wait and waste more time, or they could go inside.

Holland had a sudden image of her friendship with Chance catching on fire and Vic VanVleet calling henchmen to throw them out of the studio. Holland doubted that Vic VanVleet actually had henchmen. But then she thought of Cat's reaction when Holland had mentioned wanting to visit this bungalow, and the idea didn't seem that far-fetched.

"Maybe we just wait a few—" Holland stopped mid-sentence as she saw Chance stand up and shake Vic VanVleet's hand.

And suddenly Holland had a third terrible idea. But it seemed a little less terrible than the two ideas that had come before.

"Come on," Holland whispered to Adam. Then she was pulling him to the side of the building.

Chance rounded the corner with a swagger to his step.

Holland's palms were sweating, and her voice came out a little high as she said, "Hey."

Chance stopped abruptly. He looked at her, then at Adam, then back at her, and his expression went from stunned, to happy, to what-the-hell-is-going-on. "What are you doing here?"

"I can't explain right now," Holland said. "But I really need you to do me a favor."

Chance laughed, a bitter sound she'd never heard him make. He looked at her as if he didn't even know who she was anymore.

"I know in the last twenty-four hours I've seemed like a different person. But I swear, there is a good explanation for everything."

"What is it?"

"I can't tell you right now."

"Of course you can't." Chance started shaking his head. "I've gotta go."

Adam stepped forward, took his hands from his pockets and reached for Chance's arm.

Chance immediately jumped back. "Don't touch me, man!"

"Sorry," Adam said, but he looked ready to try again.

Holland put a hand on his arm, stopping him. She couldn't let Chance leave. Holland needed his help. But letting Adam erase his memories wasn't the way to do this.

Holland took the deepest breath she'd ever taken in her life. She had been living under the delusion that if she made it through today, her life would just go back to what it had been, but that was never going to happen. And maybe that was for the best. She didn't love running for her life, but she did love being able to talk about her dad, and she wasn't sure she wanted to go back to hiding that part of herself.

"Chance, wait," she called. "This has to do with my father."

Chance immediately stopped and turned. Holland could see all the questions in his eyes.

Is she manipulating me? Is she finally about to talk about the parents she never mentions? Can I even believe a word she says?

"My last name isn't actually St. James," she said. "I was born Holland Tierney. My mother is Isla Saint, and my father is Benjamin J. Tierney. I'm sorry I never told you. I never tell anyone. My sister and I changed our last names when we went to college. The reason I'm telling you this now is because yesterday, I found out my father left me something, and I believe it's in his old bungalow. Number 17."

"I don't know that I believe you." Chance said. Once again, he looked ready to walk away.

"I'm sorry I hurt you," Holland said. "But you know me. My father is the whole reason I've been so obsessed with finding the devil. I think he made a deal with him, and that's why he died. I would think you, of all people, would understand why I wouldn't ever want to talk about it. And if that's not enough for you, you can search it online. Ben and Isla had twin daughters. I don't have my phone, or I'd pull up an old family picture."

Chance ran a hand through his hair. He looked torn, as if he actually did believe her but wanted to stay mad. "Does this have anything to do with what happened last night?"

"Yes." Holland wished she could leave it at that, but she could see Chance wanted more. "The person I was with last night was a mistake. He was only after the same thing I'm looking for right now."

"What about you?" Chance tilted his chin toward Adam.

"I'm just trying to keep her alive," Adam said.

Chance continued to eye him warily, his dislike for Adam nearly palpable. But when he looked back at Holland, his anger had faded. "What do you want me to do?"

"I just need you to get Vic VanVleet out of her bungalow and distract her for half an hour while we search."

"Have you ever met Vic VanVleet?" he asked.

Holland shook her head.

"I can probably get her out of there, but only for fifteen minutes, tops."

It took Chance less than a minute to step into the bungalow and then step outside with Vic VanVleet.

Whatever he said was enough of a distraction that she didn't even lock the door. Although maybe she just planned on returning very soon.

"We need to move quickly," Holland said to Adam.

The bungalow was clearly decorated in Vic VanVleet's personal style. Everything was bright pop art. Even the movie posters on the walls were versions that Holland had never seen, all neon and oversaturated color.

Vic VanVleet was the sort of director that Holland always felt she should have loved. Her production company VX3 was most well-known for rich mystery films that combined smart dialogue with slick storytelling and painfully bittersweet romances. They were the kind of films that were always a little too commercial for the critics to praise, which made them just the right kind of entertaining for the public.

Her newest film with Chance was getting a lot of buzz. And yet, there was always something about the movies that struck the wrong chord for Holland.

Adam started at the desk, while Holland went over to the bookshelves.

Vic's bookshelves were full of Funko Pops, ball caps from films, and other miscellanea, along with an old photograph of a glowing couple. Holland bent closer. One of the people in the picture was Vic VanVleet, and the other was Holland's father.

"My dad knew Vic VanVleet," Holland said, stunned.

Adam looked up from the desk, which he'd turned into an absolute shambles. "What did you find?"

"It's a picture of my dad and Vic, and it looks like they were a couple." Ben looked so young, and Vic looked absolutely radiant. Her hair was longer, and she was smiling as Ben kissed her on the cheek.

"Did you know about this?" Adam asked.

"No. I don't know. Maybe." Ben and Isla's love story had eclipsed everything else. But Holland knew there had been another woman in his life. "Before my mom, my dad had been dating Jericho Monroe's great-granddaughter, Victoria Monroe."

It was a name most people probably didn't know. Victoria Monroe was a footnote on Ben Tierney's Wonderpage—but it was a page Holland knew by heart.

"Isn't Vic a nickname for Victoria?" Adam asked.

It was. And Holland also knew VanVleet wasn't Vic's maiden name.

When Chance had first started working with her, she was all he'd talked about for a full month. Holland remembered him telling the story of how Vic had been married for only forty-seven days to Simon Van-Vleet, lead singer of the Poisonberries. It was one of those sensational stories that made Vic VanVleet famous for nothing. Holland had been unimpressed, but Chance had been awed. He'd thought it was a gutsy move, something she'd done so she could have the triple *V*'s for her production company. And maybe it was.

Or maybe the wedding was the reckless response of a jilted woman who'd been madly in love and publicly humiliated.

Holland couldn't know for sure. But she did feel as if she knew one thing. This picture hadn't originally been Vic's. The photo frame was dark and masculine, the one thing in the office that wasn't in Vic's pop art style, which made Holland wonder if the photo had been her father's. Something he had left on purpose, because he'd known Vic wouldn't have been able to get rid of it, even after all this time.

"I think this is the clue." Holland flipped the frame around. It was so old it didn't want to open, but after almost a full minute of prying, she managed to pull the backing off.

A slip of paper fell out.

Hold

JME: *Property Department*

Show *Name: Alchemy of Secrets*
Set:
Contact: *Ben Tierney*
Phone:
Date: *2/2011*

Special Instructions: Someone who needs it but doesn't want it. Someone who will only use it once for their need and then never use it again.

"What is that?" asked Adam.

"It looks like a hold slip. They use them in the props department," Holland explained. "I think they're for renting out items."

Adam came out from behind the desk to take a closer look. "What do you make of the special instructions? Do you think your dad is saying that whoever finds the Alchemical Heart can only use it once?"

"We can worry about that later," said Holland. "But I think you're right that this slip is our clue. We need to go to the props department."

"I hope you're not running off because of me?" said a high, melodious voice.

CHAPTER FORTY-ONE

Holland wasn't sure if Vic VanVleet had ever made a deal with the devil, if she had a really good skin care routine, or if she was simply a believer in plastic surgery, but she looked as if she hadn't aged in over twenty-five years.

"You must be one of the Tierney twins," Vic said. "I would recognize Ben's daughters anywhere. Which one are you? January or Holland?"

"Um . . . Holland," she said, surprised, although she supposed she shouldn't have been, since Vic still had a picture of Holland's father in her office. The photo Holland was still holding.

Vic appeared to notice it then, or maybe she'd noticed it right away. Holland had the feeling that very little got past this woman. Vic probably went to bed in crisply ironed white sheets and woke up looking sharp enough for a photo shoot.

And yet, everything about her softened as her eyes drifted down to the photo. "You're probably wondering why I have that in here."

If she'd been anyone else, Holland would have just said yes to be agreeable, but Vic VanVleet seemed like the sort of woman who appreciated it when people left out the pleasantries and bullshit. "Because you were Victoria Monroe. My dad's first love."

Now it was Vic's turn to look surprised. "A-plus to you," she said. "I'm not too proud to admit I never stopped loving him. When I inherited this bungalow, the photo was inside the desk. I couldn't bring myself to throw it away. Ben was a brilliant filmmaker and a good person. I wish I could say the same for your bitch mother."

Holland flinched. And then her hands clenched into fists. She had always been closer to her father, but she loved her mother in a way that made it painful for her to think about. Isla wasn't on her mind nearly as much as Ben, but she felt viciously protective of them both.

"There was something about your mother that didn't sit right with me, you know, even before she stole my fiancé. I don't like to speak ill of the dead—"

"Then don't," Adam interrupted. "I think Holland has been through enough." He gave Vic a withering look, but it only seemed to harden her resolve.

"Hiding from the truth doesn't help anyone," Vic spat. And now there was a nasty gleam in her eyes that made Holland feel as if she and Adam needed to get out of there with the hold slip quickly. Vic reached into her pocket and pulled out her phone. "You know, I wonder what the press would think if they heard Ben Tierney and Isla Saint's unhinged daughter broke into my bungalow. Or maybe I should call the police first, and then the press?"

"Don't do that—" Holland said.

But Vic was already pressing buttons. The phone was on speaker, and Holland could hear someone answer. Then Adam was grabbing Vic's wrist.

Her eyes went distant, just like Cat's had.

Adam hung up Vic's call and looked at Holland nervously.

It was still terrifying to watch him use his magic, but this time she didn't feel any guilt. "It's okay."

A hint of his familiar smirk returned. "I'm not actually asking for permission. I need you to leave for this one."

"But—"

"If you're here, I'm going to be tempted to rewrite more of her memories than I should." Adam's fingers tightened on Vic's slim wrist. "Please, Holland, go."

Holland didn't make him ask a third time. She dropped the photo of Vic and Ben and quietly left the bungalow.

She waited around the corner, standing in the shade next to a fountain she was fairly certain she'd seen in the background of a dozen movies.

According to her watch, it was now 4:37. Poor Cat must have been wondering what had happened to them.

One minute passed.

Two minutes.

Three minutes.

Now Holland was also starting to worry about Adam. Why hadn't he come out of the bungalow yet? It had only taken him seconds to use his ability with Cat and the others at the hotel. Holland wondered if maybe something had gone wrong.

Then, finally, Adam emerged.

He jogged around the corner, holding keys to a golf cart. "Courtesy of my new friend, Vic VanVleet."

Adam didn't tell Holland exactly how he had managed to get the keys, but she could see that the encounter with Vic seemed to have cost him. His face had lost some of its color and his brow was damp, though the latter might have just been from the heat.

It was late enough in the day that the studio was starting to empty out as Adam drove the golf cart toward the props department warehouse.

The building looked large enough to house a plane.

Holland could hear a low rumble as they started up the stairs, the noise growing louder as they neared the door. Two large industrial fans were blowing air into a room that made her feel as if she was stepping into a bazaar that existed only in the world of movies.

Bicycles hung from the ceiling, there were bookshelves full of busts, and a giant golden turtle rested on the ground. Another wall was entirely covered in ceramic hands posed in various positions—open palm, thumbs up, middle finger. On the floor in front of them was an enormous ceramic right foot. There was a crystal chandelier shaped like a pirate ship, a statue of Poseidon, a Vespa, and a grand piano. Holland recognized a row of masks from an unfortunate movie she'd watched on an even more unfortunate date.

The head of the props department was standing in front of a sweaty-looking tour group, telling them about the taxidermy animals. "If you see one of these at the start of a scene"—he motioned to a small collection of taxidermy wolves—"you're probably meeting a villain."

Every tourist pulled out their phone and took pictures, before the man concluded the tour with a *Happy Halloween*, followed by *goodbye*.

A half dozen selfies later, Holland, Adam, and the head of the props department were the only people left.

The prop guy had longish gray hair tied back in a ponytail and more smile lines than anyone else in Hollywood. He turned to Holland and Adam with a look that said he was about to kindly kick them out. But then he seemed to think better of it. "You look familiar," he said to Holland. "Have we met?"

He had the kind of smile that tempted Holland to ask if he'd known her dad. The man definitely looked old enough. But after the way Vic VanVleet had responded, she hesitated.

"I don't think so," Holland said. Then she introduced herself and Adam.

"I'm Tom," said the man.

"How long have you been at JME?" she asked.

"Oh." He rubbed a bit of the gray stubble on his jaw. "I've been here about thirty-nine years."

"So, you must have known Benjamin Tierney?" she said.

His smile could have lit up the entire warehouse. "Of course, I knew Ben. I met him on his first film."

"*Time Warrior?*" asked Holland.

Tom's eyes narrowed. "How'd you know that? That film never even made it to theaters."

"We're film students," Holland lied, taking a page from Adam's book. "I'm writing my thesis on Ben Tierney."

Holland had never been good at lies, and she felt as if Tom was seeing right through her. But then his friendly smile returned. "Ben was the real deal. Smart. Cared about storytelling. In my opinion, he was the kind of visionary storyteller that comes around once in a lifetime. But . . . I'm guessing you two are here for more than my anecdotes, since I just gave a lot of those on the tour."

"We were wondering if you could help with this." Holland offered him the hold slip.

Tom rubbed his jaw. "Where did you find this?" He looked back at Holland. Really looked at her. The kind of stare that made her go still, as if he was taking a mental photograph. It lasted so long, she was almost certain he'd figured out who she was.

A part of her wanted him to. She wanted to hear stories that he might not tell a pair of random students but might share with Ben's daughter.

"I found it," Adam finally said.

Tom looked at him with a hint of alarm, as if noticing him for the first time.

Adam gave the prop master a self-deprecating smile, which seemed to put him more at ease. But Holland swore that Tom continued to look a little baffled as Adam said, "My dad was a huge film collector, and this was in the back of a framed photo of Ben. But we don't know what it's for."

"It's a hold slip," Tom explained. There was a slight wobble in his voice, but it went away as he continued. "We don't exclusively rent props to people at JME. Anyone in the industry can rent whatever they want, as long they have the right permits and insurance. Slips like these are used to hold the items until they can be picked up."

"Do you know what this slip was used to hold?" Holland asked.

Tom rubbed his chin again. "I don't know what it was used for—if it was even used for anything. These instructions are kind of strange and I've never heard of this film before. But I do remember the last time Ben

Tierney came in here. It was shortly before he died. I remember because that was the final time I saw him, and he made an unusual request."

"What was it?" asked Holland.

"It's better if I show you. You two okay with a little walk?"

CHAPTER FORTY-TWO

T he stuff up front is the sexy stuff for the tours," Tom explained. "It gets less exciting the farther back you go."

After about twenty feet, Holland could see there was less variety, but she still found it all fascinating.

Walls of motorcycle helmets. Enough guitars for all the freshman boys at a college campus. More taxidermy animals, cats this time, from a movie she'd loved as a child called *The Nine Feline Lives of Calliope Canyon.*

Then there was the Oval Office.

The replica was nearly perfect—it didn't just have desks and chairs, it had windows and curtains and a view of the lawn so real that Holland would definitely have stopped if there had been time.

But there wasn't. In fact, she could see Adam beginning to grow impatient as Tom paused in a room full of lamps. "The finance department always puts on the best Christmas parties," he mused. "Last year, they rented all these." He waved toward the ceiling, which was covered in crystal chandeliers.

"Are you sure you don't want to just tell him the truth and then I can make him forget?" Adam whispered.

"No," Holland said, followed by a look she hoped clearly told him that using his ability on this man was not an option. With Vic VanVleet, it had felt justified. But Tom had been nothing but kind and helpful.

Tom took them up a set of stairs and past a series of telephones: rotary phones, '90s phones, emergency phones with only one button. After that, there was a disturbing number of doll heads. Just the heads.

On the third floor, there were desks and chairs and various bits of bedroom furniture. Tom stopped at an ugly plaid couch and proudly said, "This is my top moneymaker."

"Oh, really?" Holland tried to sound polite. The couch looked like a thrift store reject. There was stuffing coming out of one arm, and the plaid smelled as if it had been around from the '70s.

He smiled as if he knew what she was thinking. "This guy has character. People like things with character."

They passed a few swords, though not nearly as many as Holland would have expected.

"Weapons are difficult for liability reasons," Tom explained. "But, fun fact: There used to be a gun range underneath the yellow house from *My Neighbor Next Door*. There's a trapdoor in the house's kitchen that leads down to the range, or there used to be. The house is obviously part of the JME tours, so the trapdoor might be gone now. But if you get a chance, it could be worth exploring."

Adam gave Holland a look that said *don't answer him and maybe he'll stop talking.*

I don't want to be rude, she tried to reply with her eyes. But she was growing impatient as well.

"Are we getting close?" Adam finally asked.

"Don't worry," Tom said. He paused at another staircase and waved Holland and Adam up first. "Just one more floor."

Holland really hoped he was telling the truth. She hoped she hadn't made a colossal mistake in trusting him because of his easy smile and his anecdotes.

Her skin was prickling and her heart was pitter-pattering in a way that made her feel as if something was waiting right up ahead—either that or she'd just walked through the world's largest thrift store, and she was now on the fourth floor with no easy escape.

"Don't give up on me now," Tom said affably. "And don't eat any of those," he added as they passed a giant gumball machine.

This floor must have been where all the horror movie directors shopped.

After the inedible gumballs was a series of disturbing carnival games, naked mannequins, a very lifelike clown, and then—

Tom stopped abruptly at an antique desk, and the smile fell from his face.

"What's wrong?" Holland asked.

"It's gone."

CHAPTER FORTY-THREE

Tom looked nearly as upset as Holland felt. They were standing in front of a dusty desk with nothing but a large rectangular mark in the center.

"What used to be here?" Holland asked.

A loud crash sounded in the distance, and Holland jumped.

Tom waved it off. "That sort of thing happens all the time. I'm always telling the tourists not to touch anything, but then they do, and crash! Bam! Bang!"

"I thought you said tour groups didn't come past the front," Adam said.

"They don't, usually, but there's a private tour going around today for some well-connected rich guy." Tom shook his head as he looked back at the empty desk. "I still can't believe it's gone. This one rarely gets checked out."

"What was here?" Holland repeated.

"It was a book. An old, medieval-looking thing. The last time Ben came in here, he was holding a set of chains, and he asked if he could put them on it."

Holland shot a glance at Adam. His expression made her suspect he was thinking of the Professor's Chained Library myth, too. Only he didn't look excited. He probably thought a hiding place like this would be too obvious for the Alchemical Heart.

"Can you find who checked it out?" Holland asked. *If* someone had actually checked it out. If it had been taken or stolen, if someone else had found it first, then none of her father's clues for the Alchemical Heart mattered at all.

Tom checked his watch. It was now nearly six. Then he pulled out his phone and made a call. "Hey Devon—real quick. Do you know who checked out the old chained-up book?" He murmured and nodded as Devon said something on the other end. "Thanks, man. Have a good Halloween." Tom hung up and smiled at Holland. "I didn't tell you this. But the book is on the set of *Knife and Cross*. Stage 10. Sounds like they wanted it for the season finale."

"Thanks for all the help," Adam said.

Tom startled. "Where did you come from?"

"He's been here the entire time," Holland said patiently, although she was feeling unnerved that this was the second time Tom had been surprised by Adam's presence. Adam wasn't exactly a forgettable person.

Tom scratched his head, further mussing his long gray hair. "I must be losing my mind. Of course, you've been here. I don't know why I thought . . ." He trailed off as he pulled his hand from his hair.

His fingertips came back red.

Blood dripped from his nails.

"Your hands," Holland said. But the poor man didn't seem to see them. He just stood there, repeating the same motion. Running his fingers through his gray hair and then pulling them back out, staring as if he'd forgotten about more than just Adam.

"We need to get out of here," Adam said.

"But—something is wrong with him."

"I know," Adam said. "But unless you know something I don't, there's nothing we can do for him."

Holland tried a final time to get Tom's attention, but it didn't seem to help. She told herself that he would be fine, the same way that the Professor and the Watch Man had both recovered. But she still felt terrible that it had happened at all, and she couldn't help feeling it was somehow her fault.

Holland wished she could talk to the Professor. If anyone would know what was happening, it would be her. Holland felt as if she was turning into a story that could have been one of the Professor's myths: *Holland St. James: The Girl Who Broke the World.*

But the Professor would undoubtedly want something in return for her help, and Holland knew exactly what that something would be.

Outside, the world was still oppressively hot. The sun should have been setting, but it appeared stuck in the sky, bright as the center of an egg. Round and glowing and wrong. And then . . . it was gone.

There was no sun. The sky went from blue and bright to shades of purple and fading light. Holland suddenly felt as if she was losing her mind.

"Hey, I don't know what you're thinking, but it's going to be okay." Adam reached out and took her hand.

"No!" Holland felt suddenly panicked. She might not have understood what was happening to her or the people around her, but she felt that she was broken somehow. "You shouldn't touch me." She tried to pull away, but Adam held her fingers tight.

"You're not going to hurt me, Holland."

"You don't know that."

"Or maybe I just don't care." He took a step closer and put his other hand on her cheek, fingers cool against her flushed skin.

"You really shouldn't touch me."

"Then pull away." His thumb slowly grazed her jaw.

Her heart raced and she wondered how the world would be different if time was kept by heartbeats instead of minutes. She imagined moments like this making the world spin faster, turning minutes into hours.

It made her feel as if she needed to pull away. She was wasting time she didn't have. And Adam was a dangerous person to waste time with. He might have been charming and beautiful, but Holland had seen what he could do with his hands. She didn't think he was using his powers on her right now. But she knew it was a bad idea to put herself in a position where he easily could.

"We should go." She pulled away as the last bits of light began to fade from the sky.

CHAPTER FORTY-FOUR

Stage 10, where *Knife and Cross* filmed, wasn't far from the props department, but they still took the golf cart to save time.

Adam eyed the door to Stage 10 with the same wary expression he'd worn in the props department, like he wanted to tell Holland not to get her hopes up. But all she had was hope and a handful of hours. The hours were slipping through her fingers like sand. She couldn't lose her hope as well.

Adam opened the door and let her enter first.

Stage 10 was enormous, larger than Holland remembered any of the stages being when she had visited as a child. Yellow fire lines around the edges were empty, but the rest of the stage was full of sets and props and cameras and lights. And it was amazing, like standing inside a vampire court. Decadent and beautiful. Even the coffins were pretty.

Any other day, Holland would have wanted to explore every inch.

"I take it you're a fan of the show?" Adam murmured.

"What makes you say that?" she asked.

"Everything," he said, and he was smiling. "You look like you're one heartbeat away from asking me to participate in some vampire role-play."

Holland felt her cheeks go warm. That hadn't been what she was thinking. At all. But as soon as Adam said it, she had a sudden image of Adam's teeth sinking into a place that definitely wasn't her neck. "I actually prefer the human on this series."

"So you're a Cross fan?" Adam said.

She turned to him, surprised. Since meeting him yesterday, Adam had told her a number of incredible things, yet she found this the hardest to believe. "You watch the show?"

"Of course I do." He smirked. "Isabella is hot."

Holland felt an irrational flare of jealousy.

Adam's grin widened.

"You're the worst," she said. Then she suggested they split up.

Holland knew splitting up was generally considered a bad idea in situations like this. But Stage 10 was just too large, and she felt that getting some distance from Adam would be a good idea.

The vampire court was divided into two distinct sections. The upper court was all glamour and gold, with ballroom-like settings and beautiful cages. Adam took that portion, while Holland searched the lower court. This was full of deadly gardens, glittering black flowers, and velvet-lined coffins.

Holland's steps echoed as she debated opening up one of the coffins in search of the book. She knew there weren't actually vampires inside. But her skin was prickling, her blood humming.

There was magic here. She could feel it. How had nobody else sensed it? Or maybe they had, they'd just mistaken it for a different kind of magic. But Holland knew this wasn't Hollywood stardust. This was the Alchemical Heart. It had to be close.

Holland quickly wove through a maze of standing coffins until she saw two chalk outlines on the ground, shaped like humans. Then, just beyond the chalk, sitting on top of an iron pedestal, she saw it: the book her father had wrapped in chains.

"Adam, come here—" Holland cried. "I found it." And it did not look like a prop.

The leather was older than anything she'd ever seen. The pages peeking out were a color she didn't have a name for. The book smelled like earth and must and metal. She touched the chains, and she could feel the magic pulsing from them like a heartbeat.

Adam cursed under his breath as he approached. "These are Bank chains."

"What are Bank chains?"

"They can't be picked or broken. These can only be unlocked with the proper key."

"But—the screenplay didn't say anything about a key." Did it? Holland was about to take out the pages and quickly see if she'd missed anything, when she remembered something else. "What if—" Holland knew it was a long shot, but she pulled out her sister's key, which had turned back into a plastic Motor Hotel key.

"That's a key to the Regal," said Adam.

"I know. But what if it also opens the book?"

"Why would it open the book?"

"I found it in my sister's things, and I just had a thought—what if my father left two different sets of clues, in the hopes that my sister and I would come together to solve his mystery?"

"That's actually not a bad idea," Adam said.

Holland put the key inside of the lock.

Sparks flew. The lock hissed.

"No!" Holland tried harder.

The chains on the book blazed red.

"I think you need to stop," Adam said.

"But there has to be a way to open—"

A door groaned open. The door to Stage 10.

Holland and Adam both froze. They were surrounded by a maze of haphazard coffins and black rose trees, but there was enough space for them to see through the trees, for Holland to see who had entered.

One of them was a young woman dressed like a tour guide, but Holland didn't pay much attention to her. She was too afraid of the man beside her. As soon as she saw him, she couldn't think straight. She wanted to hope her mind might be playing tricks, but it seemed Adam could see him, too.

He grabbed her arm and mouthed, *We need to hide.*

Holland tried to take the chained book, but the volume was too heavy to lift.

We don't have time, Adam mouthed.

Then both his arms went around her middle. He hauled her backward and tucked her inside a coffin with him.

CHAPTER FORTY-FIVE

There was a crack in the coffin. Everything else was dark and Adam. It felt as if he was being careful with his hands, but she was so aware of him. She could feel his fingers wrapped around her rib cage, his chest pressed to her back, his lips at the corner of her ear. Yet her thoughts kept going to the man just on the other side of the coffin.

"I love this show so much," said Gabe. His voice made Holland's stomach churn with terror.

Adam held her tighter, his lips still pressed to the side of her ear. They didn't move. He didn't say a word and yet she swore she heard him whisper, *I won't let him touch you.*

"How can I be an extra?" Gabe asked. His voice was saccharine. The same insincerely enthusiastic voice he had used with Chance last night.

"I could probably pull some strings," said a chirpy female voice.

Holland peeked through the crack in the coffin. The tour guide with Gabe was short and slender, or it might have just been that she looked small next to Gabe, who seemed to become taller and more menacing with every step.

He was dressed more casually than when he'd abducted Holland. Dark jeans, black shirt, black boots, backpack on his shoulders. It was almost the exact same way he had looked in her vision.

"What's this?" Gabe asked, stepping closer to the chained book while Holland could do nothing but watch.

"I shouldn't be telling you this," said the tour guide, "but I think it's for the season seven finale."

Gabe touched the book and the chains glowed red.

"Um, what are you doing?" said the tour guide.

"I won't tell if you don't," Gabe said, but his voice was back to normal. Unkind. Unfriendly. Unenthusiastic.

Then the lights all over the stage started flickering.

The tour guide took a wobbly step back. And Holland watched in fear as Gabe pulled out a key.

Adam tensed behind her. Holland told herself it was going to be fine. Her key hadn't worked. This key wouldn't work, either, but the lock didn't spark as Gabe slid it inside. *How did he get a key?*

A ring sounded from Holland's purse.

Gabe's head snapped toward the tour guide. "Is that your phone?"

"I don't think so," trilled the guide.

Holland panicked and scrambled to silence her phone. *Who was even calling her?* Gabe was the only one with the number and he was occupied.

The good news: He'd already stopped looking for the ringing phone.

The bad news: The chains had fallen from the book.

Holland's heart raced furiously as Gabe reached for the book's cover and pulled it open.

Adam held her tight. "It's too late," he murmured quietly.

"No," Holland breathed. They could still stop him. Gabe was now just standing there. Staring. Not moving.

Wait—why wasn't Gabe moving?

"Huh," he finally said.

The petite tour guide now looked bewildered.

Holland's heart had been racing, but now it felt as if it was sinking because neither Gabe nor the tour guide was looking as if the book contained the most powerful object in the world.

The tour guide laughed nervously and said something, but Holland couldn't hear it. She couldn't hear anything. All she could do was watch through the crack in the coffin as Gabe walked away, hands in his pockets.

"He didn't take anything," Holland whispered, and then she was stumbling out of the coffin. Adam shadowed her, and for a moment the two of them stood there, much like Gabe and the tour guide had.

They stared at the open book.

It was fake. The pages inside were blank. A hole had been cut in the center, leaving a slender rectangle that hid one very ordinary object.

CHAPTER FORTY-SIX

A yellow pencil.

It felt like a joke without a punch line.

Holland picked up the pencil. "I don't understand."

"We must be missing something." Adam picked up the empty book and shook it, but all that fell out was dust.

"It can't end here," Holland said.

She took the pencil and started to scribble in the book, hoping magic words would appear, but it seemed that all the magic had been in the lock Gabe had opened. Holland wondered again how he'd even gotten a key. Then she remembered the mysterious phone call she'd received in the coffin.

Quickly, she reached into her purse and pulled out the phone.

**Missed call First Bank of
Centennial City**

Voice Message

Adam suddenly looked nervous.

"I don't even know how they got this number," Holland said.

"Ignore it," Adam warned.

But Holland was already pressing *Play* on the message.

"Hello, my dear," the Professor's familiar voice flowed through the phone. "Your friend Gabriel and I had an interesting chat, in which he gave me this number. If you could call me back, I would greatly appreciate it. But since I'm doubtful you will, I'm going to speak plainly. While I was conversing with Mr. Cabral, I became aware of your very alarming bleeding episodes.

"I know what's happening to you, Holland, and I know how to save you, but you must bring me the Alchemical Heart. You can find me tonight, at the Hollywood Roosevelt Halloween Ball—and I hope you do. Please let me help before it's too late."

"You can't trust her," Adam said as soon as the message was done.

But the problem was, Holland was tempted to believe her. She had thought earlier that if anyone knew what was wrong with her, it would be the Professor.

"If you find the Alchemical Heart, you won't need her."

"But what if we don't find it?" Holland looked down at her watch. There were only five hours left. And her father's latest clue didn't feel like much of a clue at all. Gabe hadn't even bothered to take it. But Gabe didn't have her father's screenplay pages.

Holland pulled out her father's pages, and instantly she saw it. Her father's familiar handwriting—*in pencil.*

"This is it," she said excitedly. "My father wants us to look at the notes he made in pencil."

She pointed to the first set of pages.

EXT. A GRAVEYARD. SUNSET

A hand (the hand of Red Westcott) sets a bouquet of flowers in front of a grave covered in spring-green grass. The tombstone reads:

Sophia Westcott
Beloved Wife. Beautiful Soul.

```
        This is only temporary.
```
My neighbor next door?

```
There is a moment of perfect silence, except for the
sound of a breeze rustling leaves on a sycamore tree.
Then . . .
```

```
Red plunges his fist into his wife's grave and pulls out
a handful of dirt.
```

"Look at the words he's written in pencil: *My neighbor next door?* And then look at this."

Holland shuffled the pages to get to the ones from the Watch Man and pointed at the bottom of the final page. Her father had penciled the words: *Be certain you're going in the right direction before you dig in.*

"So, back at the hotel, I was right about the digging," Adam said.

"Yes, it looks like my father buried something. And I think this is telling us where to look."

She showed Adam the pencil marks on the first page again. "The houses used in *My Neighbor Next Door* are part of the JME tours. I think that's where he buried his next clue."

Holland just hoped it would also be the last clue.

Holland could acutely feel the change in time when she and Adam exited Stage 10.

The studio looked empty.

There were no more buses of tourists.

The sky was as dark as it ever got in the middle of a city.

The whirl of the golf cart seemed too loud as Holland and Adam drove through the studio back lot and then to the houses for *My Neighbor Next Door.*

The set felt like a different version of reality. A neighborhood from the days when doors were never locked, all phones could do was make calls, and most problems could be solved with a good heart-to-heart with Mom or Dad.

Holland knew that in the daylight they would all be as pretty as pastel candies, with crisp white shutters and overflowing flowerbeds. But tonight, the neighborhood felt eerie. The lampposts cast all the houses in a soft glow that made it impossible to distinguish their colors.

"Everything looks the same," Adam muttered. He looked up and down the perfect street as if he didn't understand the appeal.

"You don't like *My Neighbor Next Door*?" Holland asked. Although she had to admit, right now it looked more horror movie than wholesome. And she had no idea where they were supposed to dig. Before leaving Stage 10, Adam had grabbed a large shovel, but it would take all night to dig up all the yards.

"Can you pull out the screenplay again?" Adam asked.

Holland stopped under one of the streetlamps and held out the page where her father had penciled *My neighbor next door?*

"'Red plunges his fist into his wife's grave and pulls out a handful of dirt,'" Adam read. "Are we supposed to look for a grave?"

Holland raised an eyebrow at him. "There aren't any graves on this street." She continued to flip through the pages, but the only words written in pencil were *My neighbor next door?* and *Be certain you're going in the right direction before you dig in.*

"Let me see a few of those?" Adam asked.

Holland handed him the set of pages from the Watch Man, while she combed over the pages she'd found in the safety deposit box.

The first page already held a clue, so she focused on the second, wondering if there was something she'd overlooked.

INT. A BOWLING ALLEY. EVENING.

Red slams the jar full of dirt down on a table. The jar now says the word *Ball* instead of the title of the film.

In the background, balls are rolling, pins are falling.
When someone gets a gutter ball, a neon sign inside of
a heart lights up with the words *Not Your Lucky Day*.
Think Cassius Marcellus Coolidge meets Spanish colonial
revival. The neon sign is on as Red walks in. He
approaches a vinyl table with a group of stylish older
women in matching bowling shirts. The word *Hollybells* is
monogrammed on the backs of their pink-and-green shirts.
Five of the women are sipping sodas from vintage glass
bottles with striped straws. The sixth is stitching a
yellow house on a needlepoint pillowcase.

Holland's heart started racing. "I think I found the next clue." She
pointed to the final paragraph. "See this bit about the needlepoint pillow? It's totally unnecessary to the story. I think it means we're supposed
to go to the yellow house."

"How do we find the yellow house?" Adam asked. All the colors
looked the same in the dark.

But Holland didn't need the light. Anyone who'd ever watched *My
Neighbor Next Door* knew the yellow house had a tree with an old wooden
swing where arms were broken, love was confessed, and tears were shed.
And now she wondered if this was where her father's secrets were buried.

CHAPTER FORTY-SEVEN

This way." Holland led Adam to the end of the street.

The wind rocked the old wooden swing and rustled the leaves of the tree it hung from.

"Let me see the first page again," said Adam. "I think there's a line about rustling leaves."

He was right. He used the flashlight on his phone to show Holland the words on the bottom of the page.

```
There is a moment of perfect silence, except for the
sound of a breeze rustling leaves on a sycamore tree.
Then . . .

Red plunges his fist into his wife's grave and pulls out
a handful of dirt.
```

"Maybe this means it's buried at the base of the tree," said Adam.

"There should be another clue here," Holland said. "My father wouldn't have us dig up the entire base of the tree."

More leaves rustled as Adam moved around the base of the tree with his flashlight, looking for a sign that—

"There!" Holland pointed down, near the bottom of the trunk, where two initials had been carved into the tree. They were small but deep, half an inch, if Holland had to put a figure on it. Deep enough that the years had warped but not erased them.

$$B + I$$

"Those are my parents' initials," she whispered. And for a second, Holland's throat felt thick. Every little thing her father left behind felt like an arrow to her heart, but this hit differently because it wasn't just a clue. It was a tiny love note to her mom.

For a second, she saw Adam eyeing the initials. His expression was inscrutable. Holland wished she could tell what he was really thinking.

Back at the Beverly Hills Hotel, Adam had said he didn't know if her parents had made a deal with his brother Mason. But she wondered if Adam had just been saying that because he didn't want to tell her the truth.

Holland believed in the truth. She wanted the truth. But she could see there was no truth Adam could tell her that was going to make her feel good. If her parents had made a deal with Mason, then Mason was the reason they had died, and if they hadn't made a deal with him, then her mother was the reason.

If Adam did indeed know the truth, Holland wondered if it was his kindness that kept him from telling her—or his fear.

"Looks as if this is our clue to dig," Adam said. He held out the shovel he'd grabbed from Stage 10. "Do you want to or should I?"

Holland wanted to take the shovel, but one look at Adam's arms confirmed he was clearly stronger.

She rocked from foot to foot as she watched him dig. Shovelful after shovelful. It felt like the start of her father's screenplay.

Then—the shovel hit glass.

It was quiet and loud all at once. The ring of hope. The sound of buried treasure. The moment of absolute truth.

Adam tossed the shovel aside and started brushing dirt away. Holland was already on her knees, holding his phone like a flashlight. Her heart fluttered with nerves, and for a second she feared she was about to get a nosebleed.

Not now. Not now. Not now.

Adam finally pulled a jar from the ground and handed it to her. "I hope this holds more than a pencil."

"It will," she whispered.

Although there wasn't much inside. Just a thin scroll of paper tied up with a thread.

Adam held the phone up as Holland unraveled it. There were two pages.

On the first page, she recognized her father's scrawl immediately.

I know you'll make the right decision, kiddo.
You already have everything you need. You just have to see it.
I wish I could be there to tell you I love you.

Dad

And Holland was choked up again. She could have reread this one page over and over. She could have sat on the old wooden tree swing with it until she'd memorized the words.

But there was a second page to look at. Another screenplay page.

`INT. BOWLING ALLEY`

`A black bowling ball rolls down a lane toward six pins`
`with letters that spell the words THE END.`

"I think this is the last clue," Holland said.

"Can I see?" Adam asked.

"Actually, I'll take that," said another voice.

Gabriel Cabral stood under the streetlamp, holding a gun.

Horror tripped down Holland's spine. This must have been why he hadn't taken the pencil from the book. He'd wanted Holland to find it so he could follow her to where it led. Gabe was more calculated than she'd given him credit for. It made her wonder if he had also traded information about her to the Professor in exchange for the key that had undone the chains on the book. For someone who said the Alchemical Heart was a myth that got the people who searched for it killed, he seemed quite skilled at the searching part.

Gabe pivoted by a fraction and pointed the weapon at Adam.

"Give me the scroll," Gabe said, as easy as he'd told her to get into the car with him last night.

"Don't do it—" Adam said to Holland.

"That's also an option," Gabe said. "I really wouldn't mind shooting him again. And this time, I'll do a better job."

"No one is getting shot." Holland glared at Gabe. Or she tried to glare. It was difficult to make herself glare at a murderer holding a gun. "Here." She held out the scroll with a shaking hand.

Gabe shook his head. "You need to come to me, sweetheart. I'm not getting near your new boyfriend." For a brief second, Gabe's eyes cut to Adam and then back to Holland, giving her a look that almost resembled a warning.

Slowly, Holland walked toward him. She wasn't sure he could do much with the scroll in her hand without the other pages. But she didn't want to give anything to him. And before she could think about what she was doing, she started to run.

"Go in the other direction!" she screamed at Adam. Gabe couldn't shoot Adam and chase after her.

No gunshots went off, but she did hear Gabe's footfalls, heavy behind her.

Holland darted into the yellow house, desperately hoping Tom had been telling the truth about the trapdoor in the kitchen.

Holland raced frantically around the stairs. The kitchen was on the other side, all shadows and dark windows. She found the outline of the trapdoor and a little ring to lift it, just as she heard Gabe enter the house.

Holland dropped down to her knees and pulled.

Red light illuminated a ladder that didn't look safe on a good day. As she started down it, Gabe ran into the kitchen. She nearly fell as she descended as quickly as she could.

Everything was dark save for red lights pointing toward a neon exit sign.

She didn't see a shooting range, just a tunnel with a few errant cleaning supplies. They must have converted it to get around the studio. There were two directions she could go, but neither had places to hide, just long forbidding corridors.

She darted to the right. Hard cement beneath her feet. Nowhere to hide. She pushed herself to run faster. She could do this. She ran every day. She wanted to live. That had to count for something. Desperately, she continued to look for somewhere to hide. A way out of the tunnel. But there were only glowing red exit signs, taunting her as she ran.

She took an abrupt turn to the right. And then she felt a pair of hands wrapping around her waist. "No! Let me go!" Holland kicked and screamed.

"I'm not going to hurt you," Gabe growled.

"Too late," Holland cried.

For a second Gabe's hands stilled. Then he was spinning her around, bringing them face-to-face. His jaw was clenched and his eyes were dark. "I don't know what they said to you in the Bank," Gabe said, "but I didn't murder my wife."

"Then how do you know they told me that?"

"Because that's what everyone believes."

"But—"

"I didn't kill her, Holland." Gabe held her a little tighter, pulling her close enough to feel his pounding heart. His expression was impossible to read, but his rapid heartbeat told her he was far from unfeeling. "If you want to know what happened, come with me."

"You just pointed a gun at me."

"I pointed it at *him*. You can't trust him." Gabe looked at her as if this was the one thing she needed to believe. This was the only truth that mattered.

"You're the one I can't trust. You told me the Alchemical Heart was a myth, one you didn't believe in, but you obviously want it more than anything!"

"I don't want it, I need it. But that doesn't mean I want to hurt you." Gabe pulled her even closer. His eyes were pained, and they were *red*. Bloodred.

Holland saw blood pooling in the corners of his eyes. "No!" She tried to wriggle free, watching in terror as the blood began to pour down his cheeks. "You have to let me go."

Gabe shook his head. "You keep making the same mistake."

"You're bleeding," Holland said. But like the others, Gabe didn't hear her.

"You keep making the same mistake," he repeated.

"What mistake?" Holland asked. But suddenly, Gabe wasn't Gabe. He was Adam. And he was looking at her as if she was the one who was scaring him. And that's when she felt the blood pouring out of her own eyes.

CHAPTER FORTY-EIGHT

Holland was on the ground when she came back to herself. The tunnel was humid, sticky. She shoved up to her feet. Gabe was gone and so was her satchel. *Bastard.* He'd taken the last two pages she'd just found along with all her father's other pages. But it seemed he'd left something else behind.

January's backpack was on the ground, right by where Holland had collapsed. She quickly opened it. Everything was still inside, including the Professor's journal.

Dimly, she wondered if returning this was Gabe's twisted version of a moral code. But if he'd had any sort of moral code, he wouldn't have pulled a gun on her and taken all her father's clues, leaving her to die tonight.

Holland looked at her watch. It was 8:03. Just under four hours left. She needed to find Adam. Or did she?

You can't trust him, Gabe had said. And though Holland knew she couldn't trust Gabe, his words had planted a seed of doubt. A question that made her wonder if it wasn't better to go this last part alone.

Gabe might have stolen all her pages, but Holland knew where her father's last clue was telling her to go. She knew where to find the Alchemical Heart. And she wasn't sure if she could afford to search for Adam.

"There you are!" Adam called.

Something like guilt clenched inside her.

Adam had one of those faces that didn't look as if it worried often, but she could see worry all over his face as he jogged toward her. "Did he hurt you?"

"I'm fine," Holland said. "But he took off with all my father's pages."

"All of them?"

"It's okay."

Adam gave her a look that said he didn't understand in what world any of this could be all right. And Holland continued to feel terrible that she'd trusted Gabe over him. Adam had never pulled a gun on her, or stolen from her, or kept it a secret that he'd murdered his wife.

Gabe was the only reason she'd briefly felt like she shouldn't trust him. And yet, Holland also couldn't let herself forget there were other reasons she needed to keep her distance from Adam. His ability still made her nervous. And once this business with the Alchemical Heart was over, Adam would go back to simply being January's partner and Holland would return to a life that didn't involve him.

"Gabe might have all the pages, but I know where we need to go."

Then she started walking down the tunnel, following the glowing red signs for the exit. "There was one last screenplay page inside the jar. It had one final scene, a bowling alley with six pins that spelled out *The End.*"

"There are a lot of bowling alleys in Los Angeles," said Adam.

"Yes, and hopefully that's what Gabe is thinking. But I know which bowling alley my father meant. In his opening pages, right after he mentions the bowling alley, his description says *Think Cassius Marcellus Coolidge meets Spanish colonial revival.*"

"How did you remember that?" Adam looked at her as if she had suddenly turned into a dictionary or an encyclopedia or some other book people didn't usually read for fun.

"Within the last few hours, I've read those pages about twenty times. I don't know who Cassius Marcellus Coolidge is, but I know Spanish colonial revival."

Adam looked impressed.

Holland didn't tell him there was actually only one Spanish colonial revival building she was familiar with. "One of my favorite places in Los Angeles was built in this style, and it just so happens that it has a gaming parlor with a bowling alley."

"Where?"

"The Hollywood Roosevelt."

Adam's face went suddenly pale.

"What's wrong?"

Adam ran both hands through his hair and briefly closed his eyes. "That's where my brother Mason is."

Holland flashed back to the night before, when she'd had a vision of Mason on the mezzanine. That had been her second nosebleed. Suddenly, it felt even more significant. "How do you know he'll be there tonight?"

"Because he's always there," Adam answered. "Mason can't leave that hotel."

"What do you mean he can't leave?"

"When I tried to take away his abilities, I couldn't quite do it. The best I could do was to trap him in that hotel and prevent him from using any magic."

"If he can't use his powers—"

"He's still dangerous," Adam cut in. "And if Mason sees you with me, he'll try to hurt you."

"Then we can split up."

"No," Adam said sharply. "I don't want you out of my sight."

Holland prickled, his tone and words both setting her on edge.

But was it really that, or was it the seed of distrust Gabe had planted? Adam was her ally. Gabe was her enemy—he'd lied to her, stolen from her, left her to die.

Finally, Holland and Adam reached the end of the tunnel. The last glowing red exit sign was positioned above an industrial-looking door, and Holland tried to shake off any lingering distrust of Adam as she walked through.

The door opened into a hall that looked as if it was part of the JME tour. On either side were displays of mannequins dressed in costumes from classic films and hit television shows, guarded by velvet ropes and decorated with little plaques explaining their significance.

Holland saw an entire setup for *Knife and Cross*, and then there was a dazzling display for *Mirrorland*. It was all silver and snow and twinkling lights, and in the center of it was the famous gown her mother had worn.

Holland stopped abruptly in front of it. "Before we go to the Roosevelt, there's one more thing we need to do."

CHAPTER FORTY-NINE

Holland had never wanted to be an actress like her mother. She'd always wanted to be a storyteller like her father. But now, standing there in her mother's iconic *Mirrorland* dress, Holland could understand the appeal.

The dress was a little otherworldly, a little speakeasy-romantic, with a pale blue-violet fur that draped around her shoulders and long strings of pearls that went around her neck. The fitted bodice was covered in a sheer overlay that flowed out at her hips and turned into a short skirt covered in iridescent blue and violet beads that shimmered as she walked.

Adam was dressed like Cross from *Knife and Cross*, in dark leather breeches, tall boots, a loose brown shirt with sleeves rolled up, and two belts of weapons slung low on his hips. He was twirling another weapon around his fingers—a knife with an intricate hilt. The blade fell from his hands as soon as he saw Holland.

She tried not to smile.

It was late when they arrived at the Hollywood Roosevelt. Holland didn't want to look at the time, because she already knew it wouldn't be enough.

She could feel the feverish Halloween energy as soon as she and Adam stepped out of the car and approached the double glass doors.

On the other side, a new row of red velvet curtains obscured the view into the hotel, but Holland could hear music playing. Jazzy, big band music that made her picture swinging skirts and strong drinks in fancy glassware.

A man dressed like a butler from the 1940s stood in front of the curtains. His pants were pinstripe, his suit coat had tails, and he was holding a silver tray in his gloved hands. On one side of the tray stood an old-fashioned liquor bottle with a large glass stopper, and on the other was a stack of cream-colored cards with embossed gold writing.

"Take one if you wish to play," said the butler.

Holland didn't have time for games. But Adam picked one up with a cheerful "Thanks." Then he took another and handed it to Holland. She started to brush it aside, but the words on the front stopped her:

_____ *did it in the* _____ *with the* _____.

"It's from the game Clue." She flipped over the card. *The murder happens in a room with a secret passage.* Below the clue was a grid, like the ones that came with the actual board game.

"I would have loved this on any other night," Holland told Adam. But tonight, the clue hit a nerve. "I don't know if I should feel as if this clue is trolling me or if it's trying to warn me."

"I wouldn't worry about it." Adam grinned, but it was one of those smiles that didn't touch his eyes.

Animated chatter mingled with the music, growing louder as Holland and Adam ventured up the stairs and down the hall to the lobby, which had been transformed into Clue's conservatory.

Holland once again thought about her ominous Clue card, since the conservatory in the game was one of the rooms with a secret passage.

A dizzying array of flowering plants had been brought in, filling the room with even more color. Not that it needed it. The hotel was packed with people in costume, taking pictures and flirting, drinking and kissing, spilling drinks, and trading clues. It was the time of night when the entire party was tipsy. Holland felt like the only sober person. Even Adam had somehow managed to grab a cocktail within minutes.

"Do you see your brother?" she asked.

"No. But he's here somewhere." Adam took a long drink as both of them surveyed the room.

From the corner of her eye, Holland thought she saw the Professor. Quickly, she grabbed Adam's arm.

"What's wrong?" His drink sloshed as Holland dragged him to the staircase leading up toward the mezzanine, although tonight there were signs for the library, the billiard room, and the ballroom.

"I think I saw the Professor," Holland whispered. "She's in the lobby, dressed like Mary Poppins."

"Mary Poppins, really?"

"It's actually kind of fitting. She's magical and not very nice."

This earned Holland a laugh from Adam as he finished off his drink. She wondered if he was drinking because he was just that confident they'd find the Alchemical Heart, or if he was nervous about seeing his brother.

The stairs were full of more people. Holland and Adam passed a couple dressed as Knife and Cross; another partygoer dressed as a French maid was lying on the ground, posing for a photo as that evening's dead body. Carefully, Adam and Holland stepped around her.

The mezzanine was somehow teeming with even more people. The band must have been playing in the ballroom, because up here the sound was deafening. Holland could barely hear anything else as she and Adam moved through the crush toward the bowling alley.

She stilled at the sight of a man in a white dinner jacket. Thankfully it wasn't Mason. But then she saw another man who made all her anxiety bubble back to the surface. "Adam—it's Gabe."

He was the only person not in costume. Instead, Gabe was dressed in the same exact clothes he'd worn at JME, and he was moving swiftly toward the bowling alley.

The carelessness left Adam's expression in a flash. "I'll take care of him. Just stay here, out of sight."

"I thought you didn't want to split up."

"I don't. But I also don't want you to have to go near him again."

A second later, Adam was gone. Holland watched him move through the crowd until he was lost. And then she started moving, too. According to her watch, she had less than two hours to find the Alchemical Heart. She wasn't just going to stay—

A strong hand grabbed her shoulder and spun her around.

Holland yelped and drew back her fist. But it was only Chance.

He was dressed like a pirate from the cover of a romance novel, wearing a wig with long golden hair, golden hoops in both his ears, and a very frilly shirt he'd left almost entirely unbuttoned. A long curving sword was tied to his waist. It was a fantastic costume. But all Holland's nerves were on edge. Not even seeing Chance in this costume could calm them.

"You just scared the hell out of me," she breathed.

"Sorry," Chance said. "I need to talk to you." His eyes darted around the crowded mezzanine. "There's something I need to show you. Can we go somewhere more private?"

"Chance, this really isn't the best time." Holland started to push past him, but he blocked her way, smile vanishing.

"You owe me. And you need to see this." He took her hand before she could protest and started toward the elevators.

"Hey! Are you Chance Garcia?" someone called.

Chance ignored him, pulling Holland into the open elevator and then shutting the doors before anyone else could step inside. She'd never seen him act like this. "Chance, you're making me nervous."

"Good." He pressed a button to an upper floor. Then, just as the elevator started to ascend, he pushed the emergency stop. The elevator jolted to a sudden halt. Holland reached for the wall to steady herself, but Chance just stood there, eerily calm. "You should be nervous. There's something very wrong with that guy you were with."

"Adam?"

Chance nodded. "There's a reason I took the job on that new Vic Van-

Vleet film, and it's not because I wanted to return to acting. I've never stopped being haunted by that last day on *The Magic Attic*. I wanted to go back to JME to look into what happened. For months, that's what I've been doing. I've tried to make friends with people all over the studio, so I could look through old pictures and hear old stories and try to make sense of things. Today, when I saw you with Adam, it wasn't the first time I'd seen him." Chance held out his phone and showed her a picture of a framed photograph. "This was the first day of *The Magic Attic* filming. See anyone familiar?"

Holland, of course, recognized the cast, including a younger Chance.

"You look so happy," she said.

"I'm not talking about me. Keep looking."

Holland studied the photograph, and this time it only took her a few seconds to see a face she knew all too well.

Adam Bishop.

"He was the one person in this photo who I couldn't remember," said Chance. "I asked around and no one at the studio remembers him, either. But I found him in dozens of other pictures."

Chance showed her several more photos of Adam. In every one, he hadn't aged a day. But the part that most unnerved Holland was that every picture of Adam also showed someone she had included in her thesis—a different person in each photo, but every one was a person who had died under tragic or mysterious circumstances.

"There's one more photo you should see," Chance said a little reluctantly. "After I left you at the studio today, I found this one from the set of *Mirrorland*.

CHAPTER FIFTY

think your friend might be the devil," said Chance. But there was no excitement or playfulness in his voice. No victory that they had finally found him.

Holland's head spun as she stared at the picture. Her parents were in the middle, standing next to each other, and right behind them was Adam Bishop.

She reminded herself that Adam had told her he'd once been the devil. But he'd also promised he'd never made a deal with her parents.

She searched the photo for Mason. She looked for him in all Chance's photos, but there was only Adam.

This didn't prove that Adam had been lying about Mason, but what if he had been? What if Holland had it all backward and Adam really was the villain?

Holland reminded herself that January trusted him. She could trust him, too. But what evidence did Holland actually have for this? Now that she thought about it, only one person at the Bank had mentioned Adam's name: Padme. That should have been enough, except that Holland had seen Adam not only erase memories but change them. If he really was the acting devil instead of his brother, it would have been easy for Adam to figure out whose memories at the Bank he'd need to change in order to convince Holland he was January's partner.

Suddenly, Holland was desperate to find the Professor—to ask if she knew Adam Bishop. But there wasn't time for that. As soon as Holland exited this elevator, she had to decide whether to go find Adam or look for the Alchemical Heart on her own.

Holland restarted the elevator. Chance now looked as if he didn't want to let her out of his sight. She wasn't sure how she was going to get out of this without hurting him yet again.

Thankfully for Holland, Chance Garcia was easily recognizable, even in a pirate costume. Just minutes after she and Chance exited the elevator, partygoers were asking for selfies, and Holland was slipping away from her friend.

The night had gone from tipsy to drunk. The floor beneath her shoes felt sticky, everything smelled like liquor and sugar, and what had been jazzy music now just sounded like noise.

Holland heard a familiar laugh and spun around to find Cat near the entrance of the ballroom, talking to Eileen. Holland felt a pang of guilt for how she'd parted with Cat earlier, but she couldn't risk talking to either of her friends now. After she found the Heart. *If* she found the Heart, she would make all this up to them.

Holland was almost inside the Roosevelt's Spare Room—the gaming parlor and cocktail lounge where the bowling alley lived—when she realized she had no idea where to search. But then she remembered the words in her father's note. *You already have everything you need. You just have to see it.*

Holland could do this. She might not have solved the mystery of exactly why her parents had died, but she'd confirmed what kind of person her father was. Everyone she'd met on this treasure hunt had painted a picture of Ben Tierney that not only made her feel proud of him but also made her feel closer to him.

Ben was a good person.

He had a heart, and he was one of those rare people who only became better at using it throughout his life.

Ben was the real deal. Smart. The kind of visionary storyteller that comes around once in a lifetime.

If her father believed she could do this, then she could do it. Holland had faith in her father, and he had faith in her.

The music faded as soon as she stepped into the gaming parlor, and suddenly she felt as if she could have been walking into her father's unfinished movie. Balls were rolling and pins were falling and people in outlandish Halloween costumes were sipping cocktails like they were sodas. The double lanes had been painted green for the night, and single-digit numbers had been stuck on all the balls, making every lane look like a giant billiard table.

You just have to see it, her father had written.

Then she saw *him*. Mason Bishop.

Every single hair on her arms stood up.

Mason was reclining in the cocktail lounge, dressed exactly as he'd been last night: dark pants, white dinner jacket, undone tie around his neck.

She still thought he looked like the looking-glass version of Adam: harder, colder. His hair was darker, but his skin was fairer. He probably had an inch of height on his brother, and he looked as if he hadn't smiled in a century.

Holland watched him taking in the bowling alley scene and looking bored as hell. Then his eyes were on her. Holland felt it again—the same electric charge as last night crackled through the air.

Suddenly, Mason no longer looked bored. Then he was there, right in front of her. "You're running a little late tonight."

Holland took an involuntary step back. "How—how did you do that?" Her eyes went to the far side of the cocktail lounge, where Mason had just been reclining, then back to the man in front of her. Adam had said his brother couldn't use his abilities. But clearly, Adam was a liar.

Mason's expression darkened. "Yes, my younger brother is a liar and a number of other unfortunate words."

"How did you know what I—"

"I can't read your mind," Mason interrupted. "And I didn't need to. We've had this conversation before."

CHAPTER FIFTY-ONE

All the bowling pins crashed at once. A collective roar of drunken cheers took over the gaming parlor. Everyone was high-fiving, saying words like *Halloween magic* and looking around in wonder— everyone except for Holland and Mason.

Mason looked at Holland as if he didn't want to have this conversation *again*. And Holland felt dizzy and sick and more than a little angry as she considered his words. That somehow she'd had this conversation before and she'd forgotten. Although if she really had forgotten, she doubted it was a lapse of memory. It was Adam.

"When did we have this conversation?" she asked.

"I'll tell you. But we need to leave before my brother comes in."

"I can't—"

"You're not going to find the Alchemical Heart in here," Mason cut in sharply.

Holland bristled at his tone. There was something about Mason that made her feel as if he was the kind of guy who should come with a warning sign: *Likes shiny toys. Bored easily.*

"I'm impressed with your little magic tricks," said Holland, "but—"

"I can tell you why you keep having nosebleeds and visions," he interrupted.

"Already heard that one."

"From your Professor? Did she also mention the Watch Man, poor Tom, and that depressed bastard Gabe?"

Holland tried to stop herself from asking how Mason knew all this. She hadn't even told anyone about Gabe bleeding.

We've had this conversation before, Mason had said.

But when could she have told him about Gabe?

"What do you know about my bleeding?" Holland asked.

"This never goes well unless you follow me. We only have about ninety seconds before my brother walks in here. He'll come straight for you. As soon as he touches you, you'll forget this conversation. You won't find the Alchemical Heart, and an hour from now you'll be dead." He sounded annoyed, as if her death would be a colossal inconvenience to him.

But it was the words *never goes well* that finally caught her full attention. "What happens if I go with you?"

"You get a chance." Mason started toward the bar in the cocktail lounge. In the game Clue, there was not a secret passage in the billiard room, but in the Hollywood Roosevelt, there was a hidden door right by the bar. Mason pointed toward a handle that blended in with the wood paneling. Holland turned it, just as she caught a glimpse of Adam in the bar's mirror. Then she was slipping through to the other side.

Mason leaned one shoulder against a wall of books, somehow having entered the tiny library before Holland. She wondered again exactly what his magic was, but that wasn't her most pressing question. "Tell me about my nosebleeds."

"You're feisty tonight." Mason regarded her with a subtle cock of his head. "I like this for you."

"Why do you keep talking as if we know each other?"

"Because we do. Or—" His mouth twisted as if he'd just bitten into something unpleasant. "I know you. You never remember me."

"Because of your brother?"

"Sometimes. Not always." Mason sighed and leaned a second shoulder against the bookcase. "It's mostly because of *you*."

"Why would it be because of me?"

"Because you die. You never find the Alchemical Heart, because it's not hidden in this hotel. You die at one minute to midnight. Then at exactly a quarter after midnight, time turns back to Halloween Eve, and we do this dance all over again."

"No." Holland staggered back. "I don't believe you."

"You say that every time. Then you tell me that your father wouldn't steer you wrong."

"He wouldn't!" Holland said. She believed in a lot of impossible things. She believed in time loops and magical objects and the dead coming back to life, but Holland could not believe that her father would fail her.

Mason shrugged as if to say *sorry*, but Holland didn't think he meant it. She didn't think Mason felt much of anything except bored and annoyed that he was forced to relive the same forty-eight hours over and over again. Although she still wasn't sure if she believed him.

"You think I'm a dick," said Mason.

"I didn't say that."

"We've had this conversation before," he reminded her. "I don't know how or why the time loop happens. But I know the nosebleeds didn't start right away. We think they're a side effect of the time loop. Time wants to move forward, and since it hasn't, it's started to break."

As he spoke, Holland felt a drop of blood fall from her nose. She waited for Mason to disappear, for the library to go grainy. But all she saw was Mason frowning at her.

Holland quickly swiped it with her hand, hoping it wouldn't ruin her mother's dress, although if Mason was right, the dress was the least of her worries. "Why am I not having a vision right now?" she asked.

"Your visions aren't visions, they're memories of past timelines," he said. "I don't know why you don't have them with me. I imagine it has something to do with the fact that I exist outside of time, which is why I remember all this, and no one else does."

"How is that possible?" Holland asked.

"The same reason it's possible for me to do this." Mason shoved off the bookshelf, took one step and then—

He was gone. Holland didn't even see him walk through the wall, he just disappeared. Then, he reappeared, only slower, as if he was turning from mist to human.

Holland reached out for Mason's hand, but her fingers went right through him, and she suddenly understood why Adam had said Mason couldn't leave this hotel or use his powers. "You're a ghost."

Mason clapped slowly, his hands making no noise as he pressed them together. If Holland's mind hadn't already been fractured into a million spinning pieces, this might have truly surprised her. But learning Mason was a ghost simply seemed to fit in with all the other disturbing details of her night. Of course he was a ghost, his brother was the devil, and Holland was going to die, though she was determined to change that.

"If you're a ghost, why can I see and hear you?"

"Because you've died."

Holland still couldn't wrap her mind around this, but she wanted to know more. "How many times?"

"If I told you, it would just depress you."

"I still want to know."

Mason leaned back against the bookcase. "You say that almost every time."

"How many times have we had this conversation?"

"I don't know. A lot. But it's not always the same. It depends on whether you go with Gabe when he abducts you in the parking lot. Occasionally, you run away and find my brother. That usually means it's Adam you betray to the Professor when you're at the Bank, and then you somehow come in here with Gabe, and you and I don't ever talk on those nights."

"But I still die?"

Mason nodded grimly.

"How?"

"I'll tell you on one condition." Mason took a slow step toward Holland. Earlier, she'd thought he had an inch of height on his brother, but she'd been wrong. He had at least two, maybe more. Mason might have been a ghost, but he was still formidable. "If you do find the Alchemical Heart tonight, I want you to make me alive again and I want you to kill my brother."

Holland shook her head. "I can't do that."

"You say that every time, too. But you can. Trust me. And when I tell you why you die, you'll want to do it."

"You're wrong," Holland said. After everything she'd learned tonight, Adam definitely felt like the villain in her story, but she still didn't want to kill him. She didn't want to kill anyone. "I think it's time for me go."

"My brother," Mason said.

Holland froze.

"That's who kills you. Between the time you leave this room and midnight, it's always my brother who murders you."

CHAPTER FIFTY-TWO

Y ou never find the Alchemical Heart, because it's not hidden in this hotel. Holland felt haunted by pretty much everything Mason had told her, but this was perhaps the most haunting thing of all. She couldn't believe her father would let her down. But she didn't know where else to search if not the Roosevelt, and she had only twenty minutes left.

The party had gone from drunk to dying. The crowd had thinned, making it easier for her to keep an eye out for Adam—and for him to find her.

Holland wanted to be more shocked by Mason's warning about his brother, but if she actually paused to think about it, she just felt incredibly stupid for ever trusting Adam. And now she only had nineteen minutes left. There had to be something she was missing.

Or maybe she was thinking about it wrong. Her father had written, *You already have everything you need. You just have to see it.*

What if he wasn't saying she had all the clues? What if he was saying she already had the actual Alchemical Heart?

Holland had forgotten about her sister's backpack, but suddenly she became very aware of the weight of it on her shoulders. She would have preferred to take it off and search through it in a bathroom, but the line she saw was out the door. A dark corner in the gaming parlor would have to do.

Carefully, she unzipped it. She didn't know what the Alchemical

Heart looked like, so she would have to go by touch. As she started to reach for the bag's main zipper, she felt another zipper, hidden on the back. A secret compartment.

Fingers trembling, she opened it. Inside, she found an impressive stash of cash, an even more impressive fake passport, a thin golden necklace—

The noise of the party faded as she touched the chain. *Magic.* Holland tugged it out of the pack and instantly recognized it. This was her sister's sulfur necklace, the counterpart to the one Holland always wore. January always wore hers, too. Why had she taken it off and hidden it away?

Instinctively, Holland put her sister's necklace on. For a second, both necklaces were warm, then suddenly they were burning hot. She reached up to wrench them off. But just as soon as the burning had started, it stopped. And when she touched the necklaces, instead of two there was only one. The golden chain had formed a choker around her neck. She turned, taking in her reflection in a paneled mirror.

There was still a charm hanging off the end of the necklace, but it had shifted from a delicate thing to a thick shimmering piece of gold shaped like the symbol for the Alchemical Heart.

Every inch of Holland's skin buzzed. She was excited and scared and felt a million emotions all at once. This had to be it. Mason was wrong. She wasn't going to die. She might have had a fleeting thought that the most powerful object in the world was supposed to feel a little more magical than this, or perhaps that it should do something slightly more impressive than just sit on her neck. But Holland could worry about that later, after she got out of the Hollywood Roosevelt alive.

She had ten minutes now. She was still upstairs in the gaming parlor. If she moved quickly, she could go downstairs, go outside, and then maybe even get in a waiting cab before Adam could find her.

Holland's heart raced as she put on her sister's backpack and made her way to the balcony overlooking the lobby, with all its flagging decorations and tired costumes. The band was gone, but someone was playing a piano in the ballroom—a guest, probably, from the way the song would fumble and pick up, its tempo just a little off.

Holland quickened her pace as she reached the stairs. The lights were dimmer now, shadows replacing guests who had gone for the night, although there was still a number of partygoers. She didn't recognize anyone. She saw no sign of Chance, or Cat, or—

A hand landed on her shoulder, soft and warm. "There you are, Bright Eyes. I was worried I wasn't going to find you before midnight. But now I can see you've been looking for me, too."

The hand slid down to her wrist, sending shivers across her skin. Then she was being turned around. Adam looked down at her with an expression she'd never seen on him. His lips were pressed into an angry line, his eyes flat, unsmiling. But when he spoke, his voice was pure music. "You were worried that you weren't going to find me, either. But now that I'm here, you're so relieved you don't ever want me out of your sight."

"Yes, I was looking for you," she said. Relief washed over her. She'd go anywhere with Adam, as long as he didn't leave her sight.

His grip tightened on her, almost painfully, but she didn't really mind, as he led her down to the lobby, which still looked like the conservatory from Clue, albeit a slightly haunted version. More shadows, fewer guests, and the guests who remained were passed out on the chairs and couches. Holland saw a sleeping Statue of Liberty lying on top of a passed-out skeleton.

Adam led her toward a dark corner, next to an installation that looked like one of the game's glass conservatory walls. It was a strange, fuzzy sort of walk. In fact, Holland couldn't remember how it started. The last thing she clearly recalled was entering the hotel with Adam, losing him, then frantically searching for him. But even that was fuzzy.

She must have had something strong to drink. She cursed herself. How had she wasted the entire night? Holland looked down at her watch, suddenly remembering what she needed to do. "We only have seven minutes until midnight."

"It's all right. You don't need to worry," Adam said, in his beautiful, musical voice. "Unless this building is about to crumble, you're not going to die before midnight."

He pulled her closer.

"What are you doing?" Holland asked. "We need to find the Alchemical Heart."

"All you need is me," Adam said. Then his lips were on hers. Holland's mouth parted easily. He tasted like brandy and citrus, and she felt a little drunk as his tongue gently touched hers. His kiss was softer than his touch, but Holland enjoyed the rough way Adam pulled her closer. She liked the powerful feel of his hands as his lips continued to play with hers, tasting, drinking, licking, making Holland's head light with pleasure. Her eyes were closed, but she imagined that if she opened them, everything would be a blur of light and midnight colors, except for the two of them.

"I've been wanting this," Adam murmured against her mouth. Then he was taking the kiss even deeper, tugging her further into the dark corner of the Roosevelt lobby, pressing her back against a wall.

He brought a hand up to the front of her throat. Her heart started beating faster. This wasn't a place she liked being touched. Then she felt his fingers on the chain around her neck. A flash of memory came back to her. The necklace. Something about this necklace was important.

She tried to pull away, but her back was to a wall and Adam's grip was far too tight. One hand was like iron around her back, and the other was still at her throat, and he was pulling, yanking, tearing at the necklace.

"No," Holland cried. But Adam's harsh lips were still on hers.

The hand at her neck had moved to her scalp, keeping her lips pressed to his as he murmured, "This is going to hurt." And then he stabbed her in the back.

Nothing in Holland's life had ever hurt so much.

She cried out against Adam's mouth as he kissed her one more time.

She cursed and screamed, and he took it all with his lips and his tongue, pressing them one last time to hers before he finally let her go.

Her vision was swimming as he released her.

For a second, she thought he looked sad.

Then he was walking away, holding her only hope in his bloody hands.

CHAPTER FIFTY-THREE

Holland tried not to crumple to the ground. A stab to the back wouldn't kill her right away; she knew this from the research she'd done when writing *Knife and Cross* fanfic. But this didn't feel like an ordinary wound. It felt toxic, poisoned.

She thought about Jake, how he'd died the same way. Now she knew for certain who had murdered him, but there was nothing she could do.

Holland coughed as the hotel started spinning. A blur of memories resurfaced, including all the nights she'd spent here with her friends. She saw flashes of Eileen and Chance and Cat, all buying drinks for people they thought could be the devil, like children playing with matches. Then, in the corner of her vision, Holland saw another familiar figure. A man in a white dinner jacket. *Mason.*

As he stepped closer, more of the memories Adam had erased flooded back. She remembered their conversation in the library, the warning he gave before she left. *It's always my brother who murders you.*

Mason had been right, but he didn't look happy about it. He also looked more real than earlier, less ghostly. Holland wondered dimly if this was because she was dying.

"I've never come down here for this part. But tonight felt different, and I hoped . . ." He trailed off, as if putting words to feelings would make them more real than he wanted. Up close, Mason's expression was even more miserable. But she could already see him wiping it away, replacing whatever he might have been feeling with acceptance of the inevitable.

"I still think you're wrong," Holland choked out. She could feel the blood running down her back and the seconds running out, but she refused to give up. If anything, Mason's defeated expression made her more determined.

The Watch Man had said the only way to live past tomorrow was to find the Alchemical Heart. So, she shouldn't have been dying. Unless she hadn't actually found the Alchemical Heart.

She must have been wrong about the necklace. But she still believed her father was right about her being in possession of the Alchemical Heart. Which meant that *having* it wasn't enough, she needed to actually *find* it, like the Watch Man had said.

Holland fumbled to open her sister's backpack again, ripping out the clothes she'd shoved inside. As soon as she touched the Professor's journal, her fingers began tingling. The journal was upside down as she pulled it out, revealing the Alchemical Heart symbol embossed on the back. Now she could feel the tingling down to her toes.

Suddenly, it felt so obvious. The longer Holland held it, the more she could feel the magic—pulsing like a living thing, wanting to be used. Gabe had repeatedly told her that no one knew what the Alchemical Heart looked like, and that some people suspected it could even change form. Holland imagined he must have been right about it changing form. She couldn't imagine it always looked like this journal.

She wondered how her father had managed to send it to her. But she would have to puzzle that out later. The Alchemical Heart was now glowing in her hands.

The drunken skeleton perked up a little on the couch.

"Is that—" Mason stepped closer, his words cutting off as he took in the book.

Holland needed to move. She couldn't risk drawing more attention, not when Adam was still nearby.

She was in so much pain, she didn't think she could run again. But maybe she didn't have to. Not far from her was a temporary wall for the party with a little arrow and two life-saving words etched into a sign: *secret passage.*

Holland pressed on the words, and suddenly she was in another room. Actually, she was just in a sequestered part of the Roosevelt's lobby, but it had been made to look like a little sitting room, with two wingback chairs and a small table with a glowing Tiffany lamp on top.

Holland slumped into one of the leather chairs, unable to stand any longer. The Heart was still glowing, but it didn't seem to be doing much of anything else, including healing her.

Then Mason was there, towering over her. "You need to use the Alchemical Heart now."

"How am I supposed to do that?" she wheezed.

"Nobody told you how to use it? Of course they didn't," Mason muttered. Then he started rapidly talking. "The Alchemical Heart was taken from another world where objects are sentient. It's not simply an object. It's capable of thought and choice and action. If you want to use its power, you need to ask for it, specifically."

"That's a lot of words," she said. Everything in the world hurt, and now her vision was going black around the corners. Aside from the glowing book, she couldn't see much of anything. But she hoped she understood what Mason had just told her. "I need to live," she said to the book in her hands.

"No," Mason said sharply. "Tell the Alchemical Heart what you need it to do."

"You don't need to yell," Holland murmured. She spoke to the book again. "I need you to heal me."

"Be more specific. Tell it to keep your heart beating and stop the bleeding."

Holland repeated Mason's words. "And could you get rid of the poison, please?"

As soon as she spoke, the Alchemical Heart glowed more brightly and she started to gag. Her throat, her stomach, everything felt as if it was on fire, and then she was spitting the foulest thing she'd ever tasted onto the table.

Immediately, Holland's pain vanished and her vision returned. She could see the half-finished drinks on the table before her and every spill that had been made throughout the night. The world was coming back into focus, except for Mason. He was looking faded, more ghostly again. And he still looked miserable.

"Would it be too much to ask for a smile?"

"You're still not safe."

Holland looked down at her watch. She was seconds away from midnight. Five. Four. Three. Two. One.

She half expected fireworks to explode or a great unseen clock to chime, celebrating her victory. She wanted to cheer or cry or throw confetti. But mostly she found she just wanted to sit there quietly, without anyone trying to kill her, or steal from her, or pull any types of weapons on her. She was safe, and she just wanted to feel it.

Around her, the lobby had gone unnervingly quiet. Even the music had stopped, magnifying the sound of someone approaching on the other side of the wall.

Holland froze.

Mason disappeared, reappearing a few seconds later. "It's just Gabe," he said, a little disdainfully.

Clearly, Gabe didn't have the best reputation in this world. But Holland found she was relieved he was alive. She still didn't know whose side Gabriel Cabral was really on, but he had tried to warn her about Adam. That counted for something. Still, she knew how desperately he wanted the Alchemical Heart, and she didn't want him to find her here with it.

"You can relax," Mason said. "He's gone. He just frowned for a few seconds at the clothes you left behind, then he walked away."

Holland checked her watch again. It was now two minutes past. "I think this means I'm officially safe."

Mason shook his head. "Adam will come back for the actual Alchemical Heart when he realizes his mistake."

Holland swore she had never met someone so pessimistic. "How do you know that if this has never happened?"

"Because I know Adam." Mason met her gaze like a challenge. "Don't underestimate him because he has a pretty face."

Holland made a show of looking offended. "He just tried to kill me." She no longer thought Adam was pretty. He looked like a poor imitation of his brother. In fact, looking at Mason now unnerved her a little because it was obvious they were related.

"I'm not my brother," he said.

"I thought you couldn't read minds?"

Mason cocked his head as if to say, *You might not remember me, but I remember you.*

"I know you still don't want to hurt my brother, but if you have any sense of self-preservation, you need to do something about him now."

Mason eyed her watch and Holland remembered what he'd said about time resetting at a quarter past midnight. It was only five past now. Ten minutes left until they would know if the loop was truly broken. And Holland feared he was right.

She knew he was at least right about her. Despite everything, she didn't want to hurt Adam, but she knew he needed to be stopped. She just wasn't quite sure how.

She wished she had more time. And that's when she realized she still had the Alchemical Heart, the most magical object in the world.

Holland cleared her throat and looked down at the journal. "I need you to please pause time."

Instantly, the journal transformed into an hourglass. It was similar to the one in the Professor's office, except this one was gold with beads of green sand. From the amount of sand, Holland surmised she had only a few minutes.

Mason scoffed. "I told you, if you're going to be successful at using magic, you need to be confident and decisive with your requests."

"Just because I'm being polite doesn't mean I'm not—wait," said Holland. "Aren't you supposed to be frozen?"

"Ghost," he reminded her. "Time and magic don't affect me the same." His gaze shifted to the rapidly falling sand, his expression difficult to read. "There's not much time in there. If you don't want to kill my brother, ask the Alchemical Heart to have him take my place."

Holland hesitated. Turning Adam into a ghost actually sounded like a good idea. But she was less sure about making Mason human. He might have known her, but she didn't know him. And while she no longer believed the stories Adam had told, she didn't have any other information about Mason. "If I do that, how do I know you won't kill me for the Alchemical Heart?"

"If I wanted the Alchemical Heart, I wouldn't need to kill you." He said it almost casually, as if murder was so beneath him the idea wasn't even worth entertaining. "And I'm nothing like my brother. I'm a man of my word, and if you give me my life back, I will not take the Alchemical Heart. I don't even want it. I just want to be free of this place."

The last of the sand ran through the hourglass as he spoke.

Holland wondered if ticking clocks would now make her nervous for the rest of her life, because as soon as time started moving again, she felt it.

The Alchemical Heart was still shaped like an hourglass as Holland addressed it. "I don't want Adam Bishop to hurt anyone ever again. I want Adam to take his brother Mason's place. Turn Adam into a ghost that will forever haunt this hotel and never harm another living soul."

The hourglass started to glow, and so did Mason.

Holland barely breathed as she watched him transform into something that was almost there, almost real, almost human, into someone who felt more human than anyone she had ever seen. She remembered Adam saying Mason was the center of the universe wherever he went, and she could definitely feel that gravity now.

If Cat had been there, she would have said there was something about a guy in a white dinner jacket. Eileen would have said it was because he was tall. January would have said it was because Holland had tragic taste in men. Holland would have said it wasn't any of those things. And yet it was all of those things, along with something else she couldn't put a name to. She just knew it scared her a little.

She felt a little bit of relief as she saw in his eyes that Mason Bishop was just as eager to say goodbye to her as she was to him.

"I still think you should have killed my brother when you had the chance," he said.

"That was a lovely thank you. You're welcome."

"I'm just trying to give you some advice. Adam won't be able to do much now, but I became stronger over time and so will he. You need to be careful. And—" He took a step closer.

Holland put her hand protectively over the hourglass.

"Relax, St. James. I'm keeping my word. But others won't hesitate to take this. You should get out of here while you can. That thing is just asking for people to come after you."

CHAPTER FIFTY-FOUR

Mason didn't say goodbye. Not that Holland had expected him to. Well, she might have expected it a little. Along with the *thank you* he never gave her.

She wondered if there was a version of yesterday that would have ended with Mason thanking her. She hadn't fully wrapped her head around the idea that she'd lived so many yesterdays. She imagined it would probably take a lot of tomorrows for her to sort it all out. And she had other things to sort out at the moment.

Mason Bishop might have been rubbish at goodbyes, but she knew he was right about the Alchemical Heart. Holland had made sure Adam couldn't hurt her again, but he wasn't the only one who wanted the Alchemical Heart.

She needed to get out of there. Although the last time she'd tried to escape with what she thought was the Alchemical Heart, it hadn't gone well.

"What would January do?" she wondered aloud.

"There's a reason your sister didn't find me."

Holland jolted at the sound of an unexpected voice. She turned and saw Manuel Vargas, dressed in the same hat and checkered suspenders he'd worn the other day, sitting on top of the table.

"How did you get here?"

"I've always been here. I just thought you might feel more comfortable talking to me in this form." He smiled, but it wasn't quite a human smile. It was a little too much. Every part of his face seemed to move, from the wrinkles on his cheeks to his eyebrows and hairline.

That's when she noticed the hourglass was gone, and he was sitting in its place.

"It was you all along." Holland remembered the intense bolt of déjà vu she'd felt when she'd first met him, and how he'd been the one who had handed her the package she'd mistakenly thought was from the Professor. But the package had never been sent in the mail. It had always been part of him, or maybe he was part of the package. Holland was a little fuzzy on how it all worked, but she was fairly certain there had never been a Mr. Vargas. Mr. Vargas had always been the Alchemical Heart.

"Bingo!" it said animatedly. "I can take on any form I wish, and multiple forms if need be, but only if those forms are in close proximity."

"So I'm right?"

"Quite." It grinned, clearly enjoying talking about its magic. "Now, let's talk about what you want to do."

"What can I do?"

"You *can* do whatever you want." It smiled wider, in a way that made her think it hoped she'd choose to do something exciting.

"Can I bring my parents back?"

Its smile faded. "You can. If you wish. However, I would not recommend it. There's always a cost to using magic. It's the whole keeping-balance-in-the-universe bit. For example, when your father used me to see the future, he thought he was sending you on a fun, final treasure hunt. But in doing so he created a new future he didn't foresee, with a much darker ending." The Alchemical Heart's expression continued to sober.

"If you think this was bad, there's nothing that upsets the balance more than bringing someone back from the dead. If you really want to bring a loved one back, the best way to go about it is to turn back time, but the cost to that is forgetting. So you wouldn't remember the last fifteen years of your life. And that is a great many years to turn back. If your parents had died only a few minutes ago, that would be a different story." Its eyes gleamed.

For a second, Holland thought about how she kept dying and time kept restarting, and she couldn't help asking, "Is this what happened with me?"

The Alchemical Heart kicked its legs back and forth. "I really can't answer that question, because if you're correct, part of the cost for whoever saved you is that you could never know. So, again, I don't recommend turning back fifteen years, because it will be quite messy for everyone. But entirely your choice," it added cheerfully.

Holland couldn't help thinking about it for a minute. But then she remembered a scene from her father's screenplay, when Alma was talking to Red. *The dead are meant to stay dead. When they come back, there are always consequences . . . Do the right thing. Leave what's better left untouched in the past, think about the future, and move on.*

Maybe the screenplay wasn't just a treasure map but a warning. Her father had seen the future, and he knew exactly what Holland would want to do when she reached the end of his treasure hunt.

It made a lot more sense, now, that he hadn't actually hidden the Heart somewhere anyone could find it. He'd stacked the cards to make sure she would be the only winner. And even though there had been unforeseen consequences, Holland was still thankful he'd done it. She was glad she'd gotten the chance to feel close to him again, to hear stories about him, and to finally talk about him.

Her father was so intentional, putting Easter eggs inside of Easter eggs like little nesting dolls. Maybe he'd always known this treasure hunt would have more than one story inside of it as well.

She wanted desperately to bring him and her mother back. Holland felt that after what she'd just been through, she could handle the consequences of anything. But she knew her father wouldn't want that. She imagined that he'd sent her the Alchemical Heart so she could keep it safe, because he trusted her not to do anything dangerous, even if she was extremely tempted.

"For the record, I don't mind being used at all." The Alchemical Heart grinned, and again she noticed that there was definitely something inhuman about it. "Magic is meant to be spread. However, your father didn't want that." Its smile abruptly turned to a frown, and Holland imagined that if someone else were to come for the Heart, its loyalty might quickly shift.

If she wasn't going to use it, she needed to get rid of it. And yet, she hesitated. There had been a time when all she wanted was to go back to her ordinary nonmagical life, but she knew too much had changed for that to happen.

She wasn't sure if she would ever go back to the Regal or the Bank, but if she did, she didn't want to be powerless. She knew her father didn't want her to use the Alchemical Heart to bring him and her mother back from the dead. But that didn't mean she couldn't use it at all.

"I want an ability," Holland said, before she could change her mind.

It looked disturbingly pleased, lips stretching Cheshire-Cat wide, all the way to its ears. "I was so hoping you'd ask."

Holland hesitated. Its excitement made her feel that perhaps this was a bad idea.

"Don't tell me you're having second thoughts."

"I just want to make sure I pick the right ability," Holland hedged.

Its smile vanished. "Sorry, but I don't work that way. There are certain things you can tell me to do. But I'm afraid this isn't one of them. Each human is made with a unique, inactive ability. I can activate this power. But you can't choose what it is. And you won't know what it is until after it's been activated."

Once again, Holland felt as if this could be a mistake. The Alchemical Heart had also just warned her that there was always a cost to magic, and she wasn't even sure what this magic would be. But if she didn't do this, she knew she would always wonder about what her magic might have been, what *she* might have been.

"Do it." Holland closed her eyes as she said the words, like a child making a wish.

When she opened her eyes, the Alchemical Heart was kicking its legs back and forth again, smiling even wider. "It might take a few days or a few weeks for it to activate, but I think you'll be pleased when it does." Its face turned mischievous.

Holland wondered exactly what she'd gotten herself into. But she didn't regret her choice.

The truth was, Holland St. James simply wasn't capable of turning down a chance at having magic.

Now she only had to decide what to do with the Alchemical Heart. She still didn't imagine she'd be able to walk out of here with it easily—or at all.

She thought about asking it to self-destruct. Then she remembered what Gabe had said about that possibly destroying *all* magic, and she didn't want to be responsible for that.

She needed to hide it, like her father had. Except her father hadn't hidden it. He'd sent it to her. He'd sent it into the future.

He'd believed it was too powerful for any one person to possess. And he must have known it was too powerful to simply hide. Then she wondered if it wasn't just her father who had sent the Alchemical Heart into the future, but if that's what the others had done as well. If that was why the Alchemical Heart would disappear and then reappear decades later.

The Alchemical Heart looked at her sadly, as if it knew what she was thinking. "Is this where we say goodbye?"

"I'm afraid so," said Holland. "It's time for you to find a new home in the future."

"And where might that home be?"

For a second, Holland didn't know. Then she remembered one last thing her father had written. His special instructions on the hold slip. "I want you to go to the future, to someone who needs you, but doesn't really want you. Someone kind, who will only use you once for their need and then never use you again."

CHAPTER FIFTY-FIVE

There is a bench outside the Hollywood Roosevelt where a statue of Charlie Chaplin sits. Tonight, he had a companion, dressed like Mary Poppins. She sat on that bench straight and proper, in a manner that would have made the actual Miss Poppins proud.

The air had finally cooled to a temperature appropriate for November, which it officially was now. But this woman didn't shiver. She was used to waiting. Usually, she was the one who made others do it. But there was nothing usual about tonight. Everyone at the Roosevelt had felt it—the strange pauses in time, the surges of energy, the feeling that perhaps this party wasn't just smoke and mirrors—but no one had felt it more than Holland St. James.

"I don't have the Alchemical Heart."

The Professor peered at Holland from the bench. "I know. It's past midnight now, officially November. The Heart will have gone into hiding again, until the next date on the list."

Holland realized she knew something the Professor didn't, but she only said, "You don't seem upset."

"Have I taught you anything, my dear? There are always magical objects to be searched for in the world." The Professor primly pushed up from the bench. "May I offer you a ride?"

"I think I'm okay." Holland was fairly certain she looked anything but okay, especially if you took a look at the back of her dress. But to her credit, the Professor tactfully refrained from mentioning it.

"Well then, I suppose this is goodbye for now, my dear. My job offer still stands. I can no longer promise you a very good ability, but I think you'll still find it worthwhile."

Holland was tempted to tell the Professor that she was no longer in need of an ability. In fact, she had to suppress a smile at the thought that she'd soon have one. She didn't need a job at the Bank, and she meant to say as much, but "I'll think about it" came out instead.

A number of things might have changed for Holland St. James tonight, but she still couldn't quite close the door on a rabbit hole.

Epilogue

The next morning, Holland could feel all the real again. She could feel the minutes tick by, fresh unlived minutes, crisp as that first breath of early morning air.

She went for a run to drink it all in. The weather had fully changed, and the cold was knife-sharp, cutting away all the dirt and the smog, making LA feel blissfully clean.

Holland ran faster, chasing the feeling of an unlived-in moment as if it might disappear. She ran until her lungs couldn't take it, until her legs burned and she was covered in sweat, which cooled too quickly as soon as she slowed, leaving her chilled and out of breath. But for one perfect minute she wasn't haunted by thoughts of yesterday. Or the yesterday before that and the yesterday before that.

Normally she stuck to the sidewalk lining Santa Monica beach, but today she wanted to take off her shoes and sink her toes into the sand. As soon as the sand felt slightly damp against her feet, she plopped down onto the beach, right on the edge of the damp and the dry.

Holland gazed out at the water and tried to hypnotize herself with the sound of waves. She knew there were so many things she needed to do. Starting with getting a new phone, and then getting in touch with her sister and her friends. She really needed to talk to January in particular.

But for this one simple moment, she didn't want to worry about any of that. She wanted to believe everything would work itself out. She curled her toes in the sand as a wave crashed against her ankles and splashed her calves, dampening her leggings. She tried to just think about how good it felt to breathe in and out. To be alive. To be cold and taste salt on her tongue.

She sat there feeling the water ebb and flow, until she started to wonder how yesterday could have gone differently. She knew there wasn't a version where she could have walked out of the Hollywood Roosevelt with Adam, but she did wonder if there might have been a version where she left with Gabe.

She wondered about him more than she wanted to. After the events of yesterday, she was wondering again if January had actually sent him. The only way to know for sure was to talk to her sister. January still hadn't texted Holland on the burner phone Gabe had given her, which made Holland think he'd been lying.

Another wave crashed, and in that moment, Holland felt a sharp pinprick of awareness, right between her shoulder blades.

Someone was watching her.

She turned around, but it was only a couple of beachgoers. They dropped their towels and ran toward the ever-cold Pacific. And she told herself she was glad no one was watching. That no one had found her there. It was good to have this moment alone.

Another wave crashed. Children squealed as they ran from it. And Holland felt it again, a pinprick of awareness followed by a shift in the air.

She turned, hoping maybe her sister had found her. But it was Mason Bishop, walking toward her. He'd changed out of his white dinner jacket into expensive jeans and a pale blue shirt, which looked even better on him than the jacket.

He sat down beside her, and again she was overwhelmed by the humanness of him. By the power he seemed to carry. As he sat there, she played that game where you wait for the other person to break the silence. At first because she felt oddly nervous and unsure, but then because it was surprisingly nice to sit there in the quiet and watch the waves crash with someone else.

"I missed this," he said finally, looking at the ocean. "You think you can remember the sound and the smell and the way it feels when the sun burns through the fog. But memories are never quite as good as the real thing."

"No, they're not," Holland agreed. She thought about her parents then, and for a second, she regretted that she hadn't brought them back.

"You're wishing you used the Alchemical Heart," said Mason.

Holland's head snapped his way.

He responded with another look that seemed to say, *I know you, remember?*

"I actually did use it again," she said.

He raised an eyebrow. "You gave yourself an ability?"

"I did." Holland hoped that as she said this the magic power would finally appear, but she didn't feel any different. And there was still no tattoo on her wrist.

"Good for you," Mason said. "But don't tell anyone else."

"Why?"

"People treat you differently when they know. If they think you're ordinary, they leave their guard down a little more. People will figure it out eventually, but even when they do, don't tell them what it is."

"Do people know what your ability is?"

"No, and I prefer it that way."

"Will you tell me?" Holland asked.

He gave her a look that said *not a chance.*

"I'll figure it out," she told him.

"Good luck with that." Mason looked back at the ocean, watching the waves crash and retreat, until Holland's curiosity finally got the better of her.

"Is there a reason you came here?" she asked. "Of all the beaches, in all the world, why did you choose to sit on mine?"

"You could say this is my version of a thank you." Mason shoved up from the sand. "You brought me back to life yesterday, and now I owe you a debt."

He reached toward his back pocket, just as Holland's phone rang. Her heart gave a sudden jolt. She pulled it out and looked at the name: January.

Her sister was finally calling.

She looked up to tell Mason to just hold on. But apparently guys like Mason don't wait. He was already walking back up the beach. Again, he didn't say goodbye. But he had left something in the sand. A matte black business card with a gold art deco border.

Closing Credits

I thank God I was able to write this book. This might have been the most challenging book I've ever written, and it feels like a small miracle that it's actually done.

I spent years working on this story and there have been so many amazing and wonderful people who have helped and encouraged me along the way. Thank you, Caroline Bleeke, for being all around brilliant and so patient with me. Thank you to my amazing agent, Jenny Bent. As I type this it's our ten-year anniversary and I continue to be so grateful for you and everyone at the Bent Agency!

Thank you so much to my incredible and loving family who have put up with me talking about this book for years. Mom, Dad, Allison, Matt, and Matt—I love you all so much!

I couldn't be more grateful for all the amazing, beautiful people in my life! Thank you.

Isabel Ibañez, Anissa de Gomery, Mary Pearson, Margie Fuston, Brandy Ruscica, Stacey Lee, Sarah Barley, Nancy Trypuc, Rachel Griffin, Adalyn Grace, Adrienne Young, Jenny Lundquist, Shannon Dittemore, Katie Nelson, Amanda Altamirano, Kerri Maniscalco, Kristen Williams, Richelle Latona, and Kyle.

I also want to give the biggest thank-you ever to the so real Victoria VanVleet—this book literally wouldn't be the same without you. Another special thanks to Bill, Robert, and Michael for the amazing tours!

Thank you so much to my fantastic US publisher, Flatiron Books, and to all the amazing people there who worked on this book. Thank you, Maris Tasaka, Laywan Kwan, Marlena Bittner, Jane Haxby, Donna Noetzel, Frances Sayers, Morgan Mitchell, Emily Walters, Vincent Stanley, Steve Wagner, Mary Retta, Malati Chavali, Louis Grilli, and Megan Lynch. I am so grateful for my brilliant UK publishing team at Gollancz! Thank you so much, Katie Espiner, Bethan Morgan, Cait Davies, and Anna Valentine.

About the Author

Stephanie Garber is the #1 *New York Times* and internationally bestselling author of the Caraval and Once Upon a Broken Heart series. Her books have been translated into more than thirty languages. *Alchemy of Secrets* is her debut novel for adults and will be published around the world.